A Distant Sunset

WORDSWORTH ROMANCE

A Distant Sunset

VIRGINIA IRONSIDE

WORDSWORTH EDITIONS

The paper in this book is produced from pure wood
pulp, without the use of chlorine or any other substance
harmful to the environment. The energy used in its
production consists almost entirely of hydroelectricity
and heat generated from waste materials, thereby
conserving fossil fuels and contributing little to the
greenhouse effect.

First published by Arrow Books Limited

This edition published 1994 by
Wordsworth Editions Limited
Cumberland House, Crib Street, Ware,
Hertfordshire SG12 9ET

ISBN 1 85326 513 6

Printed and bound in Denmark by Nørhaven

1

Everything was quiet in the bedroom except for the crackle of the fire in the grate. When a log fell with a crunch, a flame briefly flickered up, illuminating the room. A girl sat in front of a mirror, her face immobile as an old woman brushed her hair. Apart from the persistent swish of the silver brush, the only other sound was the caw of the last rook in the darkness outside the old manor house.

'They'll be here soon, dear,' said the old woman, leaning over to turn up the oil lamp.

The girl said nothing, just stared ahead into the ancient blue-grey glass, nervously clenching her fists from time to time and occasionally reaching up to smooth parts of her silk dress. The old woman stretched across for some pins and started to put up the girl's hair, her hands stiff but still skilful.

From downstairs came the sound of a knock on the door, the stamp of feet and the creak of rusty hinges. The girl's expression changed as she listened intently to hear exactly who had arrived; then, on hearing the brash tones of a Northern voice, her face fell.

The old woman paused for a moment, putting her hand tenderly on the girl's shoulder.

'You are very, very unhappy, Elizabeth,' she said, more of a statement than a query. 'What a pity young Mr Applevale is going! Ah, I wish you were going to India with him, if only circumstances were different.'

Lizzie shook her head. 'He says India is no place for women, Nannie,' she replied in a low, lifeless voice.

'And indeed he's right!' exclaimed Nannie, her eyes flashing protectively at Lizzie in the mirror. 'Nor, if I may say so, is Penworth Court any place for a young woman. Cooped up with your father without a mother and nobody to organize a proper season for you! Why, Mr Applevale will be back from India in time, anyway.'

Lizzie looked distressed. 'But he doesn't love me – or not enough to remember me by the time he returns,' she cried.

'Doesn't love you? What utter nonsense, child! It's clear as the nose on your face! And not just him, neither, the two of them loves you, not just Richard but Mr Whittle, too, that's *clear*! Why everybody who sees you love you, you silly nonsense!'

'Don't mention Mr Whittle, for heaven's sake! The very thought of him makes me utterly sick!'

Nannie stepped back and tilted the lamp to view her work. 'Very nice,' she said. 'You're a real beauty, just like your mother. And as for Mr Whittle, you'd better get over your sickness since that were him arriving two minutes ago, and it's in your father's interests you're nice to him.'

'Father seems intent on destroying himself, whatever I do,' said Lizzie, ruefully, getting up and brushing down her dress. She looked in the mirror and set her expression more cheerfully. 'Thank you, Nannie. If I am beautiful it's certainly because you make me so.' And she hugged the old woman warmly before leaving the room to go downstairs.

Whatever Lizzie's doubts on this last evening, there were none in Richard Applevale's mind as he galloped towards Penworth Court down the avenue of lime trees. He was a good-looking young man, with a fine seat on a horse. He was dark with blue eyes, and a nose that had once been broken while boxing at school gave him a faintly aggressive air. He had a bruise of a mouth that emphasized his very even, almost translucent white teeth, and his figure was lean and wiry, with a natural life and grace that gave him elegance even in his oldest riding jacket.

This had been a difficult, testing year for him. His father, Lord James, had wanted him to follow his elder brother into parliament, but he himself had wanted to enter the army in India. There had been arguments, threats, silences, but in the end, as usual, Richard got his way. He was leaving for

6

London the following day – and now he could not help but look around the courtyard, darkening in the evening light. This was his last night in Devon. He felt poignantly touched by the chill English mist against his face, the smell of rotting leaves, and the cold leafy fronds that seemed to dip out of the night to flick the dew on his face.

And it wasn't just Devon that he was leaving; it was Lizzie, his childhood friend – who had grown to be more than that. For in the last few months their friendship had changed, despite all he intended. When had it started to become clear to him? Perhaps during the days he'd ridden over from his father's house, bringing with him maps of India which he would lay out in her father's study and browse over with her in the long summer afternoons. Then he'd practised his Hindustani on her, lying on the cliffs and repeating, '*Chotahazri* – breakfast, *charpoy* – bed, *dudh* – milk,' as the seagulls cruised around in the clear blue sky above. And later, indoors, they would sit together after supper as he showed her his small but treasured collection of Indian miniatures – and tried to explain his fascination with the vast sub-continent. Was it then that he'd decided? No, it had been even more recent than that, if he were honest with himself.

They'd been lying on the rock on the beach late one afternoon and he had been talking of India. 'I can't wait to be away from here,' he'd said, enthusiastically. 'I'm longing to be riding over the plains, to see the temples, find out about the people and their language, even go on a tiger hunt. I'll bring you back a skin and you can recline on it – it would certainly suit you. And they say the Indian women are fascinating . . . and the dancing girls –'

But Lizzie had suddenly turned away at this remark. Quickly she recovered herself and turned back, using a voice of cool and friendly detachment that infuriated him. 'I see! You plan to lose your life in drink and debauchery. That'll be fun for you!'

At that he'd reached out and grasped her wrist and looked at her with frightening intensity.

'Oh, is that what you'd like, Lizzie?' he'd heard himself

7

saying, bitterly, almost sarcastically. 'That I'd forget . . .' He'd been about to say 'forget you', but changed his mind. Perhaps he'd misread what seemed like the tones of jealousy in her remark. And anyway, just before leaving for India – this was no time to fall in love! But, perhaps it was already too late to warn himself against it.

He took his hand away brusquely, angry with himself for getting so involved. He looked grimly at the sea in an attempt to recover his composure, but as he turned back he found her looking at him. Their eyes met briefly, but long enough for him to be certain that he saw a lot more than just friendship in her gaze. He remembered her colouring slightly and his sudden longing to take her in his arms and kiss her.

As he saw the dim yellow squares of light from Penworth Court in the distance, he brought his thoughts back to the present and kicked his horse to spur him faster for the last few yards. He dismounted and as he did so he noticed, to his anger, another horse tethered in the stables. With annoyance he recognized it as George Whittle's horse. Surely that wretched trader was not coming to dinner? He scowled as he knocked on the door, and was let in.

Lizzie paused at the top of the stairs before going down to dinner. There in the hall below stood the unmistakable figure of George Whittle, on his way back from the gun-room. He had stopped momentarily and was fingering one of the old tapestries that hung on the walls. Lizzie gripped the banister. Here was the man who had ruined her father through gambling; couldn't he wait for his money rather than handle their possessions as if they were already his own? He moved slightly, then examined a bronze bust that stood on an oak table, his rough hand stroking the smooth surface with interest.

It wasn't so much that he was an ill-looking man; more that he was ill-bred. His red smoking jacket was too garish, his cummerbund was pulled over a figure that betrayed the opulence of his living, his hands were covered in extravagant rings that were far too ostentatious and which, far from making him appear more aristocratic, only served to emphasize his vulgarity.

As she stepped down, a stair creaked and George Whittle turned sharply and looked up.

No man could fail to be arrested by the sight that met his eyes. The faint light fell on her features, highlighting her cheekbones, her full mouth and her rich, dark hair, parted in the middle of her forehead and rising to a pile of intricate curls at the back. Her dress was deep blue, watered silk, cut in a straight line across the shoulder, only dipping slightly to reveal the curves of her full breasts. Her head was held high and her skirt rustled slightly as she glided down the stairs.

George Whittle's eyes were fixed on her as he stretched out a hand to help her down the last step. He coughed and bowed slightly.

'Good evening, Miss Shawcross,' he said.

'Good evening, Mr Whittle,' answered Lizzie coldly as she took his hand. She was about to walk on and then changed her mind. She stopped as if struck by a thought. She turned to him and looked him in the eyes. 'Mr Whittle,' she said in a voice uneven with despair, 'is there nothing I can do to stop you? If you could just delay demanding payment for a few months, then I am sure my father would be able to borrow some money to pay his gambling debts. . . .'

George Whittle smiled, showing a gold tooth. 'I don't believe in delay, Miss Shawcross,' he said flatly. 'I didn't get where I am through delay. I am sure you understand my position. But an arrangement would not be impossible,' he added, smiling knowingly at her with far too much familiarity. 'You must understand my meaning. . . .'

Lizzie pulled her hand away sharply and was about to speak when she was interrupted by her father's voice. 'Come on, Whittle, tell me what you think of the gun and stop monopolizing my daughter! Come and dine! Richard Applevale is already here and he's starving!'

Each time guests came, Lizzie saw the dining room with

9

new eyes. She was acutely aware of the chips on the willow-pattern plates, the silver that was wearing thin, the oak panelling rotten with woodworm, the carpet so covered with other carpets to conceal the holes that it looked like a patchwork quilt, the paint on the hatch to the pantry that had been scrubbed so hard that the undercoat showed through and, in some places, even bare wood. They had never been able to afford to keep the house up and now that her father had lost what money he had through his reckless gambling, there was even less chance that they'd ever have the opportunity.

Lizzie loved the house. Penworth Court was her home and nothing could erase the memories she had of it when her mother was alive, when the fires had crackled in the grates, nursery tea had been waiting when she came in from long walks on the cliffs, and the house, reflecting her mother's happy presence, had seemed to echo with laugher and gaiety. It would be unbearable to leave it.

Sir Henry was a changed man, too. When his wife had been alive he'd been alert, interested, and a fine scholar; but when she died part of Sir Henry seemed to die, too. He took to drinking and gambling and read nothing except occasionally *The Times*. Lizzie loved her father, loved him for how she remembered him before her mother's death, but she could not forgive the terrible urge that, despite all her protestations, led him to squander their much-needed money at the gaming tables.

The guests settled themselves at the table, and Lizzie flushed as she caught Richard's eye opposite her.

'Well, serve round,' Sir Henry growled at the maid as he drew his chair in, and helped himself to some madeira from a decanter. She hurried to serve George Whittle who had tucked greedily into the hare pâté before anyone else. Lizzie took a small portion but she found it almost impossible to eat any of it, her mouth felt so dry and dusty. She managed a small taste and then pushed the plate away from her.

Struggling to give the dinner an air of normality, she said, 'So, how is your sister, Mr Whittle?' She had missed

10

Emily very much in the past few weeks. She might have reservations about George Whittle, but his sister was different: shy, kind, loving, so trusting and gentle that no one could fail to love her, except, of course, the sort of men she met through George, men who were looking for class and status and not sweetness of nature.

'Why, Emily's having a fine old time in London,' he said, putting his thumbs into his cummerbund and stretching it to make himself more comfortable. 'Poor Emily, so bored around here, but she's doing well in the city. I got a letter from her only today full of news of an Indian gentleman she's met, Azi Khan – something like that.'

'Azimullah Khan, you mean,' interrupted Richard. 'My father met him recently in London.'

'Who is he?' asked Lizzie.

'He's the envoy of a man called Nana Sahib,' explained Richard. 'The British government paid the Nana's father a large pension, making it clear it would stop on his death. But his adopted son, the Nana, wants it to continue so he can support his retinue of fifteen thousand people. He won't take no for an answer from the governor general, and he's sent this lackey over to plead personally – to no avail. I hear he's charming the ladies in London, and everyone says he's an attractive fellow – but a scoundrel. I'd be fascinated to meet him, despite it.'

'And you may well be so lucky, sir,' said Whittle, his expression showing irritation that Richard knew so much of the situation. 'Perhaps you'll meet him in India, eh? In fact, I'm half tempted to follow you there after meeting Azimullah. He's certainly a fine businessman, and they say that those outposts are crying out for shops and provisions. His attempts to get money out of the government may not have been successful, but he's made a few good friends, like myself, who might do him a lot of good. Talking of getting money out of people, I hope you'll have mine ready for me at the end of the week, Sir Henry. I'm getting impatient!' Whittle gave a loud laugh and stretched across Lizzie for the madeira, spilling the salt-cellar in the process.

11

'What's wrong with discussing money?' said Whittle, aware of the sudden embarrassed silence that had fallen at his remark. 'The pâté may be good, but money's good too, and it's food and money that makes the world go round, eh? You'll be finding this out in India, Mr Applevale. I know you're the son of a lord, but India is one of the few countries where a man of any rank can rise and be admired for his real worth!'

'Oh, indeed,' said Lizzie, trying to avoid an argument, exchanging a glance with Richard who was about to interrupt.

Sir Henry waved his hand at Sarah. 'The joint, serve the joint! Come, there's only one thing I want to hear at my dinner table and that is the sound of good talk and the clink of glass containing good wine! Here's to your health, sir!'

During the second course Lizzie tried to alleviate the tense atmosphere by changing the subject. 'Have you read Charles Kingsley's new novel, *Westward Ho!*?' she asked brightly. 'I'm already so taken up with it in the first few pages that you're all privileged to find me even here at dinner!' She gave a rather desperate laugh and looked pleadingly at Richard as if to beg him to join in. 'I swear that any further hint of an argument between you gentlemen and I shall simply go up to my room and bring it downstairs and read it at table!'

The rest of the meal passed away in uneasy banter, until the maid came in with the coffee, tiny cups on a papiermâché tray. It was then that Whittle started again. He coughed as he lit up a cigar.

'Well, it's the end of the meal, isn't it? Now, let's talk about money, Sir Henry!'

Sir Henry stared down at his cup.

'I have a proposition to put to you, Sir Henry,' he added, gloatingly. 'No, don't go, Lizzie,' he said as Lizzie rose. 'For you are an important part of the plan I have to put to you!'

Lizzie sat down again, gripping the tablecloth. A dark look of hatred passed over Richard's face. Only Whittle relaxed, reaching out and gulping down his coffee in one

12

gulp like a Russian drinking vodka. 'You want time to pay your debts, Sir Henry. Well, I'll make you an offer. I'll make you an offer where you don't have to pay any debts, ever. *And* you'll get an allowance from me. How's that?'

Sir Henry looked anxious. 'What's the proposition, Whittle?' asked Sir Henry, in a low voice.

'The proposition is the price,' said George Whittle, a satisfied smile growing over his coarse features, 'and the price is that I marry your daughter. Now there's an easy way to solve your problems, eh? Then we're all happy!'

2

There was a long silence. Then Richard stood up and pushed in his chair with a rough scraping sound.

'You marry Lizzie! You're out of your mind, Whittle!' he said, furiously. 'I've never heard anything so preposterous!'

Whittle smiled tauntingly at him, drumming his fingers on the table. 'Don't you think the lady herself should answer? I'm sure she's old enough not to need you speaking on her behalf.'

Sir Henry dragged a fresh glass over to himself and poured another drink with a shaking hand.

'Whittle, I think there must be another way we could resolve this . . .'

'Ah! I'm not good enough for her, is that it? Good enough for your gaming tables, but not good enough for your daughter, eh? Well, I'll tell you when I've got every debt out of you, Sir Henry Shawcross, I'll be good enough for anyone and you and your daughter will be good for nothing!' Whittle pounded his fist on the damask tablecloth on these last three words and the cutlery jumped.

Richard's eyes narrowed, and he started to walk round the table, his fists clenching involuntarily. Lizzie started in horror, and tried to stop him, but he pushed her arm roughly aside.

'I'll tell you one thing, George Whittle,' he said, coming up to him and staring into his face, 'You'll never have anything to do with Lizzie Shawcross as long as I'm around!'

He pulled Whittle up out of his chair by one hand on his lapels, shaking his fist in his face. Whittle's expression changed, and he looked anxious; then he laughed.

'But the thing is, Richard "son-of-a-lord" Applevale,

14

you're not going to be around!' He pushed Richard away from him, and Richard was just about to attack him when Lizzie stepped between them and forced them apart.

'For God's sake, stop it!' she said. 'I won't have fighting in this house!' She was trembling. To her relief Richard relaxed, and walked a few paces back. Then he leant forward, shaking a warning finger at Whittle. 'Watch out, Whittle,' he said, threateningly. 'You make one threat against this family, and I'll deal with you, even if I have to come back from India to do it!'

Whittle laughed. 'Sensitive young man, isn't he?' he remarked mockingly to Sir Henry. 'Come, let's go and discuss our affairs without the presence of hotheads like Applevale. Come on, d'ye hear me?' He helped Sir Henry roughly out of his chair and they left the room.

Richard came up to Lizzie and put his hands on her shoulders, looking directly into her eyes. 'Why didn't you tell me?' he said, accusingly.

'About my father's debts?'

Richard nodded. 'I would never have planned to go to India had I known how grave your father's situation was. I could have delayed my passage. I could have helped. Can he really have lost everything to that man?'

'It only happened last week,' said Lizzie, looking down. 'I felt too ashamed to talk to anyone about it – even you.'

'How do you think I feel now?' Richard said, throwing his hands into the air. 'I can't call myself your friend and leave you in this position. But it's too late. If I delay now my father will never again let me leave the country.'

'You're a good friend, Richard, but I'll manage. I promise you that.'

'I'm more than a good friend,' said Richard, looking at her tenderly. 'You know that.'

Lizzie looked away. She couldn't speak. It was unbearable that this was the last time she would see Richard for so long.

'I'll come tomorrow,' said Richard. 'Before I go. I'll think of something. I'll telegraph my father tonight. Please,

Lizzie, don't worry. I'm sure I can help you.'

Lizzie looked up at him. 'I hope so,' she said. Their eyes met again, as they had the week before, and each knew what the other was thinking. They instinctively moved closer – but then Richard put a finger gently on her lips. 'Tomorrow. I'll see you tomorrow,' he said. And, collecting his cane and his coat, he left the room.

Lizzie went into the drawing room, put another log on the fire, pulled up a chair and settled uneasily to do her needlework, her eyes brimming with tears, her hands tense, holding the tapestry awkwardly, the needle slipping through her fingers as she jabbed it furiously into the pattern.

It was unbearable to think of leaving Penworth Court. It meant everything to her. Not for a single, mad moment could she contemplate marriage to George Whittle, even to save her beloved home. The very thought made her mind recoil. She loved Richard, and to give herself to any other man would be inconceivable. But, much as she understood Richard's desire to prove himself in the Indian army, it was only natural she should secretly wish he wanted a life more conventional to the younger son of a lord. If only he would be happy to settle in England now, to take her into his care. But she hastily pushed such thoughts aside: they were a betrayal of Richard's character, of the stubborn streak of individuality that she treasured so much, his burning desire to make something of his life and to make an impression on the world around him.

A voice interrupted her thoughts, startling her.

'Needlework, eh? Very fine.' George Whittle stepped in. 'I hope I'm not disturbing you. But I think you and I need to have a little talk, for everyone's talking at cross purposes here.'

Lizzie looked at him coldly, then gestured for him to sit down opposite her. Whittle rubbed his hands by the fire, staring at her all the while.

'You're a handsome woman, Miss Shawcross, and a sensible one,' he said.

'Thank you.' Lizzie's voice was like ice. She continued to

stitch away. Then her work was suddenly snatched from her and she started up.

'Put that damn work down when I'm talking to you, miss!' Whittle had got up furiously, and threw the tapestry into his chair. 'I won't be talked down to by the likes of you. Look at me, now!'

Lizzie looked up, dumbly insolent. 'Yes, Mr Whittle?'

'That's more like it, you hussy! More "Yes, Mr Whittle" and less "No, Mr Whittle" is what I want. Now look here! I suggested marriage to you this evening. I put up a proposition to your father. You know what the alternative is, I suppose? I'll get the bailiffs in if I have to, and the whole house will be made over to me! Now stop being so stubborn! Have some sense! And not just sense, either, but some affection for an old friend of the family.' Here Whittle looked away, slightly embarrassed and his voice dropped. 'For you must know how I admire you, Miss Shawcross. You must have noticed how much I think of you, how I long for you to be my wife – it's my only wish. And I'd be glad if you told me you'd agree, that I would.' Here he turned completely towards the fire, as if overcome with emotion.

Lizzie rose, sparks flashing from her eyes. 'Well, I'll tell *you* something, Mr Whittle. I don't admire you, you must have noticed *that*. I don't think much of *you*, and I don't even think of you at all – except with loathing! So don't come crawling to me with your propositions! You'll never take Penworth Court from us! I'll die first!'

George Whittle slowly turned around, and his face had a grim and bitter expression etched on it. His eyes looked like cold marble set in his white, fleshy face.

'We'll see about that, miss!' he said. 'We'll see! I won't forget your words, and you'd best not forget mine, because when I want something I usually get it, more often than not, and in this instance, I'm determined. And so, Miss Shawcross,' he added, stepping back and holding out his hand, 'I shall wish you a very good night.'

Lizzie turned on her heel, shuddering, unable to touch his hand. She heard the door close behind him as he left, and the house was silent, except for the slow tick of the grandfather clock in the hall. It was a familiar sound and one she dearly loved. It was a sound she knew she must treasure, for surely she would shortly lose it. She shook her head and sighed deeply. Bending, she pushed the logs to safety with the tongs, put up the fireguard, and wearily put her needlework in her walnut workbox. Then she turned down the wicks on the lamps and stepped outside into the hall.

As she moved towards the stairs, she saw a slit of light coming from beneath the door of her father's study.

'Father?' she said softly.

She turned the handle and went in. The whole room smelt musty and dead, a smell of snuff and old tobacco smoke. Sir Henry sat in a green leather chair, a picture of despair. In one hand he had a piece of paper with a list of figures on it, in the other a large brandy. His feet rested on the brass grate. In the corner, Lizzie could see the drawers of the bureau open, as if he had been searching for bills or deeds.

'Father?'

Sir Henry looked up. His face was utterly careworn. He looked beaten. His white hair was in disarray and his eyes were bright with anxiety.

'Lizzie, there's no hope for us, there's nothing we can do,' he said, his words pouring out in a helpless jumble. 'I've ruined myself – and you with me. God forgive me!'

Lizzie went up to him and, kneeling, put her arms around his knees. 'It can't be that bad,' she said. 'I am sure we can find a way out. Richard promised he would help. Perhaps his father would loan us the money.'

Sir Henry shook his head. 'No, there's no hope, it's too much. We'll only have enough left for a small cottage, if that. Oh, Lizzie, what have I done?' Self-pity merged with anxiety as the papers he was holding fell to the floor.

'Go to bed, father,' said Lizzie, rising. 'Things will look brighter in the morning.'

'Oh, what would I do without you, dear girl, what would I do!'

'You're not going to be doing without me, father,' said Lizzie, helping him to the door. 'We'll be all right. You'll see.'

But after she had led him to his bedroom and had then, in her own bed, extinguished the light, she wondered fearfully what on earth would happen to them.

The next day dawned bright and crisp. From her window Lizzie could make out the horizon between the sea and the pale blue sky. There was still a light dusting of frost over the fields that led to the cliffs, all of which made up part of the Penworth estate. True, the stone walls were crumbling and the gates swung open, their hinges rotted by the salt air, but it was still a beautiful place. Far away on a small hill-top a group of rooks circled round and round their nests, black dabs in the leafless trees. And the sun, a watery yellow, was battling with the chill to warm up the day.

That morning after breakfast, Lizzie walked round the garden that surrounded the house. Once the vegetable garden had burgeoned with luscious tomatoes, ripe peaches, raspberries and strawberries; now it was a wild, overgrown cemetery of weeds. The flower garden had bloomed with sweet peas, rambling roses, lines of wall-flowers and borders of lobelias; now it was straggling, each plant encroaching on another's place. The drive had been clear and smooth – now it was marked with pot-holes, and ragwort and groundsel ravaged the once immaculate paving of the terrace. The head of a stone lion that had once stood proudly guarding the steps to the fields now lay cracked in the grass, a nostril eaten by rot, a tooth chipped by frost. And yet all this made it no easier to think of saying good-bye. If anything, it was even harder. To leave Penworth flourishing and healthy – that would be bad enough; to leave it when it needed love and care – that was impossible.

She walked slowly back along the box-lined path and sadly returned to the house.

After the light outside, the hall seemed dark and gloomy.

When would Richard come? She looked at the steadily ticking clock. It was only nine o'clock. On any other day she would have saddled up her horse and gone for a ride along the cliffs, but today she felt chained to the Court lest she should miss Richard.

It was a long, long day. She worked on her needlework with no enthusiasm for the task in hand, and lunched with her father in silence. In the afternoon she took a restless nap, and later attempted to continue *Westward Ho!* but the print danced before her eyes and she found it impossible to concentrate.

When she finally heard a horse's hooves on the driveway, she flung open the front door.

'Richard!' she said, kissing him warmly on the cheek. 'I thought you'd never come!'

He stood, flushed with riding, his eyes sparkling. 'Let's walk over to the cliffs, Lizzie. I want to have you to myself as this will be the last time we'll see each other for a long time.'

He took her arm and they walked briskly together away from the house. When they'd reached a favourite, secluded spot in the trees near the cliffside, they sat down.

Richard stared silently out at the sea for a few minutes. 'I'm sorry I've come so late, Lizzie,' he said finally, turning to look at her. 'I've been waiting for a telegraph from my father and I'm happy to say that he'll look after you while I'm gone. You don't have to worry, Lizzie. At worst he'll buy Penworth to raise the money but let you and your father live here.'

Lizzie clapped her hands in excitement, her eyes sparkling. 'You can't mean that, Richard,' she said, but she was smiling hopefully. 'It can't be true! It is news too good to be true! But why should he? Poor man, he's not well, he doesn't want to be saddled with an estate to care for . . .'

'He can employ someone to manage it, that's not a problem . . .'

'But why should he be so generous?'

Richard looked steadily at her. Then he put his hands on her shoulders. 'I'll tell you why he's prepared to do this,' he said slowly. 'Because I have explained that – that when you marry, you are going to marry me!'

'Marry you?' Lizzie asked, unbelievingly.

'I'm not going to India for ever, Lizzie. I shall come back. And you'll be waiting for me . . . you will do that, won't you, Lizzie?'

Lizzie could feel his warmth and closeness as he drew her to him. She felt completely in his power, and closed her eyes as she felt his arms around her and his lips on hers.

In a moment, she whispered, 'I will be waiting, you must know that.'

Richard looked at her. 'When you love someone as much as I love you,' he said, 'you know everything about her – as if she belongs to you . . .'

'I do belong to you, Richard,' Lizzie whispered. 'I am yours.'

And then it felt as if a tremendous power had been unleashed – a power that had been building up for weeks and weeks. Lizzie could never remember much about what happened next except that they were suddenly helpless to keep themselves from holding and caressing each other. She felt an excitement she had never felt before as Richard pulled her to the ground. Losing all sense of time, Lizzie was soon only aware of Richard within her, of a sharp jag of pain followed by a feeling of total joy. In the days to come when she was to look back on that evening and wonder why she had not been able to say 'Stop!' she knew that it was because at no moment did she even think of the word, for as Richard wanted her, so she wanted him, wanted his body, wanted him all so completely that once they had begun there was no stopping.

Later, Richard lifted himself on one elbow and stroked Lizzie's cheek. 'I should be sorry, but I'm not,' he said, smiling wickedly. 'I love you, you know that? I love you.'

'I love you, too,' whispered Lizzie, softly, putting her hand up to stroke his black hair. 'I'm not sorry either.'

'We are married now,' said Richard, softly. 'We may not be married in a church and you may not have yet taken my name, but here –' he touched his chest where his heart was, and then touched her breast, leaning for a moment to kiss it — 'here we are married. We are married here, too,' and he touched his head and hers. 'And we are married here, too.' He took her hand and gently guided it down, wrapping her fingers around him so that she could feel the new warmth and strength in him.

Everything would be all right, now. Even when Richard was gone, at last, Penworth Court would never be taken away from them. They would never see George Whittle again. As Lizzie went to bed that night she felt as peaceful and happy as she ever had in the whole of her life.

3

Dearest Lizzie,

I'm writing you a last letter before my servant goes down to the port tomorrow — and I hope I'll find your first letter waiting for me. These packets take such a long time — I've been in India for months now and not a word from anyone at home.

I've at last got my uniform made . . . perfectly stitched and with gleaming buttons. Poor Patcham, who I share quarters with, made the mistake of getting his uniform made in London and when he opened up his trunk here he found the buttons all damaged by the air and his smart gold lace utterly tarnished. Poor man! He's quite ashamed to be seen out with me, tells me the ladies here all eat their hearts out over me simply because of the state of my buttons — not that there are many ladies in Calcutta and certainly none worth talking to.

Richard put his pen down on the rickety table that served as a desk, and stared out of the small window in front of him. It was four o'clock. The whole of Calcutta slept and even here in Fort William the usual sounds of parade-ground bustle had stopped. All morning he'd heard the stamp of boots and the endless orders: 'Pose your firelock! Cock your firelock! Present! Fire! Half-cock your firelock! Handle your cartridge! Shut your pans! Change with cartridge! Draw your rammer!' The barked instructions that rattled across the forecourt every morning from 6 a.m. was now replaced with the sound of the continual swish-swish of the punkah pulled by a thin, dead-eyed young boy.

It was a fairly wretched-looking room. The only furniture consisted of a couple of dusty basket-chairs, and a side table on which stood a half-empty bottle of soda. In the corner were a couple of rifles and spears, and two old cigar boxes that lay tossed on the wooden floor the night before. Hanging from a pin, slightly askew, was a withered photo-

23

graph of the whole of Patcham's school with an inked arrow pointing to the head of a small, smiling boy who sat cross-legged on the grass in front of the headmaster. The cool, leafy, ordered scene was a far cry from their quarters at Fort William, a magnificent building surrounded by water, near lush fields, the best sight in Calcutta. Richard did not live in the main building but in a set of rooms built off the ground above a verandah, consisting of two bedrooms and the main, dark room where Richard now sat.

He gazed ahead. Through the haze that shimmered up from the forecourt he could make out the white outline of the stone lion that stood, with its paw on a gigantic ball, over the entrance to Government House. Behind it was the silhouette of a temple; it was always there, this contrast of cultures, and how uneasily they lay together. And how uneasy he felt, too, settled between the two worlds of Britain and India. He'd exchanged his father's castle, with its cool lawns and cold, musty library, steeped in the smoke of old wood fires, for these small quarters, hot and mosquito-ridden that looked out on to a patch of burnt earth. He had swapped his father's tenants, ruddy, full-faced Devonshire peasants, for the hollow-cheeked, half-naked and burnt-skinned Indians who begged at the roadsides and thrust out their crippled children for alms. He had exchanged his light reading of Dickens, Thackeray and Kingsley for the study of *The Stranger's East Indian Guide to Hindustani*.

The pin-prick sting of a mosquito on his cheek startled Richard from his thoughts and he slapped his face angrily, brushing the black and red stain it left on to the floor. He took up his pen again.

I think of you all the time – and yet I'm glad you are not here, fascinating as it is. Not only is India rife with disease (not to mention corruption) but there are rumours here of mutiny among the sepoys – the native soldiers in the East India Company's army. It's hard to explain to someone so far away from this strange place, but I'll try. The Indians feel we are taking over their country. We are bringing progress – putting in new railways, new telegraph wires, stamping out the customs of Thugs and suttee – widow-burning. But this results in mixed feelings. Some Indians feel we are a great help to their country, that our introductions of medicines and law and order and mechanical improvements will help their country which is in a pretty sorry state at the moment. But the majority believe we are breaking up their old ways of life and destroying their religion and their society. There was an incident recently at Barrackpore where some fool of a British officer had insisted the sepoys bite the bullets for the new gun. What's wrong with that? There were rumours that these new bullets had been greased with cow or pig fat. It's against the religion of the Hindus and Muslims to touch anything of a cow or pig, and they believe they'll be damned eternally if they do. But this British officer insisted and the Indians refused, quite naturally. The upshot was violence that led to one of the more rebellious sepoys, Mangal Pande, who was wild with *bhang* (a kind of drug they smoke), being shot from a cannon by the British.

Of course this is no way to treat a man who is fighting for his religious beliefs – and the result is unrest all over the country. Even the servants are becoming shifty and rude. I heard a woman telling how her ayah had started to look through her jewel box, and ask the worth of the contents – as if she's already choosing what to take when the time comes. Most of the British here think it will come to nothing, but those of us who believe otherwise are worried. It's now 1857, when it's rumoured that the Indians shall be free of British power. Amulets to protect the wearers from danger are appearing in the bazaars. A strange practice of circulating chapattis from village to village seems like a bad omen now and you often see signs on the walls saying: 'Everything will become red.'

I only hope the optimists are right. Myself, I'm not at all convinced. But I don't want to worry you unduly. I will survive, I promise you that. Apart from all this, we have a gay time here, visiting the tea or 'tiffin' rooms, and the ladies here have an excellent time completely out-numbered by the men . . .

A light knock on his door alerted Richard that Arjun Gohar was on his way to the port. He stepped inside at Richard's 'Come in!' – a slim, dark-skinned, handsome young bearer with a fine white turban and dhoti. Richard had acted on good advice by ignoring all the servants who swarmed around him when he'd arrived at the dock at Calcutta with cries of 'Me very good servant, me good bearer' and had waited till he had received advice on a suitable servant. He had chosen Arjun Gohar for his loyalty and good references.

'I go to the dock to buy provisions and await your letter,' he said. 'Is there anything else you are desiring, sahib?' He stood motionless, his hands pressed together in front of him in an act of subservience.

Richard nodded and gestured briskly at his letter. 'Wait a moment, Gohar,' he said, 'you can take this down to the port with you. It might catch the *Elizabeth*.'

'And perhaps you would like me to bring Gita to you this evening?'

There was no sound of disapproval in Gohar's voice, no emotion, certainly none of the ribald laughter of the young British officers. From the moment most of the cadets arrived, they indulged in an orgy of 'nautch' girls, or dancing girls – though the word 'dancing girl' was something of a euphemism. The nautch girls were a strict class of Indian who had either been born to that state or bought as infants and brought up to attend the various devout ceremonies of their religion and yet submit to the desires of any man who wanted them. Richard had entertained Gita a few times, but only to keep up appearances with his colleagues. While his friends were taking their girls to bed, Richard would be practising his Hindustani on Gita, to her obvious astonishment.

He turned to finish his letter.

I must finish, as Arjun Gohar, my bearer, is waiting to take this letter. I hope to God that Whittle is no longer a danger. But I know my father will keep his promise to you. If this letter sounds unduly pessimistic, don't be alarmed. I at least will *have* to return – to make you my wife. I love you – Richard.

He sealed the envelope and handed it to Arjun Gohar. 'No, I won't see Gita tonight,' he said. 'She's a fascinating girl but I ought to spend the evening reading some more.'

'Perhaps you would like a boy?' asked Gohar, still persistent.

Richard laughed, turning round in his chair. 'Not a boy! Look, I'm here to work, not play around with your girls – or boys!'

Arjun Gohar bowed silently, with a puzzled look on his face. 'There are very few British like you, sahib,' he said. 'I wish there were more. I fear for the bad ones – and the good.' And with that ominous remark he left Richard to continue his studies.

4

While the crew of the *Elizabeth* were just putting the finishing touches to their preparations for the long journey back to England, another packet, the *Beacon*, was on its way to take the *Elizabeth*'s place at Calcutta. The passengers had boarded it two months before at Gravesend and now they were all either accustomed to life on a boat or had taken to their beds and rarely appeared for meals.

One of the better sailors was Emily Whittle, who was reclining in a chair on the deck, her skirt covered with a tartan rug; she was sitting next to a young girl with long, dark hair. Emily was a rather plump, thirty-year-old with the slightly strained and over-cheerful look of a woman who has not yet found a husband. She was watching the sun sink – and the waves were already starting to reflect a pinkish glow from the sky. A troupe of dolphins suddenly sprang up out of the water, the last playful romp of the day, and above them the still persistent seagulls keened and wailed around the mast, their eyes bright for any scrap that should be flung overboard.

'I wish you could have met him,' said Emily shyly to her friend. 'I still can't believe we're on our way to see him! I know an Indian isn't quite the thing, but Azimullah Khan is quite different. Quite exceptional – so talented and fine looking. And he has met the Queen, after all, which is more than you or I have.' She spoke with a slight North Country accent, with the affected tone of one who had been trying to disguise it for years. 'I'm sure you think I'm very foolish to persuade George to bring us out to India to start trade there, but Azimullah's letters are so full of promise – he was so impressed by George's ideas. I gather the Nana is quite mad on fancy goods and loves good china – it is just the chance for George and being so clever it is small wonder he took it up. He'd never come just on my account, I'm sure, dear as he is.'

The girl beside her was about to open her mouth, a look of knowing scorn passing over her face. 'Don't be silly, of course he . . .' she began, but thought better of it, and leant forward to brush a cockroach from her foot. As she bent from her seat she gave a slight start, leant back and put her hand on her stomach.

'My dear, are you all right?' Emily put down her needle-work and adjusted a cloak around her friend's shoulders. 'Why, I'm sure you must be . . . well, you must be in a *condition*, you know,' she chattered, gaily. 'After all, you've been married quite a few months, it'd not surprise me at all – you're not looking well.'

Her companion started nervously. 'Oh, please, Emily, don't go on so! I know what's what. You're fancying things.' She pulled a hand wearily over her forehead.

Emily stopped for a moment to throw a concerned look at her friend. Then she continued. 'What I just can't understand is why people like your friend Mr Applevale had such a low opinion of Azimullah. He was only coming to London to get more money out of the government who have been so terribly cruel to break off their pension to the Nana, just because he was the adopted son of the old Peshwa of Bithur and not the real one. Or was it Mr Applevale's father who thought so badly of him? Poor Lord James,' she added. 'I hope he has recovered from his illness, what shocking news that was to be sure.'

The girl beside her turned her head wearily. She had heard the story of Azimullah so many times that she was tired of it. On top of that she was still feeling slightly sick. She had to face another month on this boat that seemed to her to be permanently rocking, and infested with every bug from boll-weevils to cockroaches. As she turned her head she caught the pungent smell from the end of the ship where the farm animals were kept and her stomach lurched. The pregnancy had made her particularly suscep-tible to smells of any kind, and this boat seemed designed to upset her. If it wasn't the bitter, rank smell of the coal burning, it was the heavy smell from the sweating crew who passed by, or the stench of another meal being cooked from the small galley below deck. She sighed. She wouldn't be able to keep her secret from anyone much longer; her petticoats were already getting so tight she was having to leave four hooks undone at the back. Luckily she had brought clothes slightly out of fashion that pulled in just under her breasts, so nothing was visible and her secret was still safe.

'I think I'll go downstairs for a rest if you'll forgive me, Emily,' she said, rising and smiling as kindly as she could at her chattering friend.

'Of course,' said Emily, 'but you must let me help you down the stairs.'

'Allow me . . .' A young clergyman who was passing by offered his assistance and taking her arm escorted her to her cabin where she collapsed gratefully on to the bunk.

It was a small cuddy, airless but welcoming with its furniture of polished brass and wood. Even the bolts that screwed the small table and chair to the floor, so that they would not slide around in bad weather, gleamed brightly. She could see the greenish-blue sea through the porthole. She longed to open it, to let in the fresh air, but it was firmly clamped shut.

Loosening her dress which was intolerably uncomfortable, she looked into the case that lay beside her bed, checking that her papers were still intact. There were such stories of passengers' papers being stolen that she always checked when she returned to the cuddy. With relief she saw that they were still there. For a moment her eyes rested on the piece of paper. The awful words were still fresh enough to fill her with disgust:

Passengers: three

Names: Miss Emily Whittle, Spinster
Mr George Whittle, Tradesman
Mrs George Whittle, *nee* Shawcross

Reaching down she turned the paper over as if to try to deny the facts and then lay full-length on the bunk, head turned into the pillow, sighing deeply.

How could she have done it? she thought wretchedly. And yet what else could she have done? She remembered her trip to London to see Lord James, and the awful news that he had had a stroke and would have to rest. She had pleaded that it was important, but Richard's elder brother simply refused to let her see him in case it upset him, claiming that any disturbance could be fatal for the old man. On hearing her story he tried to help, and advanced a thousand-pound loan himself. But this sum could not deter George Whittle. He had issued a writ against Sir Henry which was due to come up in court. The bailiffs had come round. Sir Henry had been close to suicide.

Lizzie had written to all their relations but none could help, and she had resigned herself to the fact that Penworth Court would have to be sold. And then, already distraught as she was, she made that terrible discovery. She was pregnant. At first she felt a twinge of excitement that she carried a part of Richard in her, but quickly she fell into total despair as she realized the full horror of her position. She would be ruined; an unmarried girl having a child would be an outcast — an outcast whom Richard, son of a lord, would never be able to marry. And certainly no one else would marry her. She would be completely on her own — penniless, ostracized. In tears she had confided in Nannie, but the old woman, who had so often helped in the past, could make no suggestions this time.

In her desperation, she had written urgently to Richard, giving the letter to his brother to post. She had had no reply. Presumably there was nothing he could do, or cared to do.

Then, on the day before the court case, George Whittle came round to visit the Shawcrosses one last time. Again he begged Lizzie to marry him, assuring her that not only would he drop his action against her father but that he would even guarantee him a small allowance to live on, if only she would accept. He swore he loved her, that he

31

would be a good husband – and Lizzie had seen no other course. She had accepted. They had been married in Barnstaple in a quiet ceremony.

She had saved her father, and she had saved her child from the stigma of illegitimacy, but she had to live with the awful knowledge she had sacrificed herself on the altar of George Whittle whom she found so repulsive. Somewhere at the back of her mind she knew that Whittle would make the discovery, but until then she tried not to think about it. Perhaps she should have slept with him on their wedding night – but a mixture of repulsion and horror that Whittle could have any hold over this child only strengthened her pleas of fatigue and modesty. And since then she had continually fobbed him off with kisses and promises that she would change when they got to India, that she was unsettled by their plans to travel. And he, because he had been continually working, had been too tired to protest. Even now she could not bring herself to share her bed with him, and her only comfort was Emily, his matter-of-fact sister whom she could call a friend.

She was woken much later by a plump hand pulling at her shoulder. As she opened her eyes she looked up into the pitted, red face of her husband. He had been drinking.

'Come on, now,' he muttered, savagely pulling the blanket away from her. 'Y'not in your fancy Penworth Court now. You can't lie around all day.'

Lizzie yawned. 'I'm tired,' she said, coldly.

'Tired? You're always tired,' said Whittle, staring at her angrily. 'It's not good for me for the men to think my new wife's so poorly! "What are you doing to her?" they ask me in the saloon, with a laugh. "Why, nothing," I say. "*Nothing!*" they answer in joke. And I laugh back with a wink for I'm not going to let on my wife won't give me her services because she's sea-sick.'

He stared down at the lovely shapely body beneath him, the lines of the long skirt hinting at the curves of her figure hidden beneath. 'By God you're getting mighty fat, Elizabeth, for all you're not eating. When we get to India things will be different, I can tell you. A man can't last long without a woman, you know. In fact, I've half a mind to . . .'

He reached for his boot as if to take it off, but Lizzie cried almost hysterically, 'Oh, please, George, no, I beg you. I'm feeling so unwell. Wait until we are on shore, don't force me now, I beg you. I'm so unhappy.'

'Unhappy?' George paused, with a puzzled look on his face. 'And why's that? I've set your father up so he is living in comfort, married you and given you the security of a husband, I take you to India for a new life . . . but,' and his face mellowed slightly, 'I can see you're not feeling well. You've got a face like cold apple pie. Not that cold apple pie isn't very good, mind you, but not on a wife's face. But who looks at the mantelpiece when you're poking the fire, eh? That's what my pa used to say!' He gave a coarse laugh. 'I'm too good for you, Elizabeth, that's the trouble.'

Lizzie turned away to conceal the rage and contempt she felt for the man.

'I'm so tired, George, it's the travelling and the climate, so strange,' she said. She ran a finger along the cool, shining brass rail by the porthole.

Whittle looked at her disbelievingly. 'Well, you had better change for dinner,' he said brusquely. 'It's gone nine.'

He started to undress, first taking off his purple silk kerchief, then his rough garish top coat and his fancy waistcoat. He turned around with a smile that made Lizzie shudder and pulled her up from the bed. To see him without all his clothes unnerved her, for never before had he undressed when she was in the cabin.

'Come on now, don't be frightened,' he reassured her. 'I know it's strange for you and it's natural for a wife to be modest, but hurry and undress and I'll show you you've no reason to be anxious.'

He gave a short laugh and turned down the oil lamp. Lizzie started to understand his meaning. She undressed, jerkily, feeling paralysed with fear and horror. She took as long as possible, folding each garment carefully and laying

33

it out on the bed. Finally, naked, she stood with her back to him. George put his hand on her shoulders and she could smell the whisky on his breath, and the acrid whiff of an old cigar. He thrust his cheek close to hers, and she felt the coarse texture of his skin. Then he stroked the back of her neck with nicotine-stained fingers.

'You're a beautiful girl, Elizabeth,' he muttered into her ear. 'I've waited long enough for this moment.' Lizzie froze, unable to move.

'Now come, Elizabeth, don't be so modest. I'll not take no for an answer tonight. Turn around and let me see you, for I've imagined this moment so many times . . .'

But as Lizzie turned slowly, Whittle's voice faded away. He stared at her, first in astonishment, then in horror and finally his face turned black with anger.

'So *this* is why you've been so modest, you whore!' he shouted, pushing her violently back on to the bunk. 'It's *this* monstrosity you've been hiding under your skirts all these weeks!' And with a vicious jab of his fist he lashed out at her rounded belly leaving a red weal on her flesh. Lizzie winced, and covered herself protectively, terrified.

'No one ever sells George Whittle used goods!' he shouted, grabbing at her shoulders and shaking them. 'Well, I'm telling you, there's no use for used goods except to throw 'em away, sell 'em cheap or use them yourself till they break in two!'

Lizzie, terrified into fury by his behaviour, jumped up, sank her teeth into his shoulder, and grabbing her pelisse, tried to push past him to the door of the cabin to escape, but Whittle stood firmly against it, breathing heavily.

'I'd die rather than submit to you,' she screamed, pulling his hand from the cuddy-latch, 'I'd rather go to hell than . . .'

But she could say no more for Whittle had struck her to the floor in mid-sentence and she collapsed at his feet, insensible.

34

It was eight o'clock when Arjun Gohar returned from the dock to Fort William. He was not alone. Floating beside him, huddled under a red silk sari, was an elusive shape, almost like his shadow in the darkness. A high ripple of laughter that escaped from the dancing, ever-moving shape was answered by a stern wave of the hand from Arjun Gohar. He vanished into his own quarters, across the forecourt. He emerged a minute later, alone, and finding no answer to his knock on Richard's door, he left a package of papers on his desk and retired.

Richard had only drifted into the mess room for a drink to clear his head, bored with studying by six o'clock. It was cool there, a big fan slowly turning on the ceiling over the various groups of laughing cadets, some standing, some sitting at small round tables. Patcham had immediately noticed him and came over, and Richard bought him a glass of madeira. Patcham was insisting on a game of snooker, regaling Richard with a long and detailed description of an amazing night he had spent with a nautch girl.

'You only live once, old chap,' he said to Richard as he potted the white, muttering 'Damn!' under his breath. 'You'll never get such a chance again. These native girls are splendid, don't you find? You should have been here last night, too! Craven had two fighting cocks and won a fortune on them and bought us a bottle of madeira each! Then we all took palanquins into the town for Craven wanted to throw a creditor into the Hooghly. We were all prepared, but dammit, the man was out so we returned to dine and Fotheram has set a new record in snuffing out a candle with a bread-pellet. Four yards and three inches! Damn fine shot!'

'Unlike your last play,' said Richard as he took aim at the balls on the table. He leant over carefully, his broad shoulders illuminated by the light inside the square-fringed lampshade that swung over the table. His face was taut with concentration and his eyes narrowed keenly as he lined up his shot. Then he sharply tapped the ball, manoeuvring it into precisely the spot he required.

'Dammit, you snookered me properly there!' said Patcham, lining up his next shot. 'I'm glad I didn't lay money on this game, Applevale. Now why don't you come out with us this evening? We're . . . a thousand damnations!'

As his ball missed his target he stamped his foot. 'These damn cues, they become warped and bent in the heat,' he exclaimed, leaning over the green baize table and examining his own.

'It's those nautch girls, Patcham,' said Richard, wryly. 'Nautch girls and madeira. Rot your brains. I'll be glad when we leave this place and find some action.' He walked round the table, summing up the situation left by Patcham.

'I hear you're to be promoted,' said Patcham moodily as he saw the pattern of the balls left him no room to make a winning shot. 'Suppose you've got some influence here, with your old man being who he is.'

'As this is the only part of the army where you are promoted on merit and not because of your connections, I doubt it,' said Richard, a note of anger in his voice. 'Anyway,' he said more kindly, 'I'm sure you'll be promoted soon, Patcham. You're a natural leader; your men would follow you anywhere.'

Patcham smiled. 'Well, get on with it, and follow me by potting the white!' he said.

'Oh, I won't follow your mistakes,' said Richard, aiming again. 'Ha!' The red tumbled into a hole. 'Now the pink . . .' There was a rattling sound as it fell into a pocket. 'And finally, the black.' It bounced off two sides of the table before slipping into the net at the corner.

Patcham slapped him on the back. 'Well done!' he said. 'Let me get you a drink.'

'No, thanks,' said Richard handing him the cue and brushing a smudge of chalk dust from his jacket, 'I'll see you tomorrow. I'm retiring early this evening.'

He left the mess and made his way back to his quarters, realizing that Arjun Gohar must have returned. He quickened his pace, and turned up the lamp the moment he got to his room. He searched through the mail. A letter from his mother . . . a copy of the *Barnstaple Gazette* . . . and three days of *The Times*. But nothing from Lizzie. He shook his head, puzzled. He read the letter from his mother – the family was all well. There was news of the estate and snatches of gossip, but nothing that really interested him. He shrugged. It was odd there was no word from Lizzie. But the history of lost post in India was an old story. Next month would bring news, no doubt.

After ordering a cheroot and some tea from Arjun Gohar, he settled down with some nostalgia to read through the English papers. It was good to see the familiar *Gazette*. He flicked through the main items and then turned to the advertisements so familiar to its pages. He saw there had been a cavalry ball at the Assembly Rooms in Barnstaple, but there was no sign of Lizzie's name in the list of attendants. He read the comments on the Crimean War and then folded the paper to put it away. But as he put it down his eye caught the name: 'Whittle'.

George Whittle Ltd of Barnstaple, sells Glass and China and Other Useful Household Ornaments. We possess an IMMENSE stock of novel and useful Articles suitable for the season and solicit an inspection of our Stock which will be found to be VERY MUCH THE LARGEST AND CHEAPEST in the West of England. The Goods are all of the Best Quality and Workmanship and are made in plain figures at EXCEEDINGLY LOW PRICES. Dressing cases, alarums, inkstands, Bagatelle Boards, Jet ornaments . . . CLOSING DOWN SOON

Richard pushed the paper away in disgust. 'Exceedingly low prices indeed!' he muttered to himself.

He reached for *The Times* to catch up on the parliamentary news. After an hour's reading he decided it was time to turn in, but before going he allowed himself a glance at the society and obituary columns at the back.

Mr Peter Desmond . . . passed away. Poor Mr Desmond. Richard's old headmaster. Of course he would have died were Richard at home or not, he thought ruefully, but it was at times like this that he would like to have been at home, to have called on Mrs Desmond and offered sympathy. A wave of near-homesickness overtook him. Then his eye caught the marriage column. And his hand started to tremble and anyone seeing him would have been frightened to have seen the expression on his face as he craned over the print.

Shawcross: Whittle.   Miss Elizabeth Shawcross, daughter of Sir Henry Shawcross, formerly of Penworth Court, married Mr George Whittle, son of Thomas Whittle (dec.) of Liverpool at Trinity Church, Barnstaple.

In a moment of disbelief he turned to see the date of *The Times*, imagining the whole thing might reveal itself to be some ghastly hoax, but there was the date in black and white. Lizzie had married. Not only had she married, she had married George Whittle.

Perhaps it was because the Indians were so sensitive; perhaps it was because Richard, in his state of shock, had accidentally knocked over a chair and the sound had reached Arjun Gohar. Whatever it was, Gohar was suddenly before him, anticipating Richard's needs and demands.

'Bad news, sahib?' he said, straightening the chair. 'Would you like some more tea?'

Richard stood up and turned away, gesturing him to get out. The torture he was feeling was bad enough without having his own servant witness him in this reduced state.

'I think you will be liking a woman to talk to now. I took the liberty . . .'

Richard said nothing. Then he turned. Very slowly, he nodded.

'I will send Gita to you, sahib,' said Arjun Gohar, vanishing.

The girl who appeared at the door a moment later was slight and dark-skinned. A bright jewel gleamed in her nose and the red spot on her forehead made her features glow. Richard stared at her. She moved closer towards him, reaching out her arms. For a moment Richard felt a rush of tenderness towards her. Then, pushing her into his bedroom, all the rage and anguish he felt seemed to rush like currents of energy into his hands. He seized her fiercely, pulled her by the arm and flung her on to the bed. With one wrench and a rasping tear, her sari lay a tattered rag on the floor. She gave a faint but submissive whimper as he loosened his belt and entered her with a strength and fury that made her give a brief scream of pain. After a few loveless minutes Richard was satisfied and pushed the poor girl from the room.

As he put on his jacket, Arjun Gohar entered. 'I trust the girl was to your satisfaction, sahib,' he said, questioningly.

Richard turned on him. 'No girl is to my satisfaction!' He spat out his words like gunshot. 'All of them are treacherous, as treacherous as the sepoys in this regiment. They'd slit your throat or betray you for a rupee!' He pushed his way into the main room, then went out of the door, slamming it hard, and Gohar heard the stamp of his steps towards the stables. He shrugged, tidied a few papers, shut the inkwell and swept the top of the table with a small ivory-handled brush. Then he went into the bedroom, and with sure, even sweeps of his brown hand he neatened the ruffled sheet over the coarse mattress and drew the bedding over the string frame of the bed. He paused, sighed slightly. Then he closed the door quietly and heard the vanishing thud of hooves as Richard galloped off.

'Gita,' he said, in a low voice to the girl who stood by the doorway, 'do not be having fear. He is just upset. These English sahibs have strange ways with women. But he will learn to like you. Perhaps he is new to women. He is only a young man.'

The huddled shape of Gita by the door remained still for a moment, the moonlight glancing off a silver tear that fell down her cheek. She seemed immobile, staring out into the blackness as if hypnotized by the decreasing sound of hooves.

'No, he has known other women,' she said, slowly. 'He has known how to love a woman, very dearly. And now he knows how to hurt them, too.' She shuddered slightly and then, turning, she ran lightly over the forecourt towards the town.

5

The first view of Calcutta, as the transfer boat moved from the Diamond Harbour up the Hooghly – too dangerous a part of the river to be attempted by the steamship – was Garden Reach, which extended nine miles below the town. The bank was studded with elegant mansions, surrounded by groves and lawns which led to the water's edge. The river was dancing with life. American and English boats, picturesque crafts from the Persian Gulf and Arab boats with wild-looking crews and gay flags jostled for space in the dark waters. The native boats drew close to the ship and strange brown faces stared up at the newcomers, some of them holding up pieces of silk or carved tusks for the English to buy. Further down river, the boat passed Fort William and the Esplanade, a long vista of palace-like mansions. All the slopes on the fort were covered in green; for a newcomer prepared for dust and sand, the first view of Calcutta reminded him strangely of England. The copious dew-fall at night watered the ground, resulting in a carpet of bright green grass, and in the daytime the sacred cattle grazed peacefully on this luxurious growth. The skyline of temples and church spires quivered in the heat-haze that rose up from the city.

When the boat finally pulled alongside, this peaceful scene was shattered. As it scraped against the sides of the harbour, a sound of cheering went up from the people assembled on the quay. From that moment it was all yells, screams, hoots, uncanny wails and laughter. Children from the ship pointed excitedly to their parents, the people on the quay waved frantically at new arrivals, and loved ones threw their hats in the air as they sighted each other. The passengers disembarked, pushing their way through the crowd with difficulty. George Whittle forged ahead, with Lizzie behind him, and Emily protectively bringing up the rear. Emily found herself obliged to cling to Lizzie's skirts as would-be servants swarmed around them, attempting to find work. The cry of '*Jow Jehannum*!' – Go to Hell! – was frequently heard shouted by the English as they tried to protect their newly arrived friends or relations from the crowds. All around rung out the noise of the sailors hauling in the ropes, the shouts as the tin trunks were hoisted ashore, the alarming sound of frightened animals mingling with the wail of the *bheesties*, clanking tin cups on their leather water-carriers. All this was new and exciting. And the smell . . . that was what struck Lizzie most of all . . . a mixture of oil and tar, spices and leather, manure and sweat – smells suddenly swept away, perhaps, by the swish of an English lady dowsed in cheap eau de cologne hurrying on her way to greet a husband or child. Or the sudden sickening whiff of putridity – 'Don't look, don't look! That's where they throw the bodies in the river,' shouted one woman in a lavender hat in utter horror, whereupon everyone in earshot immediately turned round to stare. 'And there,' called the companion who had met her, 'see that man, he's been sitting cross-legged here for six months till his fingernails have grown into the palms of his hands and they say his heart is still beating though he's not had a morsel to eat!' The new-comers turned again, but the Whittles were distracted by a call of 'Mr Whittle! Mr *George* Whittle bound for Cawn-pore! Make yourself known, please Sir! Please, Mr Whittle!'

Whittle waved frantically and an elegantly dressed half-caste man appeared to take charge, herding them through to a quieter part of the quay where he showed the women a bench in the shade. 'Please wait here, I will organize some tiffin. Mr Whittle will have to come with me through customs before we can arrange for the transport to Cawn-pore, very pleased, very pleased . . .'

He ushered Whittle off to a low hut-shaped building, leaving the two women alone, sitting and staring in aston-ishment at the curious scene that met their eyes.

A crow's loud screeching cry could be heard above the colourful crowd mingling at the shore. A native, silent, sullen and motionless, sat woodenly by the doorway to the customs house. At his feet lay a child with no arms, covered in flies, wailing dismally. There was the clink of a rupee as a generous stranger, not as yet hardened to the sight, took pity on him.

'My Bible, my Bible!' The clergyman swept by them, his black coat already covered in white scuffs of dust. 'I have left it on the boat . . . Excuse me! Excuse me! I am a man of *God*!'

In the sky the sun quivered, shimmering in the heat as if it were suspended on a thin line of cotton by a shaky hand. Lizzie turned away from its brightness to observe the extraordinary blue of the sky, the ragged line of the horizon – palm trees stood out like solitary figures, and the city skyline of temples and elegant classical architecture intermingled in peculiar symmetry. She tried to take in the scene but the mixture of heat, smell and noise confused her. She felt faint. The scene before her started to spin and she felt as if the brilliant sun was coming closer and closer to her. A sharp spasm of pain across her stomach brought her suddenly back to awareness, and she put out her hand to Emily. Another spasm seized her stomach. With dread she realized it was starting. She opened her mouth to explain, but as she did so another fierce spasm seized her and she gasped in pain. 'Emily . . .' she said, 'it's beginning . . .'

But Emily had already jumped to her feet in panic and was running to the customs house calling for George. 'George, George! Lizzie is having the baby! Hurry! Get help!'

'My dear . . .' a nervous voice outside the room whispered after a slight knock. 'May I come in? Are you still sleeping?'

Lizzie opened her eyes slowly, and putting out her arms

to stretch, she was surprised to feel the light gauze of the mosquito net over her bed. A month had passed since they had arrived in Calcutta, and the baby boy had been born. 'What a time to choose!' Lizzie remembered Whittle complaining angrily, as it had become clear that they would have to spend six weeks at least in Calcutta before moving on. 'No, she and the baby mustn't travel yet,' the army doctor had told them. 'Especially as the baby was premature. And she must rest. She is tired out after her journey. It would be very harmful to move.'

And so Whittle had rented the small bungalow temporarily before they moved on.

It was a typical bungalow, with a thatched roof, a wooden verandah, and four large rooms, in the cantonment area. There was a small scrubby garden surrounding it, and the path up to the verandah steps was lined with plants in pots – a custom that had been started to enable the itinerant English to scoop up their plants, taking with them their precious shoots of honeysuckle or verbena that they had had shipped out in glass jars from home.

The bungalow was scarcely furnished, Whittle planning to move on soon, and the rooms were bare and unfamiliar, with the absolute minimum of furniture. And the little that there was had been arranged not for the comfort of the occupants but to prevent infestation of beetles or snakes creeping on to it. At least it was cool, though this was only achieved at the expense of a distinctly pungent and mildewed smell which was given off by the tatties – roots of scented grass soaked in water that served for blinds – as the heat tried to carve its way into the rooms.

Lizzie lifted the mosquito net from the bed and sat up. She glanced down at the baby sleeping by her side in a wicker cot and, squeezing a flannel in a bowl of water by her side, wiped away the beads of sweat on his forehead. Her heart turned every time she saw him. He was fast asleep and she paused a moment, captivated by his tiny eyelids, tightly shut in deep unawareness of all that went on around him.

The voice at the door came again, accompanied by more tapping.

'Come in.' Lizzie turned to the door, pulling her lace shawl from the bamboo chair next to the bed and arranging it round her shoulders, 'Come in, please!'

Emily came in, followed by a servant carrying a tray, which he placed on a rickety table beside the bed. She smiled at Lizzie and sat down. 'How *are* you, my dear?' she asked, dismissing the servant. Lizzie was delighted to see Emily's eyes sparkling. Ever since she had come to India Emily had looked better and happier than she'd ever seen her. Her figure was better, her hair glossier, her cheeks rosier and a look of almost girlish hope had replaced the sometimes over-pale and anxious features of the Emily she'd known in England. She had even taken on a much greater interest in her appearance – the pale green muslin dress she wore had been copied from one sent round by a new friend, Lady Chambers. This aristocratic lady had taken Emily under her wing and was forever sending her chits, folded in such a complicated style it was all Emily and Lizzie could do to unravel them.

'She is trying to marry me off, I swear it. She thinks I'm one of the fishing fleet,' Emily had said, a week ago. 'Little does she know I've already been caught. *I* shan't be a "returned empty". At least I hope not!'

As Lizzie looked at her, she found herself hoping that it was true, that Azimullah would prove exactly what Emily expected. Emily deserved some love.

'I'm feeling marvellously refreshed,' said Lizzie. 'I'm sure I'll be able to travel soon, you know. After all, I've been out quite a lot already.'

'But going out isn't like travelling,' prattled Emily, sipping her tea. 'And the journey to Cawnpore is very long and arduous. You must build up your strength here, my dear, and do as the doctor says. George is not so put out as all that. Anyway, he is away all day doing business and arranging for stocks to be sent to Cawnpore. Really I should think he is grateful to be able to make this stop, I don't know how he would have coped if we'd just gone

44

straight to Cawnpore. And anyway, who could be put out when he has been given such a darling little treasure as this?'

Emily had got up and tiptoed over to the cot on the other side of the bed and, holding out her finger, gazed at the tiny bundle as he sleepily clasped her knuckle with his fine fingers. He gave a small cough, turned slightly, and then, his small pink tongue resting on his lower lip, he settled to sleep again. 'Oh, Lizzie, you are so lucky!" she said. "He's such a little swell! He looks exactly like George, too! And I'm lucky, too, to have such a charming little nephew! He'll break a few hearts when he grows up, I'll bet! Oh, I could eat him up, he looks as delicious as a marshmallow!'

Lizzie leant over and touched his downy cheek. Certainly he would break some hearts, she thought painfully. Just as his father had broken hers. 'Yes, he's lovely,' she said, sighing slightly. 'Every time I see one of his little night-gowns I start to burst into tears – silly, isn't it! I thought I knew what love was . . .' At this Emily coloured and tittered knowingly and Lizzie felt irritated. 'But I honestly wonder if any woman can love anything more than her baby. He's my whole life. Now.'

'Ah, come, you'll make George and myself jealous!' said Emily, releasing her finger and adjusting her brooch. 'Not that I blame you. And indeed, George loves him too.' Then she stopped and stared at the ground as if she had said something wrong. She twisted her hands and there was an uneasy silence.

'Come, don't pose, Emily,' said Lizzie, in a matter-of-fact voice. 'You know he doesn't like the baby very much. There's no point pretending.' She remembered the first time Whittle had set eyes on the baby and the look of loathing and pain that had crossed his face. That was one of the reasons Lizzie had insisted on the child sleeping with her. She had a nagging fear in the back of her mind that George might try to harm him unless she kept a constant guard.

'Well, they say all husbands are jealous of their boy-children, particularly when newlywed,' said Emily nervously. 'But he does love him, you know. He came in here

45

this afternoon when you were asleep, especially to have a look at him, he said. And when he came out, I could swear he'd been crying, why, marriage is a queer do! I don't think I shall ever be used to it!'

She passed round the edge of the bed and sat down again in the chair.

'And have you heard from Azimullah?' asked Lizzie, taking the hint.

Emily blushed. 'I have. I am afraid I was forward enough to send him word I'd arrived and he sent me . . . this!' She fumbled in her pocket for her handkerchief and pulled it out. Carefully she folded back the corners. There, glittering in the centre, was a diamond ring set on a solid gold band. It seemed to shimmer even in the shaded bedroom. Lizzie felt startled, despite herself. Perhaps he really was genuine! She peered at it.

'My word, Emily, you certainly have made a hit!' she said, taking it and examining it. 'And what reply have you given him?'

'I shall reply when I see him in Cawnpore,' replied Emily, waiting a moment before taking it and gently wrapping it up again. 'When you are quite fit to travel. Here, did I show you this? It is advance news of George's shop.' And she handed Lizzie a crumpled piece of paper she had discovered in her pocket when slipping the ring back.

Lizzie took it and read:

A NEW SHOP. WHITTLE OF BARNSTAPLE. Opening shortly is a New Shop which will be a Lively Addition to Cawnpore's trade. It will stock Glass cases full of Fine French china, bijouterie, gold lace, sauces, brandied fruits, riding whips. In the central aisle will be jewellery, French clocks, Cheshire and Gruyère Cheese, hams, cases of sardines and salmon. Suspended from the ceiling will be Bird cages, Lamps and coloured French lithographs in handsome frames. We recommend our Readers to make haste to this new Shop as soon as it opens before all the goods are Purchased!

Lizzie gave a wry smile. Trust George to set up advance publicity for himself! She handed it back. 'What else has happened?'

Emily sighed and shook her head. 'The servants! You know Lady Chambers told me to watch out for their pilfering? Well, last night I took her advice and made pencil-marks on the brandy and madeira bottles and checked the larders, and this morning I ordered an inspection. Lizzie, half our stocks were gone! The brandy was down by three fingers, and there was one sack of rice where there were two yesterday! I ordered the culprit to come forward but of course no one would admit to it. I knew it must have been Indira, for only she has the key. I ordered her to go, and you know what she did? She went on her knees before me, she kissed the hem of my gown and put her hand under my foot for me to trample it! It was so terrible, Lizzie, I didn't have the heart to dismiss her, though George says I am soft-hearted. I don't understand these servants one bit! One moment they are so kind, cooing over my sketches, admiring my gowns, and behind my back they are stealing everything!'

Lizzie reached out and put her hand on hers kindly. 'You've managed so well, Emily,' she said, 'I only wish I could help you more. I will, in a week or so. It's not fair for you to have to play lady of the house when I'm sure you'd like more time to go visiting and playing cards. You must feel tired with the heat, too.'

Emily stretched out her arms, and smiled. 'Oh, I'm all right,' she said. 'You don't feel like visiting right now, do you?' she added. 'I was in the Maidan yesterday and saw so many people there, including a very nice young officer, a Mr Patcham. He is so pleasant, Lizzie. I met him the other day at Lady Chambers's. Poor man, his hat was dangling ever so, I just wished she would ask him to lay it down that he might stay to dine, for here if you are asked to put your hat down that is an invitation to dine in itself, but she had decided to dine alone that day and so his poor hat continued to dangle so on the end of his finger I was convinced it was going to drop!'

Lizzie laughed. 'No, although it's getting cooler, I'll stay in today. I'll just get up and read,' she said. On her few excursions out to sample Indian social life, she had already spent too many evenings in the company of pale, thin, yellow Englishwomen whose conversation was nothing but gossip. She had had enough sandwiches to fill her for ever and had seen enough of those ill-lit bungalows with their chintz-covered chairs, their mosquito-filled interiors, their silver bowls of English roses in the centre of the table. She was already depressed by the sight of those black bottles clothed in netted covers and tumblers, hidden by pieces of silk to keep the insects out. She already hated the sight of all the legs of the furniture placed in small bowls of water to keep the ants away. And the conversation was already tiring her — conversation about Paris fashions, servants, sketching, flower-pressing. No one had read a book in months. She preferred now to stay at home, with the baby. It really seemed to her as if her life had ended. The baby was the only thing that gave her a reason for living.

When Whittle summoned her that evening, Lizzie expected an argument. They rarely spoke these days except angrily, and since the birth Whittle had kept himself to himself. That evening he sat in the main room in a basket chair. He was smoking a hookah, a habit to which he had quickly become addicted, and was being fanned by the punkah wallah. Two servants were pulling off his boots while another carefully combed his hair and yet another paused by his side with a bottle of madeira waiting to refill his glass.

As Whittle saw Lizzie he angrily dismissed the servants except for the punkah wallah who remained tugging at the blind, an endless, silent task that he performed wearily but uncomplainingly.

'Sit down!' Whittle snapped at her from his chair. The light was already fading and his features were becoming indistinct in the dim room. When she sat, he pulled an invitation from his waistcoat pocket and flung it on to the table in front of him. 'There!' he said triumphantly. 'Good news! The day after tomorrow. We'll all be going!'

Lizzie reached forward and read the card. 'Your presence is requested by the Lord Dalhousie at a Ball at Government House at 8.00 p.m. on Thursday,' she read. In normal circumstances she would have been pleased to go out, but now her heart sank. She couldn't go to a ball. She was still too tired. She fingered the invitation reluctantly.

'I really don't think I'll be well en . . .'

'You'll be coming with us, and no excuses,' snapped Whittle, flushing. 'It's taken me enough trouble to get that invitation, and I'm not having you throw it back in my face, madam! Everyone who is anyone in Calcutta will be there, and that means you and me these days. So mind you look your best. I don't want to take any moaning minnies with me. I'd like to be complimented on my wife for once!'

Lizzie put the rose-coloured card with its gold surround back on the table. Everyone who was anyone? Although she imagined that she might meet Richard again, her common sense had always told her that among all the millions of people in India, and among the thousands of British, there was hardly any chance of their even seeing each other across the street. But this ball was a different matter. She had not counted on George's driving social ambition. Despite her efforts to control herself, she was unable to check the telltale leap of her heart, the momentary flush of her cheek.

'That's all,' said Whittle, turning to his copy of the *Hindusani Times*. 'Servants! Light the lamps! I can't read a thing! Stir yourselves!'

Lizzie got up and bowed to him. 'Very well,' she said, as she left the room. 'I will do as you say.'

6

'Oh, they are queer kittle-kattle, these natives! Their depth past finding out! It is best to treat them as children who know no better, but they seem proud of their lies and the innate *goodness* of the European is not understood by them!'

Lady Chambers was shrieking to make herself heard above the chatter of the 300 assembled guests at the ball at Government House. She held her head very high, waving a fan constantly to keep away the mosquitos. Her blue silk ball dress she had had made especially for the event, and all the ladies admired it. Lizzie had been about to join in the compliments when she noticed, to her horror, a cockroach crawling up one of the folds of the wide skirt. She had decided to say nothing.

Government House was a splendid place. The gravel on the paths outside had been specially imported from England, and the side paths were covered with crushed shells that Emily had thought charming until George had pointed out that the reason they were there was to deter snakes. The entrance hall was polished black marble, the doors polished mahogany with gleaming brass handles, each one attended by a servant, their scarlet and gold sashes over their white Maratha petticoats. George and Emily had exclaimed at the grandeur of the place, as their coats were taken by the servants, and even Lizzie couldn't help but feel quite awed in such surroundings. And yet as she looked she saw that even at Government House the British ways never quite worked in harmony with the Indian climate. The servants' eyes, always cold and distant, frightened her. Looking up to the marvellous plasterwork mouldings on the ceiling, she saw how the edges were already being eaten by termites.

And now, as they all discussed Calcutta life before going into the banquet, she couldn't help but notice the acid smell of the ammonia and glycerine mixture which the English ladies used to soothe mosquito bites through the eau de cologne. It was as if no matter how many English people were imported to India, no matter how many buildings were designed in the English style, no matter how much English food, books, pictures, styles, laws were dragged into this country, everything English would eventually be tarnished, eaten by termites, bitten by the ants, poisoned by the water, or mildewed by the damp.

'Of course you must remember they're just niggers,' a young man in hussar's uniform of dark blue and silver had overheard Lady Chambers's remark. 'They are quite different to Europeans. It is hardly fair to expect them to understand our ways.'

'Oh, do be quiet!' hissed Lizzie, flushing, as she noticed they were standing next to a group of wealthy Sikhs.

'Fiddlesticks, they cannot understand what we are saying!' said the young man standing next to her. 'Why, I had to explain to them in Hindustani just now about the dancing. They were shocked that the governor general's wife would dance with her husband. Nautch girls? they asked. I soon put 'em right. No, old chaps, not nautch girls but *ladies*, English ladies! In England the ladies do dance, and they dance with the gentlemen! Gentlemen? they asked. Well, I just gave up. Why they bother to come I don't know. The Hindus can't even eat the English food. They have some curry at home, then come to watch us, like monkeys!'

'Talking of monkeys,' said Lady Chambers, who had now noticed the cockroach and brushed it discreetly on to the floor, 'I visited the menagerie last weekend. It is surprisingly interesting, you know. There are tigers, elephants, all kinds of goats . . .'

'Oh, those poor things!' Emily chipped in, her eyes filling with tears, 'they are half starved. I went once but I could not stand to go again. They are so thin their bones stick out!'

51

'But did you see the insects?' continued Lady Chambers. 'I am so interested in these insects for my botanizing, I have instructed my ayah to catch me some of these delightful specimens. You know she didn't understand and after a week brought me simply five dead cockroaches! Of course I beat her for that!'

Lizzie fingered her programme, printed on blue and white satin and edged with lace, and looked around the room. There were officers in gold and scarlet, ladies in red and yellow satin, their hair piled on top of their heads, men in dark bottle-green dinner jackets, and the governor general, Lord Dalhousie himself, resplendent in gold-encrusted uniform. She tried to remember every detail of the room in her mind so that she could describe it when she next wrote to her father. There was the American jewel-dealer, Mr Araboun, who had given an emerald necklace to the wife of a major and caused an awful scandal. He was in the corner, turning his attentions to a new matron. 'Let me take that fly out of your champagne, madam,' he was saying, leaning over her so that his chest brushed against her shoulders, making her go scarlet with delight. There was Dr Ferrel, a great favourite among the ladies in Calcutta, too, who had a good reputation for curing malaria. 'We need more doctors,' he was saying to Whittle, 'not more shops! D'you know the cemeteries of Calcutta are full of Europeans who have died before forty?'

'But better shops mean better food, and better standards of cleanliness,' argued Whittle. 'It'd be a fine do with all doctors and no shops. What'd you do for shaving soap then, eh?'

A group of officers sat lounging in a corner of the room, and three rose to mingle with the guests. Lizzie noticed that one officer was trying to attract Emily's attention. She tapped her on the shoulder to bring her to notice him.

'But they are so black, such strange skin . . . why Mr Patcham!' Emily coloured slightly. 'How d'ye do? We thought you'd all be doing drill or whatever you do . . . and . . . and . . .' Emily's eyes rested on a figure behind Mr Patcham, a tall, elegant man with broad shoulders and lazy eyes. 'It can't be true! I can't believe my eyes! Why Lizzie . . .'

But Lizzie was standing dumbly as she looked into the face of Mr Patcham's friend. She was aware only of her cheeks, burning with a red flush that spread slowly up from her bare shoulders, transfusing her face with colour. She staggered slightly.

'It's your old friend, Richard Applevale, to be sure!' cried Emily, reaching over warmly to grasp him by the hand. 'Why, what pleasure to see a familiar face around these dusty parts! When we last met, you were riding along the cliffs, I remember well. I'm sure you look back on those days with some nostalgia, no? I sometimes long for a good old English mist! George, look who's here . . . you've heard the good news, have you not, Mr Applevale, that Lizzie and George are married now . . . and George is setting up a shop in Cawnpore . . . and I am to meet Azimullah Khan again . . . well, what chance! Now we can all enjoy the ball together! What fun!'

As she prattled on, Emily seemed unaware of the colour draining from Richard's face as he icily took George Whittle's hand and gave a stiff bow. Whittle in his turn looked murderously at the young officer. His face grew red and his eyes bulged threateningly. He seemed about to lose control when he caught sight of the governor general and regained some composure. He stood, silently trembling, his fists clenching and unclenching.

'Good evening,' said Richard. His face first showed astonishment, which soon changed to reproach and finally a kind of disbelieving rage.

Whittle grunted. Lizzie said nothing. All she could do was look at him in despair, pleading with her eyes for him to understand. But her looks met an ice-cold wall. She turned away. In his look she had seen only hatred; there was no hope.

In the distance a brass band played a small air to announce dinner. Everyone around her murmured and started to assemble their things. In despair Lizzie, her heart aching, took her husband's arm to go into the banqueting

53

hall. As she passed Richard, all she was aware of was his physical presence, his eyes burning into her, the warmth of his body almost scorching her as she passed him. She would have given anything to fling herself into his arms and kiss him. Instead her arm hung limply at her side, and her whole spirit felt utterly downcast.

When she sat at the dining table she couldn't eat. She sat motionless as course after course came in, soup, salmon from Scotland, sardines from the Mediterranean, beef, pheasant, cakes, trifles, madeira. All the while the room seemed to her in a kind of dreadful blur, with just the odd snatch of conversation drifting her way in a meaningless gabble.

'You know this floor took fifteen men *squatting* for *two days* to polish it . . .'

'She behaved appallingly, she had drunk herself quite silly with cherry brandy when Mrs Sanders threw a pastry at her to keep her quiet and we all laughed and laughed till we got home . . .'

' . . . in the middle of the street! Imagine, we had the train to catch and the natives had left us stranded in the palanquins! Mr Forbes had told them they'd not get one rupee more out of him, but we never expected such behaviour! So what could we do but call them back . . .'

'Really, the wives of the military are so vulgar, such "low toss". She was endlessly talking of suckling babies in the very room where we were sketching and her hair was curled quite shockingly . . .'

Lizzie sipped her madeira listlessly. She longed to return to the bungalow and to blot out everything in sleep.

On the other side of the room at his table, Richard was feeling no more cheerful. Patcham had already commented on his black looks and had called for more madeira. 'Come on, old man!' he yelled across the table. 'You look as if you're about to be hanged! What's the matter? Seen a ghost? Or are you still brooding about the annexation of Oudh?' The guests at the table laughed and Patcham turned to his guests. 'He gets very upset about the annexation of Oudh, does old Applevale. Thinks it was the most

54

disastrous thing we've done in India. . . .'

'Oh, come, he has a point,' argued a plain lady on Richard's left. 'My father says . . .'

Like Lizzie, Richard left his meal virtually untouched. He could hardly hear the conversation going on on either side of him. What on earth was Lizzie doing here, in Calcutta? It was bad enough she'd got married, worse that Whittle was going to Cawnpore — but to appear, to torment him, in public! And what was that look she'd thrown him meant to mean? As if trying to apologize? He shook his head bitterly and angrily. He wouldn't think of her. She was nothing to him now, nothing.

He felt a pushing at his back and, turning swiftly, saw Patcham, tugging at his chair. 'Come on, out of your reverie! The band has struck up and you will miss the first dance if you don't look smart! What a dull companion you are, to be sure! The lady on your left has been making eyes at you all evening and you have done nothing but mumble at her. Get your feet moving! It's the polka!'

Richard rose and shook his head. He put his hand on Patcham's arm. 'Thanks,' he said, 'but I'm not feeling too well.' Patcham's look immediately turned to alarm. So often in India, being ill was the prelude to death.

'Well, you don't *look* well!' he said, in concern. 'Would you like me to call Dr Ferrel?'

Richard shook his head. 'I'll get some fresh air,' he said. 'Got a cheroot, Patcham? I'll go out for a quiet smoke and then I'll feel better.' And, taking the cigar offered to him, Richard stepped on to the verandah overlooking the vast, dark gardens of Government House.

When the music had started, Lizzie had made her excuses too. So much gaiety only heightened her misery. Stepping on to the shell-covered path, she felt soothed by the cool air, and the smell of jasmine, passion flowers and honeysuckle. The sky was the deep blue-black that only an Indian sky can be, studded with pin-pricks of silver that seemed so close Lizzie felt that if she were to put out her hand she could reach for the very sky and pull it over her, like a glittering shawl. Far away a firework exploded into the sky, sending sprays of shimmering red and yellow fragments into the air. In the distance she could hear the music of the band inside; then, if she listened more closely, the rhythmic sound of interminable drums from the city. In the garden the air was alive with the noise of insects, the chirping of the frogs, the 'chip chip' of the grasshoppers, the hooting of the night-hawk.

She moved further along until she stopped in the rose garden. Turning back to look at the house, she could see the long yellow rectangles of light from the ballroom windows and the shadowy dancers passing to and fro under the dazzling chandelier. Then her attention was caught by a dark silhouette on the verandah. She smelt the slight bitter smell of a cheroot. And then, as her eyes focused more clearly in the darkness, she realized it was Richard. She stood rooted to the spot. Would he notice her? Was there any point if he did notice her? The figure started to approach. Yes, it was Richard. There was no mistaking those broad shoulders, the familiar steady gait. She could see his face, bright, expectant and loving, and her eyes filled with tears. At last she could explain. She ran towards him, expectantly, clutching tightly her lifted gown as she moved along the path. 'Richard!' she whispered. 'Please listen! It's me, Lizzie!'

He seemed to freeze at the sound of her voice, as if he had been hoping that it had not been her in the garden. For one moment they stood, facing each other, their eyes burning. A look of anguish crossed Richard's face as he saw her. He reached out his arms as if to take her, and then suddenly he let them fall to his sides in despair.

'What have you done?' he muttered, staring at her. She began to talk but her whispers seemed like dead leaves on the night air. She didn't seem to be making any sense and her words stopped in her throat. She simply wanted to look at him, hold him, be with him. She looked imploringly at him, clasping her hands in front of her. But there seemed to be no way of getting through to him. His expression was blank.

'It's too late now. There's no point,' he said. And turning

on his heel he made his way back to the verandah with a quick, firm step. He broke a cheroot in two, entered the ballroom and leant close to a woman who nodded with pleasure.

Lizzie ran after him impulsively, but was stopped near the window by George Whittle.

'And where've you been?' he asked angrily.

'Oh, looking for you,' replied Lizzie in confusion. 'And I went out for a quick breath of air, it's so hot in here. Oh, George, can't we go home now? I've got such a headache.'

Whittle laughed, and mopped his brow with his handkerchief. 'Want to go home do you, now? After I've gone to all the trouble to get us here in the first place, all the gratitude I get is a headache! You go when I say you go!'

On the other side of the ballroom Lizzie saw Richard, dancing. He was pressing the woman close to him, and as he turned with the music she caught the fury in his eyes.

'Please!' Lizzie's grip on Whittle's arm tightened and she found herself clinging to him, suddenly finding a kind of strength in his stolid, chunky build. At least she knew where she was with him. And in a strange way, knowing that made it easier. He was an ambitious, hard-working box-wallah, ruthless but unequivocal.

'Half an hour, Lizzie,' he said firmly.

Later that night when they had returned to the bungalow, Whittle did not say good night in the hall as usual. He stared Lizzie boldly in the eyes. 'You'll sleep with me tonight, hear?' His voice was rough, commanding.

In bed Lizzie surrendered completely to her husband's caresses. She felt so abandoned now, so lost, that any affection was balm. As they lay in the darkness, she started to cry, feeling totally lost. She could not even find the energy to move away from George's body.

'So, you're coming to like me more, now you see how your fancy friend behaves towards you, eh?' said Whittle, half waking from his sleep, as she shifted her position. She didn't say what she felt – that anything, anyone, would do – but her silence said it for her. With a scowl that was a

57

mixture of frustration and pain, Whittle pushed her roughly from him.

'Go and sleep in your own bed, with your little love-child!' he whispered, bitterly.

Wearily Lizzie made her way to her room, and fell into a deep sleep. One hand lay across the cot beside her bed and was held in such a tight grip by the baby that she could not bear to prise his fingers from it. She knew, after all, how he felt. And she was only thankful that soon they would be on their way to Cawnpore, leaving Calcutta and Richard Applevale behind. Perhaps there, at least, she could start to rebuild her life.

7

There is a peculiar light at dawn, in India. Perhaps it seems particularly strange to the traveller from England who is not used to rising at five to catch the only cool time of the day. To Lizzie the misty blueness of the sky and the first glimpse of the sun glinting on the dome of a temple seemed almost uncanny. As she stepped into the carriage that was to take them to Cawnpore, she was filled with a kind of elation. The doctor had pronounced her fit, Whittle had done well by purchasing good stock in Calcutta, Emily was in a fever of excitement at the prospect of meeting Azimullah – and, perhaps most important of all for Lizzie, she would be away from Calcutta, and away from Richard or any chance of meeting him ever again. Even in the unlikely event of his not receiving her letters, he *must* have understood what had happened, she felt. After all, his family would have told him that his father had been seriously ill – he must have been able to put two and two together, he would have known that she would never have married George Whittle except in utter desperation. He had obviously not even bothered to think. No doubt he had women in India . . . for him it had all been nothing but a cheap romance, as meaningless as a story from a penny dreadful. For her, it had been real, her whole life. However, she thought, she must now forget him. And as she looked out of the window of the carriage which was now moving along the roads, she knew that it would be easier to forget when she was away from Calcutta.

Looking down above the baggage strapped to the sides of the carriage she could see the first sleepy Indians starting to rise from their wretched homes by the wayside. Some were already squatting in groups brewing tea around fires. A mother suckled a baby on the street while her other children ran after the carriage shouting, '*Baksheesh! Baksheesh!*'. Lizzie was struck by the hatred in the woman's apparently impassive stare. She instinctively held the baby tighter to her as if to protect him from any malevolence that might come from those dead, kohl-covered eyes.

Whittle had left an hour earlier to supervise the manoeuvre of so much of his stock over the bumpy roads; Lizzie, Emily and the baby followed behind in another carriage with two businessmen for company. Now, at last, they were really drawing away from Calcutta, and, looking out of the window, Lizzie could start to see the shapes of the city finally retreating into the distance. What relief! Lizzie leant back into the silky cushions and shut her eyes.

'Going to Cawnpore, eh?' said one of the businessmen, leaning forward in a friendly way and producing a cheroot. 'Mind if I smoke? Good.' Without waiting for an answer, he lit it. 'Yes, you'll like it well enough there, I'll be bound. Small place, but lots of opportunities for men like Mr Whittle, and there are some good features there. Race course, racquets courts, ice-houses, theatricals . . .'

'And a well-stocked burial ground,' muttered his companion.

'Don't be so pessimistic,' said the other, smiling at the women and shaking his head. 'There are some entertaining people there. General Wheeler, for instance. Met him? You will. Married to an Indian girl and knows the language better than any man in India. Good friends with the Nana Sahib too – he's the Maharajah of Bithur – so you can be sure you won't find any problems there, at least.'

'Oh, we won't have any *problems*!' Emily couldn't resist chipping in, 'You see – *I* know Azimullah Khan, I met him in London. I'm sure you gentlemen have heard of him.'

There was a slight pause as the two men looked at each other. Then the first one coughed and nodded. 'Ah, yes indeed,' he said. 'We have met him – perhaps we know more *of* him. But anyway, he is a good companion to be sure.' There was another slight pause and the first man changed the subject, by leaning over jovially and patting the baby on the cheek. 'Fine little baby you've got there, too, Mrs Whittle! One thing you have to say for Indians, they may be no more trustworthy than young boys in an orchard, but when it comes to the little ones, they're kindness itself.'

His companion grunted. 'Don't be too sure,' he said, spitting out of the window after this statement. 'I wouldn't trust an Indian further than I could throw him.'

'Come now, Robert, don't frighten the ladies,' said his friend, in a jocular way. 'They're like children.' He nodded his head laughingly at the man beside them and turned back to the two women. 'He's one of these scaremongers, aren't you, Robert. One little incident, one sepoy who won't bite the bullet and has a bit too much *bhang* and Robert's saying they're all going to rise up and murder us in our beds. Why, take Raoul, my groom, my syce –' he jerked his thumb in the direction of the road. 'I've had him for fifteen years – *fifteen years* – and he's been like a father, brother and a child to me, all in one. His wife is looking after my children at this very moment in Calcutta, and I know she loves them more than she loves her own.'

His companion grunted again. '*Un* – likely,' he snorted. 'I tell you, I'm getting out of this damn country as soon as I can. It's written clear as day, you fool. They're not quiet, they're disturbed. Didn't you hear, the infantry just rose in Lucknow? Why look.' And he pointed out of the window at the broken hanging of a telegraph wire. 'They're even pulling the wires down. Think they're magic and we're trying to put a spell on them all. Think we've come to take their religion away from them. Don't like the land system. Don't like the reforms. Don't blame 'em. How'd you like it, John, if these niggers came to England and started building damned – excuse me, I do beg your pardon, ladies – building Hindu temples up and down Hyde Park? Or bringing their caste system in behind our green baize doors so the butler couldn't buttle without a second man to help him with the tea and the maid couldn't eat if a gardener's shadow passed over her food?'

The first man was now roaring with laughter. 'And just think of all those Indians sleeping out down the Mall!

Come on, Robert! I've never heard such rubbish! What if—what if . . . but they *haven't*.'

'But if—then would you be walking around Kensington Gardens in a dhoti? You'd be sending them packing! I'm damn sure I would! And that's what they're going to do to us before a few weeks is up. I can feel it in the atmosphere.'

But his friend continued to laugh and before long they had both fallen back in the corner of the coach into a snoring sleep. Lizzie craned her neck out of the window once more. Behind them there was only a cloud of grey dust swirling up; in front she could just see the endless landscape, a patch of trees, and the sun, ever-rising above them. She decided to follow the example of their companions and soon fell into a doze.

By midday it was so hot Lizzie felt she was in a furnace. It was always impossible to anticipate in the early morning quite how hot the Indian sun would be at noon. The travellers paused to take dinner in the shade under a group of banyan trees, their strange snakelike roots hanging down around the trunks like the drips from some giant candle. The bearers sprinkled water on the ground in the shade to make it cooler for them, but it was still almost intolerable. After dinner the syces slept, flies buzzing round their faces. Nearby a group of elephants that were carrying Whittle's stock shifted from heavy foot to heavy foot and sometimes, in a torment of annoyance, reached down to hurl a trunkful of dust over themselves to deter the flies. The beautiful Arab horses lay down gasping for breath, and everywhere the air hung heavy, an oppressive, dry heat that seemed to push in on Lizzie, suffocating her. She hardly knew how she would survive the journey, for it meant three more weeks travelling like this before they would arrive at Cawnpore.

But after a few days they became more used to it. The baby slept most of the time; Lizzie had got into the routine of the early rises and the swift, sudden dusks, and in the cool of the evening grew almost to look forward to the quiet chatter of the natives, the clink of their bowls as they prepared the food outside the bungalows where they lodged each night, the wailing chants that continued, night after night, despite protests from Whittle that he couldn't sleep with that 'nigger racketing' all night. Each day passed more easily than the last, helped by the fact that as they travelled further north it became very slightly cooler. It was still hardly bearable, but after the cruel heat of Calcutta, Lizzie and Emily were grateful for even one degree's lessening of temperature.

The evening before they reached Cawnpore Emily became even more excited than usual. They had stopped at a rickety bungalow for their last supper on the road. The sun was setting, casting long shadows on the ground; the sky was a hazy purple, and a pale golden dust seemed to appear on the line of thin, bony cows on the skyline. As the sun sank, the landscape became suffused with mist, like a huge bowl of rosy milk. They all sat down on the verandah and even the travelling businessmen, usually insensitive to the sights around them, were stunned into silence by the view. Finally they finished. Whittle sucked his hookah and Lizzie knitted a small shawl for the baby while staring out in awe over the grey-pink light on the sloping fields that stretched endlessly in front of them.

Only Emily was impatient. She had left the supper table early and was now below them, delightedly trying on the ayah's sari, much to Lizzie's amusement and Whittle's discomfort. The ayah grinned and smiled in the shadows at Emily, clapping her hands saying, 'Pretty memsahib! Pretty memsahib!' In minutes it got darker and darker until Emily could only be seen in the light of the fire that burnt below.

'Take that rag off, Emily!' shouted Whittle from his chair. 'You're behaving like a gypsy!'

'Oh, but George, I just want to see what it's like to look like an Indian lady! Please, she is going to show me another way of trying it, just a minute longer!'

The ayah crept forward, bent and low in the darkness, and with swift movements readjusted the folds so that the bright cotton fell in new ripples down Emily's side. The servants chattered busily in a corner, staring in obsequious delight at the European lady, dressed up as an Indian. 'Pretty . . . pretty . . . pretty . . .' they whispered, nodding their heads again and again. The ayah nodded, smiling, and then, rising, jabbed at Emily's forehead with her thumb, pressing a red holy mark in her forehead. The servants applauded again, continuing their excitement.

'Why, I am ever so Indian, George!' exclaimed Emily, revolving round and pressing the palms of her hands together towards him in an Indian greeting.

Suddenly there was the sound of laughter. The ayah started rocking on her heels, laughing and giggling; soon the whole group of servants was laughing and pointing. Emily was confused and began to take the sari off; Whittle rose from his basket chair and unsteadily started to walk down the steps of the verandah, his fists clenched. 'You make fun of my sister, you dogs, and you'll regret it!' he shouted. 'Be quiet! Take that damn thing off, Emily! Be quiet!'

But they wouldn't stop. They continued in an endless chorus, now laughing, chanting and pointing; then, with no warning, a stone cut through the air and fell, insultingly, at Emily's feet. The two businessmen got up and looked alarmed. More stones followed, and more and more, until Emily was holding her hands up to her face, crying.

'Raoul!' shouted one, 'Raoul! Put a stop to this! Syce! Where are you! Raoul!'

The noise built and built; then a tall Indian stepped forward into the darkness and with a few words from him the servants became quiet. Emily took off the sari, shaking now, and the ayah slunk off into the shadows.

'See? Just like children,' said the businessman, his hearty voice belying his lack of conviction. 'Nothing to worry about. Get a bit out of hand these days. But loyal people like Raoul can deal with them. Good work, Raoul!' he shouted, throwing him a rupee.

In the firelight Lizzie saw Raoul's face. Its impassive features split into a grasping smile as he reached to catch the coin. And as he opened his fist to seize the money, Lizzie was the only one to see a rainfall of tiny stones fall from his hand. With a chill shudder she realized the truth. No one could be trusted, after all.

Cawnpore reminded Lizzie of a provincial town – though Lizzie had come to the conclusion that everywhere in India was provincial. It was small, gossip-ridden, comfortable, claustrophobic, with all the assets and disadvantages of a small English community. Everyone noticed who went to church, and who didn't and who was late and who wasn't. Everyone noticed who flirted with whom, and gave their views on who ought, in their opinion, to be flirting with whom. The first week was passed in an exhausting round of visits from everyone in Cawnpore who wanted not only to see the new arrivals but to stare at their bungalow, criticize their furniture, tut-tut about their taste in clothes, envy their garden or give some opinion or other about everything in sight.

The bungalow was small but adequate for the family. It had a thatched roof, a newly painted verandah, and a large main room. Whittle had seen to it that it was well furnished, and so there were chintz-covered sofas, basket chairs, a leather-covered writing desk in the sitting room, not to mention a piano (although the notes stuck in the heat), brand new China matting on the floor and a bureau. He had organized the delivery of a billiard table that after a week was already warping in the heat, and had engaged a staff of fifty who all lived in small shacks at the end of the garden. When Lizzie protested about the numbers of servants, Whittle had explained tersely that because of the caste system there had to be one man to perform every single different task in the house, and that each man had a family to support.

It was the garden that was the prettiest feature of the bungalow. Whoever had lived in it before had lavished a lot of care on the garden, and there were palms and mango trees giving cool shade; and in the beds grew convolvulus, morning glory, moonflowers, passion flowers and jasmine and oleander, all of which gave off a wonderful spicy perfume in the evenings.

For a few days Lizzie felt almost content there, concentrating on polishing up the brass lamps, seeing to the curtains, working out how to run the house efficiently; indeed she could have felt quite resigned to her lot if it hadn't been for Emily. For Emily was in such a state of excitement that she had wanted to send word to Azimullah Khan the very day they arrived saying that they would welcome a call. But even George Whittle had thought this too forward.

'Wait a while, Emily,' he cautioned. 'It would be much better if he were to find out himself that we had come, and for him to visit us. You've done well for yourself so far . . .' and his eyes wandered to the large ring on her hand. 'Don't upset the balance of things now.'

But Emily could only just be restrained. She had to go out, to be seen. For the whole of the first week she continually shopped, with her servants, in the busy Chandni Chowk, the exotic marketplace of Cawnpore. She made extra efforts with her clothes, striking an odd figure in her blue silk dress and carrying her sunshade, surrounded by squatting Indians hammering at pots, offering her handfuls of herbs from large sacks and being jostled by the water-carriers with their great leather bags that dripped on to the dust. In the evening she sang louder than usual at the piano, as if she thought that by raising her voice Azimullah might be reminded of her by the distant strains of English ballads.

Everyone in the household had been slowly maddened by Emily's high state of excitement, her tension at the sound of any elephant or carriage that passed by, followed by a panicky gaiety that she would maintain while keeping an eye on the window, hoping that through the dampened rush blinds she might catch a glimpse of the dark shape of her Indian admirer. So it was with great relief that Lizzie was finally informed by a liveried native that he hoped she would accept a call from Azimullah Khan the following day.

Lizzie spent most of that day helping Emily try on different dresses and tying her hair in every different kind of knot she could imagine; later it was spent trying to persuade Emily to stay quietly indoors sewing instead of actually waiting at the window. At last, to everyone's relief, Azimullah arrived, with a retinue of servants who settled outside on the lawn like a flock of twittering birds. Lizzie went to the door to greet him.

'How delightful to meet you after we have heard so much about you!' she said, holding out her hand warmly. Azimullah smiled back a shy, delightful smile, and pressed her hand to his lips, a habit, thought Lizzie, that he surely must have picked up in Europe. She had to admit that he was a strikingly good-looking man. He had a slate-grey-brown face, immaculate white teeth and even features. His turban was gleaming white, with a single diamond set in the middle, and he wore a richly embroidered coat of brown, with thin, black trousers.

'Come inside, please,' Lizzie led the way.

'Thank you, madam.'

When he came into the sitting room, Emily blushed bright red. She could not hide her delight at seeing him. Her pleasure burst over her face and made her eyes sparkle, but she just rose and smiled, nervous and joyful.

Azimullah gazed at her, as if in awe, and suddenly fell on one knee, crying dramatically: 'What a delight! I am your obedient servant! What heaven to see you, Miss Whittle! I am thinking we will never meet again when I left England, but now my prayers are answered. . . .'

'Oh, come now . . .' Emily smiled and turned aside to hide her feelings.

'I am sincere, Miss Whittle, I am honoured and delighted . . .'

Lizzie had to conceal a smile at his behaviour. She felt he must have been to a great many romantic theatricals in London to have picked up such affectations. She gestured to him to sit, and he moved to the nearest chair to Emily, looking into her eyes all the while as if speaking secrets to her through his intense stare. Then he dropped his gaze and his sharp white eyes swept around the sitting room. His expression changed.

'I am thinking that your brother had bigger property, Miss Whittle,' he said, as he accepted a cup of tea from a servant. 'This is being very nice, very nice, but I am thinking it was bigger.'

Emily went slightly pale and looked to Lizzie for support. 'Oh, I'm sure he must have given the wrong impression by mistake,' she apologized.

'Wrong impression,' murmured Azimullah, half to himself, as if he were storing the phrase away for future use.

'You see most of his money is in his *shop* –' again Emily turned to Lizzie pleadingly.

'My husband is a very wealthy man, Mr . . . er . . . Khan,' said Lizzie speaking with confidence. That was at least true. 'We have quite simple tastes ourselves.' She stared him boldly in the eye and was disconcerted when he suddenly roared with laughter, his whole face lighting up with an enchanting smile.

'Myself, I do *not* have simple tastes!' he said, leaning back. 'I have had enough of simple tastes in my youth. I shall enjoy showing you both my own tastes – and my master's. They are not simple at all! And yet –' and here his mood changed, as he leant forward conspiratorially, 'they have to be simple, very simple, because of what your government has done to us!' Then he relaxed again, at ease. 'But we can be friends, can we not? Just because our masters are not friends, we can be friends? I am great friends with Miss Whittle in London,' he added to Lizzie, 'but of all the friends I have in London she is the only one to come and pay me a visit here! And I am so delighted I have persuaded the Nana Sahib to give a fireworks display for you! And there are so many things . . .'

'Oh, but you shouldn't . . .'

Azimullah cut Emily short and gazed into her eyes. 'No, I shouldn't,' he murmured, 'for what are fireworks compared to the eyes of a beautiful woman?'

Lizzie felt extremely uncomfortable and shifted in her wicker chair. 'We shall be delighted to attend your firework display,' she said. 'And of course we shall be friends.'

'Yes?' Azimullah turned on her with an animated face. 'And you must not be believing these tales they tell of Delhi. It is nothing. And you must remember you are safe here with me. Stay with me, and you will be safe!'

'Delhi? Why, what has happened there?'

Azimullah looked surprised. 'Why, they say the sepoys have mutinied today and have put the old king in power, Bahadur Shah! He is eighty-two! Very clever man. He can change into a fly at will and go from place to place like that, it is true. You may say it is not possible, but I have seen it for myself.'

'Mutiny? In Delhi?' Lizzie clutched at the arms of her chair in panic. 'It's not true!'

'No, no, dear madam,' said Azimullah, shaking his head, 'it is not true, it is a big lie. You must not believe it for one moment. It is wicked lie put about by some Hindus. We love the British here, all Indian people love the British, I am your friend, you will see.' And he stretched out his arms as if to include them both and smiled reassuringly at them. Emily smiled but Lizzie did not. She knew now with certainty that the mutiny in Delhi was not a lie. All her suspicions had been confirmed. The infantry had risen up in Lucknow, that she knew was true – but now Delhi! Where next? Would they be safe even in Cawnpore? Startled by her thoughts she took another look at their new Indian friend who was now deep in conversation with Emily, having changed the subject completely. Would he be any help to them? A trickle of doubt seeped into her heart. Azimullah, she now knew, was charming. And the reason he was charming was because he always said what his listeners wanted to hear. Like so many Indians, he thought that to be liked and trusted, a man had above all to please – a delightful characteristic in society, but a deadly one in the dangerous days that lay ahead.

8

Having heard so much about the terrible poverty of the Nana Sahib from Azimullah, Whittle, Lizzie and Emily couldn't help but be surprised at the splendour of his palace when they arrived for the banquet given in honour of their arrival.

'I was given to understand he hadn't a brass farthing,' whispered Whittle to Lizzie as they entered, pointing to the dazzling chandeliers and exotic carpets hanging on the wall.

Emily whispered back in his defence, 'But he has a retinue of fifteen hundred to support,' she said. 'He is used to finery, too, it is his rank. Azimullah told me the Nana is not fond of simple tastes any more than he is himself.'

Whittle gave a snort of a laugh and Emily put her hand on his arm to quieten him. 'His rank! You're getting some fancy ideas these days!' And he smiled at Emily, obviously pleased.

But indeed it was difficult to imagine what financial problems the Nana Sahib had. The palace was enormous, surrounded by four domed minarets. It was set at the top of a steep cliff overlooking Cawnpore, and it was made entirely of a pale green marble. The gates were wrought of gold, the bars being the trunks of the elephant god Ganesh, each head studded with a ruby eye. The hall was vast and domed, and the reception chamber was lit by French chandeliers that sparkled above the hundred or so guests.

Everyone was dressed in their best – dresses of shot silk and pink palamine and embroidered shawls – and the chatter of English voices jarred slightly with the whirring strains from a small band of Indian musicians who played sitting on a long, low table at one side.

They made their way to a group, and Lizzie couldn't

help but pause by a window to look out. There was an enormous garden, and she could see the corner of the Nana's famous menagerie where he kept elephants, camels, horses, dogs, pigeons, falcons, wild asses and apes. Next to it was an 'English section' where all sorts of cows, dogs, horses and sheep were kept in a paddock.

Whittle's touch on her arm made her turn back, and she surveyed the scene. On the walls old oil paintings were hung next to Indian miniatures; a large Queen Anne wardrobe, with doors warped in the heat, stood next to an ancient Hindu carving; in the centre of the room on the polished floor was an enormous inlaid rosewood table on which lay copies of *Blackwoods* magazine beside ancient manuscripts; racing magazines from London, too, were piled on a throne in a far corner with cloth woven with silver and gold. Glass cabinets contained everything from chipped willow-pattern plates to rare Indian gongs made from fine beaten gold. Everywhere there was evidence of the Nana's obsession to collect objects. The room was sumptuous and strange, the English furniture jarring oddly with the Indian architecture and the sickly sweet smell of joss sticks.

A serious-looking elderly Indian in a long white shirt politely shook their hands and introduced himself as the Nana's astrologer. He asked their dates of birth and then gestured for them to join the other guests.

Immediately another servant came up to them carrying a silver tray, and brought them chipped tumblers full of scotch, offering them pappadams as an accompanying titbit. Lizzie and Whittle refused but Emily took one and instantly declared it delicious.

'George Whittle!' A man from the group disengaged himself and came over.

'Greenway!' Whittle introduced them and Lizzie remembered that he owned a shop in Cawnpore and was eager to involve George as a partner rather than a competitor in this small outpost which served 10,000 English customers. ('Not that you need worry about that,' Greenway had told Whittle before. 'The Nana Sahib will buy

71

anything English you import. He may say he is poor but he's not too poor to give up his food from Fortnums, his stiltons, his anchovy paste, his shortbread or his jars of ginger!') 'It is good that in these troubled times there are still pioneers like you arriving, determined against all odds to come out and make an honest penny and not flee like the rest of them!'

'Flee? Who's talkin' of fleein'?' A short, grey-haired man of around sixty-five and formally dressed had turned from his conversation to join them.

'Ah – General Wheeler, the man who commands all the forces of Cawnpore,' said Mr Greenway by introduction. 'He will not hear of fleeing, I think.'

'No, indeed,' said Wheeler, and his voice had a sweet Irish lilt to it. Lizzie suddenly felt homesick. She couldn't help but see something of her father in this gentle old man, and in her mind she sent him a quick prayer, hoping that he was still well, and happy. Though the English voice should be no surprise to her, it always sounded strange and de-lightful simply because India was so very different. They shook hands. 'I cannot understand why people talk of fleein'. Here we are, the best of friends with the Nana Sahib, a man I like as well as admire – he is a fine billiard player to be sure – and yet *still* I hear talk of fleein'.'

'Many families took off this morning down the river, I hear – no doubt after that bad news from Delhi,' said Mr Greenway, but then, observing Wheeler's disapproving stare, changed the subject. 'Have you seen the Nana Sahib's collection of guns, Whittle?' he asked. 'Let me take you. He has pistols and guns made by Purdey and Egg – it would be pleasure enough to see such weapons in England, and here you find them all in Cawnpore! Ladies, excuse us!'

General Wheeler smiled at the two women, his kind old eyes twinkling. 'Well, I hope you're not alarmed by this foolish talk,' he said pleasantly, 'for I can assure you there is nothing to worry about. We have four native regiments here and they are as loyal, every man, as you would find.'

'And how many English?' asked Lizzie. Despite his kindness she didn't feel reassured.

'There's one Englishman for every ten sepoys, and some say this makes 'em even more nervous! But I say, ten loyal sepoys are worth one lazy English soldier, and I've seen some lazy English soldiers in my time, I can tell you.' He fingered his white moustache. 'Ah, they're not like they used to be, the English soldiers. They used to be good men, who respected the Indians, and wanted to learn Hindustani and the customs, too. Now they are drunk all day, and they abuse the servants. To be sure I'd sometimes rather a sepoy than an English lout!'

'You seem to admire the Indians then – like me?' said Emily nervously, and proudly.

'Well, m'dear, I'm married to one, so you cannot get friendlier than that, can you? My wife is a darlin' woman and a great friend of the Nana . . . here, where are you . . . come and meet these two ladies, dearest . . .'

But before he could introduce them, a great gong sounded, and at one end of the room the Nana stood, clapping his hands. 'Dinner, my friends!' he cried. He was a small, very fat man of about forty with a thin black moustache, a turban, and great hooped earrings hung around his ears. His mouth was ruby-red, small and wet, as if he had licked his lips a great deal; his eyes were black as a raven's. Lizzie shuddered when she saw him; he had a cruel, indolent look about him that she found repulsive.

The guests filed into the dining room, yet another sumptuous hall with walls of beaten gold and statues of Indian gods set in niches around – the blue, many-armed Rama, the black, violent Kali, the strange elephant Ganesh, and Krishna, in blue. They waited until the Nana had seated himself cross-legged on a large carved Chippendale chair at one end of a long table that nearly filled the hall, and then sat down. Next to the Nana sat another Indian, Gupta Singh, Rajah of the Lake. He looked more elegant than the Nana, small, like him, but with finer features, and a slim figure. He stared back at Lizzie as she observed him and, beckoning the astrologer who had received them, whispered something in his ear before silently picking at the sweetmeats and ginger, observing the rest of the guests. Lizzie found herself wondering whose side Gupta Singh would be on if there were an uprising – the Indians', or General Wheeler's and the Nana Sahib's. And yet, she noticed, he looked kinder and wiser than the Nana Sahib. . . .

The table was enormous, about twenty feet long, covered with a damask tablecloth from England. Lizzie was surprised to find that when she picked up her napkin to put it on her lap it was, in fact, a small bedroom towel. The soup was served up in a trifle dish which had formed part of a dessert service belonging to the 9th Lancers – or at least so the coat of arms upon the dish proclaimed – and the ladle she was offered to serve herself with was a broken teacup.

She glanced across to Emily to express her surprise, but she was deep in conversation with Azimullah and seemed not to have noticed the social peculiarities of the Nana's dinner table. But the lady on her right, a woman of very dark complexion who introduced herself as Mrs Jacobi, winked at her dismay.

'He's quaint, ain't he?' she said, sipping her mulligatawny, 'but as long as the food's good, see if I mind how it's served! I've been here ten years now and I'm used to this!'

Lizzie smiled politely.

'Well, and are you enjoying life here?' continued Mrs Jacobi. 'It ain't half fun here, ain't it?'

'It is certainly very *hot*,' said Lizzie, sipping her soup.

'The soup or the weather?' asked a lady opposite, leaning over. 'My broad beans have done so badly this year, you wouldn't believe it. I had a servant tend them day and night, they were never left for a minute, and we only got one helping from the whole crop!'

'The climate, the soup – and the situation we're in – all hot!' said Lizzie, laughing. 'Tell me, what do you think of Bahadur Shah? Has he any power?'

'Bahadur who?' asked the lady opposite.

74

'Bahadur Shah, the king of Delhi – you know,' said Lizzie.

'Oh my, I don't know anything. Didn't they say they'd make him king of all India or something? Mad. No power, he's probably just an opportunist.'

'Why certainly not,' said Lizzie. 'He's over eighty, hardly an opportunist. He had to be persuaded to accept the role of king, a lot of pressure was put upon him.'

'Eighty? Really? Well, I never. I never knew that,' said the lady opposite helping herself to some sugared almonds that lay incongruously in the same dish as some sausages, still joined together at the ends.

'Why she knows more politics than I do, and she's only been here two weeks! I'm completely and utterly uninterested. Why, I must tell you such a funny thing. I got my tailor to copy a dress I had from Paris, a very old one I was ashamed to wear and got it back today – do you know, he'd even copied the patch and the darns to the very last stitch! What a do!'

The ladies near her laughed and talked among themselves. Lizzie felt excluded. She was depressed that there was no one here to whom she could talk, no one who shared her worries about the future.

The second course was fried fish with slices of stilton with a jar of Patum Peperium at her side with a spoon in it, to be served, Lizzie assumed, like mustard.

She tried again with Mrs Jacobi. 'Tell me,' she said, as she took a piece of fish and pushed the stilton back on to the serving dish, 'do you think we are safe here?'

Mrs Jacobi shrugged her shoulders. 'I'm sure I don't know,' she said, 'but we're safer here than anywhere else in India, that I believe. General Wheeler is in mighty thick with the Nana, he's almost more Indian than English these days, eats nothing but curries, his children are half Indian, too, like myself – oh, no, you wouldn't have noticed it, I know, it is hardly visible at all, it is always such a surprise to people when I tell them, they don't half get a shock! The Nana is a generous man, too, and adores the Europeans as you can see –' she laughingly pointed at her German champagne glass which was being filled with the best French claret. 'He is surrounded by Eurasians, like Mr Todd – have you met him – who translates *The Times* for him every morning, for the Nana knows scarcely any English. Oh, of course there are rumours in the bazaar – someone told me today that the Nana's guru had told him three years ago that in three years that he'd be as powerful as his father – but you can't believe that sort of nonsense. What we need here is more British trade, like your husband brings; less soldiers and more trade, that's the answer. There's nothing Indians like more. Forget about British reforms, British good works, all the good things the British have done like bringing justice into the villages, clearing the country of Thugs, abolishing suttee – forget all that. Give Indians a bargain and they're your friends for ever.'

'I hope we can offer the Nana a better bargain than the one Bahadur Shah will soon be offering him, then!' declared Lizzie uncertainly.

'Bahadur Shah! An old, weak man! He won't even live another six months! King of Delhi – pah! Talking of old kings, I have been working on some paintings of rajahs that my husband found – took them off a trader who wouldn't pay his bills. D'you like painting? There is no more fun than touching up these terrible Indian pictures and getting the perspective right. . . .'

By the time dinner had ended and the ladies had assembled in the original hall to chatter more, Lizzie felt she was going mad with boredom. She sat on her own on a silk-covered couch, twisting her evening purse in her hands. From a group nearby she could hear the consistent jabber of silly women.

'Why, I discovered that when I give my dhobi my sheets to wash, he lets them out as winding sheets! Have you ever heard anything like it' . . . 'She thought she'd married a three-hundred-a-year-dead-or-alive man, and when she found he was only a corporal she took off her shoe and hit him over the head with it until he bled! She'd be stuck with him now, and if he died she'd not get a single rupee as pension. Did we laugh!' . . . 'She always faints at dinner, it's only an excuse, why I've seen her faint five times now, we just let her fall into the soup and get on with it, wait till she revives, we can see through her and is she annoyed! I'll tell you!' . . . 'These servants, such a lazy lot, cramming themselves with ghee and sweetmeats and smoking their wretched chillums all day and all night, that you might as well think to train pigs.' . . .

Looking around the room, Lizzie rose up. No one noticed her. She moved to the other side – and still no one thought to look up. Silently she slipped through an archway and found herself outside in the cool of the evening. It was truly beautiful. She looked over the parapet at the little lights of Cawnpore below, smelling, in the cool of the evening, the heavy scent of night-flowers that hung in the air. She could hear the distant tingling of bells, the odd cry, the crunch of wheels below, then a distant blow on a trumpet from a drunken soldier. How strange it must be to be the Nana, she thought, and look out, apparently so powerful, over this tiny community of Europeans and Indians. Did he really want to ally himself with Wheeler? She knew how she would feel if she were him. She wandered along the colonnaded corridor slowly, pausing to look down as she walked. At one stop she suddenly heard the oddly familiar tick of an English clock and, unable to resist her curiosity, she turned the handle of the door from where the sound came and went in. Standing next to a large Buddha was an English grandfather clock.

She stopped in front of it and peered through the glass. 'D. Jacobi, Clock-Maker,' she read on the front. This must be Mrs Jacobi's husband. As she stood listening to the click of the pendulum, she felt it had a different sound to the clocks at home in Devon, which had a slow, comforting, steady rhythm. Each tick of this clock was an effort; it was as if the pendulum could only just manage to get from left to right and back again by its last breath.

She turned to observe the room before leaving it, rather nervous to remain longer, and saw the rich awnings above the huge bed covered in an embroidered bedspread, the glittering golden hangings, the exquisitely cut glass ornaments, the enamelled bowls piled high with rare fruits. Seeing a book of English love poems by the bed, she couldn't resist just turning a page and saw the inscription: 'To my wonderful love, Azimullah, your own Lucy.' She flinched slightly. It must be Azimullah's room. So, there had been other English women who had loved him, loved him even more than Emily, it seemed.

And then, looking up to admire the ceiling, she saw it. It was a fresco painted on the plaster around the chandelier. A naked woman was curled around the hook of the lamp, and all around her were men with whips. Drops of blood were pouring from the terrified woman's mouth and breasts, and a dog and a bull were assaulting her from behind. One man, completely naked, was leaping into the air upon her. . . .

Lizzie looked away, repelled and sickened by the sight. She put out a hand to a table to steady herself and as she pressed down on the outer panel so the back lifted up and there, in horrible array, was a line of whips, sticks, canes, loops of ropes, irons, clips and every kind of instrument of torture imaginable. Lizzie noticed the trace of blood on one of the sticks and suddenly felt faint. Could this be what was waiting for Emily, her friend? She hurriedly pulled down the dreadful cabinet and ran from the room. So *that* was what Azimullah Khan had meant by not having 'simple tastes'! That was what lay behind the thin shell of civilized pretence. Behind the culture, the books, the surface trimmings of British life lay this – utter depravity, sadism and lust.

Lizzie ran down the corridor, her heart racing with anger, only calming down when she heard the reassuring mutter of the English voices of the guests. Any chatter, however banal, was better than what she had witnessed. The men had joined the women after dinner and the air was smoky with cheroots. Lizzie pushed through the guests to find Emily, and finally discovered her sitting on a sofa, still engrossed in conversation with Azimullah.

'Emily, we must go,' she said breathlessly, 'it is terribly late. We must be off . . . I'll find George . . . he must take us away . . .' She stared Emily in the eyes as if to try to warn her, but Emily was far too radiant to notice any anxiety on her friend's face.

'It's only ten o'clock, Lizzie,' she said, looking up. 'Come, it's not that late. We haven't yet seen the fireworks. Sit down and join us. Azimullah has been fascinating me all evening with stories of life in India.'

'I could not be fascinating without a fascinating woman,' murmured Azimullah, keeping up his droning flow of compliments, 'and what is life in India without a fascinating woman. . .?'

Lizzie felt like striking him, but only flung him a cold, despising look. 'How dare you continue like this with my sister-in-law,' she whispered, in a low voice full of loathing. 'How dare you come trying to seduce her, complimenting her . . . I know what you are like, Azimullah, and . . .'

'Lizzie, how can you say such things?' Emily started to look at her tearfully. 'What has happened? You mustn't slander Azimullah like this! You're only saying it because you despise all Indians! You've been listening to wicked gossip! He's *wonderful*!'

'And I can tell you you're not the only woman who thinks so,' said Lizzie angrily. 'He's been leading you on, Emily, and I've seen with my own eyes, now . . . he is loathsome, despicable . . .'

Azimullah had got up now and a look of hatred had crossed his usually charming features. 'I think you are right, Mrs Whittle. It is late. I am being sorry that you are finding it in your heart to misjudge me . . . Madam.' He took Emily, who was now crying heartily, by the hand and raised her from the sofa. He looked at her, his calculating eyes covering the whole of her body in one glance. Then he bowed, kissed her hand and said: 'Good-bye, Miss Whittle. I hope I shall be seeing more of you. But perhaps in happier circumstances.'

And he walked across the hall to join another group of women.

'Oh, Lizzie, now look what you've done!' said Emily,

angry through her tears, 'you interfering, horrible, horrible person! You wait till I tell George! I hate you! You're jealous of me, that's what! You never loved George, nor anyone, you just pretend! Oh, I hate you!'

'It's for your own good!' cried Lizzie, trying to hold her, but she had flounced off, and she, George and Emily went home in complete silence, the atmosphere charged with hatred and suspicion.

9

'Now, you've got some explaining to do, you interfering witch!' Having heard Emily's story when he returned, Whittle now stood in the doorway of Lizzie's bedroom, his face red, his eyes bulging with fury. When he was angry his skin became blotchy, and beads of sweat stood out on his forehead. Down the passage there were the sounds of miserable sobbing from Emily's room.

'George, there's a good reason, I promise you . . .' Lizzie looked at Whittle imploringly, twisting her hands together. She wondered if the servants were still up, for he looked so violent and mad that she felt frightened.

'There'd better be!' Whittle replied. 'One of the main reasons I came to this stinking country is for my sister's sake, because she's fallen for an Indian, an Indian with rank and money, and as far as I can tell he's fallen for her, too. I come to this God-forsaken place to set up a shop here – oh, you may think it's for money and it is, but it's for Emily as well, mainly Emily . . .' He moved further into the room, hitting one fist into the other hand to make his point. 'I go to all this trouble, I get you all invited to the Nana Sahib's palace, and I can tell you I've had some expensive dealings with Azimullah, too, on Emily's behalf – though if you ever breathe a word of that I'll see you in hell! And then you go and insult him, you offend him disgracefully, in his own residence, you not only do this, you pull Emily away at the very moment the man is practically proposing marriage. . . !'

His anger got the better of him and he subsided into a coughing fit. Then, wiping one arm brusquely across his mouth, he seized Lizzie's wrist with the other and forced her roughly on to the bed in front of him.

'I thought you at least liked Emily, Lizzie, but all the time you were planning to sabotage her future!' he said, staring down at her. 'Your kind are all the same! You don't like to see anyone else get on the rung of your ladder. And the moment you see one of our hands get on to a rung, down you stamp with your aristocratic boot to kick us off. My God, if you were a man I'd thrash you!' His grip on her wrist tightened so much that it hurt and Lizzie winced, trying to pull away. Then, finding it impossible, she finally retaliated, stung by the injustice of his outburst.

'How dare you think I'd do such a thing to Emily!' she cried. 'I love your sister, George! I discovered something at that palace tonight, and if you knew what it was you'd thank me for saving Emily from a horrible fate rather than insult me! You'd be on your knees to me with gratitude! You think I'd wish Emily any harm? It's because I care for her that I got her away. You don't trust me, do you, not one jot!'

'And why should I?' asked Whittle bitterly. 'When I marry you and find you're carrying another man's child? Why should I trust you?'

Lizzie paused. She felt defeated. Whittle would always have the last word. She should never have married him. Anything would have been better than this, this endless humiliation. She looked down; she couldn't bear to look any longer into that puffy, contemptuous face. 'Well, let my warnings go hang, then,' she said softly and bitterly. 'Go ahead, let her marry him, see if I care. Let her be maimed and humiliated. You wouldn't care, would you? As long as she marries well, that's all you care about, isn't it? Not whether she is happy or not. . . .' Her voice tailed off. Then she regretted what she'd said. She didn't mean it. She looked up again. 'No, wait,' she said. 'You may not care, but I do! I'll tell you what I found. I found Azimullah's bedroom. I wandered off after supper because I was bored by the conversation, and there I found pictures – pictures of such revolting depravity, you wouldn't believe it!'

Whittle sneered at her. 'Pictures of pretty girls? Why,

Lizzie, I would never have thought with your background you would be so coy! What a turnabout!'

Lizzie reddened but ignored the insult. 'Not pictures of pretty girls, George, pictures I can't describe. Horrible pictures, pictures of women with animals, of men with whips and devices and horrible things. And I found a cabinet and saw an array of such equipment for torture you'd faint if you saw it, even you. *That's* why I took Emily away, *that's* why you should be thanking me, not accusing me!'

For one moment Whittle's rage seemed to subside, and his face sunk slightly, like a punctured balloon. He became paler and started to tremble. He stared at her, unable to know whether to believe her or not. But at last he relaxed the grip on her wrist and flung it down. He took a deep breath, and his small eyes narrowed into slits of hatred. He pulled his watch from his waistcoat and looked at it. Then he looked back at Lizzie, his face contorted with contempt.

'I don't believe one shred of your story, Lizzie, but I know who'll tell me the truth. Mr Greenway. I'll go to see him now. If he backs up your story . . but he won't. It can't be true. And watch out, because when I return, I shall make you apologize to Azimullah Khan, you'll be on your knees begging his forgiveness, woman!' And with that he turned on his heel and walked out of the room.

The following morning there was no sign of Whittle, and Emily refused to talk to Lizzie. Whether he had been back and gone out again during the night Lizzie could not ascertain. After a morning of anxious waiting about the bungalow with the baby, Lizzie decided to find out what had happened for herself. For the first time she felt that she and George shared a common aim, both anxious for Emily's welfare. If only she could make him see that she had only done what she had for love, and not out of spite! If only he would realize that money and class were no good unless backed up by kindness . . . then he might change

83

himself, and there might be some tolerable future for them both.

Leaving the baby with the ayah she set off determinedly for the Greenways' house which was only a short distance from theirs, but was told by an impassive servant that they had both gone out that afternoon to see the Jacobis. It was a hot, claustrophobic afternoon. On the Greenways' veran- dah Lizzie wondered briefly whether to return home or not; then, with a determined shake of her parasol, she headed across the town, through the bazaar, to the Jacobis' house.

She walked through the narrow streets, past the staring dealers in *bhang* and tobacco who squatted silently sort- ing their leaves. She passed the half-naked girls who sat weighing silver and spices, and the boys boiling leather in great iron cauldrons, passed piles of sticky sweets, fruit paper flower, bright garlands of marigolds; she flinched at the acrid smell of the dye from the saris, stretched across wooden awnings to dry. She passed a temple, catching the stray strains of chanting, the strong smell of incense, as the worshippers, their yellow and red caste-marks still wet, hurried by her, muttering prayers to themselves. And through the bazaar, the other side of the town, she finally arrived at the Jacobis' bungalow, which lay down an avenue of sweetly smelling tamarind trees.

Before she had arrived at the door, Mrs Jacobi appeared with a smile. 'Welcome!' she said. 'My bearer told me he saw you coming – my dear, have you walked all this way? You must be uncommon hot! Come in and get cool, have some tea, this is a rare treat indeed. I have Mr Shepherd visiting me – the head assistant in the Commissariat. He will be delighted to meet you!'

Lizzie gratefully lay down her parasol and cloak in the cool shade of the verandah. A servant hovered by with a bowl of water and a damp cloth, and she gladly dabbed at her face.

'I really wanted to see Mr Greenway,' she said, apo- logetically. 'I understand he was here. . . .'

Mrs Jacobi looked sorry and shook her head. 'You've

just missed him. He went to discuss some business with your husband, he said. I hope there's nothing amiss, eh, dear?' she added, a gleam coming into her eye at the prospect of gossip. 'Nothing? Ah, well,' she said, disappointed. 'Come in anyway. We are talking mutiny talk. Mr Shepherd has been scaring me half silly with his tales, so I hope you will change the subject.'

She ushered Lizzie into the sitting room. The room was delightfully furnished. There was a huge bowl of roses in a silver dish in the middle of a walnut table in the centre of the room; the settees were covered in silk of duck-egg blue, and there were occasional tables of carved ivory by the arms of the chairs. By an enormous oil-painting of the Norfolk fens were a couple of small Indian miniatures that had been touched up by Mrs Jacobi.

Mr Shepherd got up as the ladies entered the room. Like Mrs Jacobi, he was a half-caste.

'Sit down, my dear, and have some tea.' Mrs Jacobi, arranging her red paisley shawl around her shoulders, sat down and clapped her hands for the servants. 'You've walked through the bazaar, have you? Have you noticed how they are already putting up their shutters during the day as if fearing looting in the future? It's not safe, not safe one bit, y'know.'

Lizzie nodded. 'I didn't like the look of that,' she agreed, 'but George says we are safe. He says that Wheeler has just sent a telegram to Lawrence at Lucknow saying "All quiet at Cawnpore". He must know, surely.'

Mr Shepherd shook his head. 'I like him, as an honourable gentleman, but I just think he's wrong. You've got to prepare for the worst, you know. I've had Indian dresses already made for the family so we can escape unnoticed if the sepoys mutiny – and I suggest you do the same. Why, the sepoys at Muttra have mutinied, did you hear, and the ones in the Bhurtpore army – and have you seen the signs in the market, those daubs saying "All shall become red"? I don't like it one bit.'

Mrs Jacobi agreed. 'Why, I was in the bazaar yesterday and the man who sells the chickens turned around and said, clear as a bell, that I'd be hacked to bits before the month was out! He was hacking a chicken at the time, and I can tell you a shiver went down my spine, even though he swore it was a joke. Not my kind of joke, I said! I'll get my chickens elsewhere in future.'

'Even at our house the servants haven't turned up for days, you know,' added Mr Shepherd. 'Either rebellious or frightened. I'm certainly glad Wheeler is setting up accommodation at the entrenchment, to be on the safe side.'

'Mighty safe!' muttered Mrs Jacobi scornfully. 'It's just half-finished barrack buildings, still covered with scaffolding! And you call that ditch around it a trench!'

Lizzie remained silent. She hadn't known all this.

'But I don't think we should worry too much,' said Mrs Jacobi, noticing Lizzie's expression. 'Even if they do mutiny, it'll only be a matter of days before they're put down. Why, they need us here, there's no point in them biting the hands that feed them, that's what I say.'

'And so do I!' said Mr Shepherd, taking an egg-and-cress sandwich from the plate that was offered him. 'Mutiny talk spreads mutiny talk, that's true, indeed.'

With this remark the conversation turned to more general topics, such as the cost of the repair of the roofs of the Assembly Rooms and who would be playing the heroine in the operetta planned for the ball later that month, not to mention whether it was true that Mrs Oates had really accepted the offer of Major Palmer's hand in marriage only hours after burying poor Mr Oates who had died of typhoid.

Lizzie became impatient. She was still worrying about what had happened with Whittle. She wanted to know, to get it clear. After sitting for an hour or so listening, she finally rose, made her apologies and left.

'You can't go alone,' said Mrs Jacobi firmly, 'can she, Mr Shepherd? I'll send one of the servants to accompany you, my dear. It's not safe out at night these days.'

'But it's not night, not nearly, it is only five o'clock,' said Lizzie pointing out of the window.

'It is late enough. Now do as I say, m'dear. Bearer!'

Lizzie set off in the direction of their bungalow with the bearer walking behind her to protect her. She didn't like the feeling. She felt followed, strange; she felt haunted by the dark, skinny figure which padded silently in her shadow. It was with much relief, then, that she heard her name being called from above, and, looking up on the road, found herself staring at the large grey head of an elephant, with purple and yellow painted ears.

'Mrs Whittle! Mrs Whittle!' Sitting in a fine jewelled howdah was Gupta Singh, the man she had noticed at the Nana Sahib's dinner. He bent down, concerned.

'Are you going home? Will you allow me to take you? Would you be comfortable on this beast? I will provide a horse if you prefer? Please, it is safer to come with me to your bungalow. . . .'

Lizzie paused a moment, then accepted. The elephant knelt down, and she stepped up to join Gupta Singh on top.

'This is very kind of you,' she said, grateful. 'I am rather hot and I need to get back quickly.'

'Not trouble, I hope?' asked Gupta Singh quietly. He stared at her disconcertingly.

'No, certainly not. I have just been visiting. . . .'

Gupta Singh nodded. 'The British are getting worried, I am thinking,' he said, impassively.

'Why, indeed they are,' said Lizzie, then felt embarrassed that she had blurted this out so quickly to an Indian. 'All mutiny talk!' she added, as gaily as possible.

The elephant slowly moved off, its cargo swaying precariously on top.

'And what do you plan to do? Take refuge with General Wheeler?'

Lizzie felt confused. Gupta Singh would not look at her. There was something, however, about his fine profile, his delicate features, the almost sculptural curve of his mouth, that touched her. There was a kindness and calm about him, a serenity that made her feel at peace.

'I don't know, everyone is in such a panic and I'm sure I don't know what we will do for the best.' She stopped, realizing she was assuming he was on the side of the British.

Gupta Singh remained silent, looking impassively before him.

'You must think we are so stupid,' said Lizzie apologetically, 'but I don't know which way to turn. One person says the sepoys will mutiny, another swears they are loyal. What do *you* think?'

'I know,' said Gupta Singh, in a low voice.

Lizzie stared at him. 'Then will we be safe in the entrenchment? What should we do? But then why should you tell me, if I am your enemy?'

Gupta Singh turned and smiled at her, his face transformed by kindness. 'You are not my enemy, Mrs Whittle, surely you know that? I am your friend, indeed your admirer.'

Lizzie blushed, and Gupta Singh's eyes grew fuller and darker as he looked at the Englishwoman by his side. He had been captivated by this pale-skinned woman ever since he had first set eyes on her at the Nana Sahib's banquet. He had summoned his astrologer to investigate her future, he felt so certain they were destined to be together, and the astrologer had said that his life was secure, and his illness would be checked, only when he married a European. Why was it that he felt so convinced that it would be this woman? She was married. She had a baby. And yet he was utterly obsessed by her beauty. Her hair was dark as an Indian's, and in the heat her skin was rosy and glistening, her mouth redder than usual with the blood that had suffused her face with anxiety and heat. He turned away, overcome by the sight of this beautiful Englishwoman who he knew would always be beyond his reach. As he did so, a servant tapped his hand, giving him a small phial. Gupta Singh nodded, emptied the contents into his mouth and swallowed. Seeing Lizzie's surprise, he smiled. 'I am not a very well man, despite my appearances,' he said. 'I must take for my sickness this medicine, powdered rubies. I have tried everything for my sickness, even tried your English doctors, but the only potion that I am told by my son that will work is this. I expect you think we are foolish, too. But I would rather take this than use one of your English leeches!'

Lizzie was irritated and disturbed about the way Gupta Singh would not keep to the point. She tried again, looking up at him as pleadingly as possible. 'I am sorry you are ill,' she said, and as she meant this, a mere polite comment, she was surprised to feel truly sorry as she looked into his kind eyes. 'But, please tell me . . . where will we be safest? Perhaps we should go to the Nana Sahib, I know my sister-in-law would be able to find a way, and if I did not let her out of my sight perhaps she would be safe. . . .'

Gupta Singh suddenly laughed. 'Safe? Safe with the Nana Sahib? The sun has driven you mad, Mrs Whittle! Mad like General Wheeler!'

'But the Nana is Wheeler's friend! He is sending his army to protect the Treasury! He has promised us aid!'

Gupta Singh laughed louder and louder, but was stopped by a spasm of pain that crossed his chest. He bent up, letting out a small cry.

'Why, I'm sure powdered rubies aren't good for you, if you'll excuse my saying so!' said Lizzie, holding on to his hand. 'I am sure there must be something else. . . .'

Gupta Singh recovered and breathed deeply, the pain only showing in lightning winces across his eyes. Then even they stopped.

'Mrs Whittle, I beg you, do not go to the Nana Sahib. He is dangerous and dangerous in more ways than one. Dangerous to the British, and dangerous to women. The barracks of General Wheeler will never last, he has chosen a place of such idiocy, you have no hope there. If you are in trouble, come to me, Mrs Whittle, I will protect you and your family. You can trust me, Mrs Whittle, because I trust nobody. I do not trust the British; I do not trust my own people; I do not trust the Nana Sahib. I only trust certain – special' – and at the word he looked at her with the same longing as he had looked before – 'very special people. People whom my astrologer tells me will be favourable to me. Your aspect is favourable to me, most favourable. So I trust you. I also trust my son, of course. I will help you. Please let me help you.'

Lizzie looked into his eyes and though she wavered for a moment, she made a quick decision. 'Very well,' she said.

At a signal from Gupta Singh the elephant boy jabbed his metal prong deeper behind the poor animal's ear and the great beast lunged ahead.

'Remember what I am telling you, Mrs Whittle,' said Gupta Singh when he left her at the bungalow, 'I am wishing you luck, and auspicious times.'

'Thank you . . .'

10

Lizzie noticed the change in atmosphere the minute she stepped inside the bungalow. The punkah wallah was fanning the room more swiftly than usual, and the normally quiet servants were scampering about their business as if under a threat. There was the sound of heavy boxes being moved, and the flapping of clothes as they were shaken out. She walked through the bungalow and found the bearer sorting through Whittle's clothes.

'What are you doing?' she asked, whipping one of Whittle's shirts from his hand and putting it back into the cupboard where it had lain. 'Stealing!'

The bearer grinned showing a mouth that displayed only a couple of black teeth. 'No steal, memsahib, pack, pack for sahib.'

'Pack? Why where are we going? What's happening?' Lizzie couldn't believe her ears.

'Not memsahib, sahib going journey, memsahib stay here, safe,' The bearer grinned again in a particularly loathsome way and gave what Lizzie could have sworn was a laugh.

She went out into the corridor and banged on Emily's door. 'Emily! What's going on?' But the door was locked. If Emily was inside she wasn't answering.

She felt strangely frightened. Perhaps it was all the talk of mutiny. She felt she couldn't trust anyone. Whittle had still not returned and Emily was not coming out of her room. That evening she was a solitary figure in the dining room, alone and embarrassed as she ate, surrounded by servants attending on her every movement. She only had to twitch towards a dish and a long black arm would emerge from the darkness and move it towards her. If her napkin slipped off her lap, it would never reach the floor. It was caught by a bright-eyed servant who would immediately provide a fresh one. She ate her meal quickly, pushing aside the offer of a mango and going quickly to her room where she tried to read. But it was too hot.

Surely George couldn't really be going? Not at a time like this? For the first time, the mutiny had become a real threat, not just drawing-room talk. It seemed inevitable. She was overcome by an aching feeling of longing for Richard, someone she could talk to, who would understand her, who would hold her and care for her. If she shut her eyes she could almost imagine his strong arms around her, the pressure of his mouth on hers, the tone of his voice – and for one moment she had one of those strange visions of him, an image in her head of his face, that she could stare at, inch by inch, covering it with her eyes like so many kisses. Despite herself, she started to cry, softly. For herself, for the baby, for Richard. She didn't know why. She just knew she was unhappy, desperately so.

When, much later there was a knock on her bedroom door, she felt almost hopeful. If it were Whittle, even if it were Whittle in a rage, surely they could be united in some way against the dreadful threat of mutiny.

'Come in,' she said, drawing her shawl round her.

The door opened. It was Whittle, at last. He said nothing, just came slowly into the room, closed the door and sat down heavily on the end of the bed, his face set grimly as he stared straight ahead at the blinds, not even moving a hand to brush the mosquitos away from his face. There was silence except for the croak of the frogs and the endless chirruping of the crickets.

'Yes?' said Lizzie anxiously, as she wriggled upright into a sitting position. She took the beaded yellow cloth from the glass of water by her bed and took a sip of the tepid water. Then she put it back 'What is it? Have you talked to Mr Greenway?'

Whittle grunted, still staring ahead. He coughed. Then he spoke. 'I'm going to Calcutta to organize some more provisions,' he said. He sounded strained and formal as if he were talking to a business acquaintance.

'Going to Calcutta? You can't be! Not at this time! Why, it's weeks away!' Fear seized Lizzie, and she felt herself exploding with a kind of terrified rage. He couldn't leave them at a time like this! 'But George, you can't go now! It's not safe here for us, even with you, but without you. . . . The whole town is in a panic, expecting an uprising any minute — you must have heard the talk! We need you! Who'll protect us if there's a mutiny here?'

Whittle turned and looked at her coldly. His face was paler and coarser than usual, as if he were very, very tired. 'You don't need anyone, Lizzie,' he said. 'You've got everything worked out. You know more about this town than anyone else put together, you clever minx. You've got a woman's brain,' he added, smiling rather cynically. 'Not much, you might say, but you've got intuition, you're sly as a cat.'

Lizzie waited. Was this an accusation? Or an admission that she'd been right about Azimullah? She risked it. She put out her hand to touch his sleeve and to her surprise he did not pull his arm away. 'I'm *not* as strong as you are, George, physically, I mean. We need a man here! Believe me!'

'Stuff and nonsense!' Whittle sounded irritated, as if he wanted to believe her but couldn't. 'I'll be back in a month, anyway, and nothing will happen in a month. I've talked to General Wheeler and he's convinced me there's no harm, no harm at all, in leaving you for a month. This talk of mutiny is just scaremongery. Anyway, I've got to go, or there'll be no more money for us. I've spent so much . . . so much!'

And here he turned away and to Lizzie's surprise she heard a cough from him that was more of a sob and she saw his shoulders rise and fall as if he were under great emotional strain. Instinctively she leant forward and put her hand on his shoulder compassionately.

'What's the matter? Tell me. And for God's sake, don't go. Not now, please.'

93

He pushed her away and buried his head in his hands. He made a sad sight, this big, brutish man, weakened and unsure. 'I've made a terrible mistake,' he said in a low voice. 'Mr Greenway, Mr Jacobi, even General Wheeler, they all knew it. Azimullah is indeed a . . . a strange man. What you saw only bore out the rumours round here. Oh, most of the men like him well enough and don't mind what he does behind his bedroom door, but *they* don't have sisters who want to marry him, do they? I've been duped. I have already given him expensive gifts worth as much as the stock in my warehouse. It's expensive to get a brother-in-law here. We have no money left! Emily still won't believe me, she won't speak to me, her own brother, despite all I've told her . . . I have to go.'

Lizzie reached out both arms and took his hands, pulling them away from his face. 'You've done the best you could for her,' she said, more kindly. 'Even now you are doing the best for her though she doesn't know it. I'll talk to her. I had no idea . . .'

He turned his face to her and she saw his eyes were red.

He looked at her suspiciously. 'You've cast a spell over me, Elizabeth Shawcross,' he said, hoarsely, 'you've done me wrong, you've deceived me, you've been a cruel wife to me, but you know I'd never regret marrying you, never one day.'

'Hush!' Lizzie found the sight of him almost too pitiful to bear. She still couldn't like him, but she felt sorrow for him. When he leant forward to kiss her, she didn't resist him, but put her arms round him to comfort him. After a while he got into bed beside her and they held and caressed each other with that odd poignancy of two who know, for one stray night, they've been given a reprieve from hatred and resentment and could, for once, be kind to one another.

For the first time, after months of marriage, they woke up together in the same bed, but by then the spell had been broken. Whittle got up immediately and bowed rather formally to her. 'I'll be seeing to the packing then,' he said awkwardly and left the room.

While General Wheeler, despite the gossip, was confident there would be no trouble in Cawnpore, he was a sensible enough man not to take undue risks. On May 24th, Queen Victoria's birthday, he had forbidden the pealing of bells in the churches and refused even a gunfire salute in case any sepoy mad enough might suddenly take it into his head that this would be a good day to defy the British. And while he was so certain of his own position that he actually sent some troops to Lucknow, where the British were now under siege, he did take the precaution of announcing that in case of trouble all Europeans should take refuge in an entrenchment near the barracks: a position that was exposed, but one that he felt most suitable since it was near the river; if anything should happen ('But it won't,' he said) reinforcements would find it easy to make their way down the Ganges to help them. He moved in some water supplies, quite a quantity of food, and had parapets and gun emplacements erected above the loose earthworks below.

When his advisers had begged him to fortify the magazine or the Treasury, Wheeler simply argued that if the sepoys did mutiny they would undoubtedly march straight away to Delhi, and that anyway the Nana was completely loyal and there was no question of anyone looting the Treasury.

It was the Nana's loyalty that reassured most of the European population, and certainly Whittle, who was forced to be away, clung to his faith as he left Emily and Lizzie for Calcutta that afternoon.

'The Nana will be loyal, have no fear,' he said, as reassuringly as he could as he stood outside the bungalow in a topee, pulling on his gloves. Nearby, the carriage stood to take him off, and the horse, a brown chestnut, gave an impatient whinny. 'Keep calm, ladies, above all things, don't believe the scaremongers. And if by any chance anything goes even slightly wrong, look to the Jacobis for help, won't you? Mr Jacobi has given me his word he'll look after you, like his own family . . . but you won't have any need to call him, you'll see, and I'll be back in a matter of weeks, and we shall celebrate, and I shall bring you presents. . . .' He kissed Lizzie roughly on the cheek, patted the baby on the head, an odd expression on his face, and hugged Emily, who clung to him pitifully, all her anger gone she was so overcome with the idea of his leaving her. Then he climbed into the gharry which took off at a quick pace, leaving a cloud of dust hanging over the garden.

Lizzie looked after it, the baby in her arms. Could it really be true that he had gone? That they were left, two women on their own, with only Indian servants to protect them, Indian servants who might well not prove loyal in the event? She shook her head disbelievingly. She could not help but compare George Whittle's behaviour with what she would have expected of Richard. Surely Richard would have stayed, Richard wouldn't have abandoned her . . . and then she remembered. He had abandoned her. Perhaps all men were the same – treacherous, untrustworthy. . . . Any kind of tenderness she might have felt for Whittle the night before faded away and much as she wished she could feel something for him, she found it impossible. She just felt lost, betrayed . . . but determined to survive if only for the baby's sake.

Lizzie followed Emily indoors, a curiously heavy feeling hanging over her. She sat down wearily on the sofa in the sitting room. It was so hot, so hot. The heat seemed to seep into the room under the blinds like molten lava, oozing into the room from any crack it could find. She put the baby into the crook of one arm and fanned herself with the other hand. Emily came and sat down. They still hadn't spoken since the Nana's party.

'Come now, Emily,' said Lizzie, wearily, 'let's be friends. Now George has gone we can't continue like this. It is bad enough being left here without being enemies as well.'

Emily paused. 'Very well,' she said, with unnatural quietness. She sat at a bamboo table, listlessly turning the pages of a book on natural history.

Lizzie sighed, relieved. At least she had broken the silence. 'And now how shall we occupy ourselves, now George has gone?' she said. 'I really think we ought to be thinking of making plans in case of an insurrection. Don't you think it would be wise to follow Mr Shepherd's example and get some Indian clothes made for us?'

'Whatever you say,' Emily's voice sounded flat.

'And oughtn't we to visit the entrenchment – just to see where it is, what is going on there? We ought to be *doing* something.'

Emily rose, yawning. 'No, not the entrenchment. I don't feel like going there. I think I shall go and rest.'

'Very well,' Lizzie looked after her anxiously as she left the room. At least Emily was talking to her but she was still resentful, and there was an air of secrecy about her.

If General Wheeler and George Whittle were convinced that Cawnpore was safe, most of the rest of the European population were now far from certain. Whole families were arguing with each other about whether to get on to the boats to nearby towns; some families left their houses at night to stay at the entrenchment and just returned to stay in their bungalows during the day. Others, less frightened, slept on their verandahs with guns under their pillows at night in case of an attack. Shops in the bazaar were now closing rapidly, some opening and shutting like jack-in-the-boxes depending on the mood of the day. There was such to-ing and fro-ing from entrenchment to bungalows and packing and unpacking of suitcases that it was impossible not to be affected by it. The fear that had started as a mere flicker a few days before Whittle left grew swiftly into a panic, inflamed by the rumours that abounded everywhere from the bazaar to the drawing room.

So Lizzie could hardly be surprised when, only three nights after Whittle had left, she got a message from Mr Jacobi.

I promised your husband I'd look after you, and I feel now that you must both come with us to the entrenchment. Please pack at once and come and stay with us tonight. I am sincerely fearful of what might happen if you stay another night on your own. For your own safety, please do as I say and come to us straight away before it is too late. My bearer will accompany you . . .

So, the moment had come. And so soon. Lizzie looked round the bungalow in despair. She had thought she'd been deserted when Whittle left, but now she was going to have to desert her only home, her things. . . . She thought briefly of risking staying on, but then, catching sight of the baby in his cot, his little pink legs kicking in the air, catching the sound of his cheerful gurgling, she knew she couldn't possibly take risks. For his sake, she had to take every precaution, even if it meant seeking refuge in the entrenchment.

Lizzie showed the message to Emily. 'We *must* do as he says,' she said decisively. 'We can't stay here.'

Emily said nothing, just turned the big ring on her finger around again and again. 'No, I shan't,' she said. 'I will stay here.'

'Stay here? You're mad! You can't!' cried Lizzie. 'Read it! Can't you see what he's saying?'

'You go,' said Emily obstinately. 'You must go – you've got the baby. I'll stay here. There's nothing you can do to force me, Lizzie, I'm not going to go to that entrenchment. I'd rather die here, if I have to. There's no persuading me.'

Lizzie put her hand on her arm in an impulsive gesture. 'Please listen to me. Come for my sake, won't you? Come to keep us safe – we'd be better off together.' She tried desperately to appeal to Emily's humanity, the only chink left, possibly, in her armour of obsessive love. Emily wavered, then pushed Lizzie's hand away, shaking her head. Lizzie's eyes filled with tears but she knew there was nothing more she could do. 'Very well,' she said, uncertainly, 'I'll get the bearer to pack and I'll go, but I shall come back tomorrow morning and hope by then you have changed your mind. Who knows, tonight's events may make you alter your views.' She looked out of the window. Firecrackers exploded into the sky as if heralding some new event. Then she turned back. 'I beg you, Emily, to forget what is past. Please, please come with me. If it weren't for the baby, I'd refuse to leave you. . . .'

Emily looked at her boldly. 'Well, you have the baby, so

there are no ifs and buts, are there? I shall be all right. I can look after myself.'

Lizzie arrived at the Jacobis late that afternoon in a complete fluster. The baby was howling, the bearer was behaving in an oddly sullen, shifty way, and had taken her on a route around the bazaar that frightened her. Dark faces had peered in at the carriage windows and made faces at her, and for some time she was frightened that she was being kidnapped until the bearer reluctantly explained that 'it is being safer this way, bazaar not being safe, mem-sahib.' The Jacobis' bungalow was in chaos, the furniture all covered with sheets, the flowerpots brought in on to the verandah, cases and trunks everywhere, and Mr Jacobi sitting anxiously on the verandah in a basket chair by a rickety table on which lay a gun and a glass of ma-deira.

He jumped up the moment she arrived. 'Where is Miss Whittle?' he asked, taking her arm. 'I sincerely hope she is arriving soon ... the situation is very dangerous, in-flammatory indeed. I am considering whether it wouldn't be wiser to take off right now. We hear such tales, such conflicting stories. . . .'

Lizzie gave her bearer a rupee, and took off her hat, sitting down in relief at seeing a sympathetic English face. 'She won't come,' she said. 'I've tried to persuade her, but she refuses. There's nothing I can do, really, she's so obstinate. I'll go back tomorrow – she might have changed her mind.'

'Tomorrow? But we'll be starting at dawn, my dear, you can't possibly go back, it wouldn't be safe. . . .'

'I've promised. You can take the baby, at least he'll be safe. I'll take a carriage, but I must drop by and do my best . . . I'll be all right, I promise you . . .'

At that moment Mrs Jacobi appeared, with a needle and thread. She was in the process of stitching all her jewellery into her petticoats, and her clothes hung limply about her, pulled down by the weight of the things she had already hidden away in her hems.

'We'll have some kedgeree, sleep as well as we can, then

go tomorrow,' she said, kissing Lizzie. 'How good to see you. What a to-do all this is, ain't it? What a palaver! Ho, I'm sure it's all a panic, you'll see, we'll be back here before you can say Jack Robinson, but to be on the safe side we must go for a while. Mr Jacobi is quite frightened out of his wits, ain't you dear?' she added, affectionately stroking her husband's hair.

'Isn't the Nana going to be loyal, then?' asked Lizzie, anxiously.

'Why, who knows, you never can tell. *I* think he will, but others say he won't. Mr Jacobi's right. It's not worth the risk staying here.'

Lizzie gratefully accepted a glass of madeira. It seemed impossible that all this should be disrupted, this peaceful life. She looked out over the Jacobis' well-cut lawn, the roses bursting gloriously in the beds, the honeysuckle sending out such a sweet smell; she listened to the whooping and chirruping of the parakeets. Then a mongoose poked its nose out of a bush and sped across the lawn.

'It's after a snake,' said Mrs Jacobi. 'I hope there won't be any in the entrenchment. I hate 'em, that I do.'

The peaceful scene had made Lizzie remember Gupta Singh. 'I had promised,' she said nervously, 'that in the event of trouble I would seek refuge with Gupta Singh. He said we would not be safe with anyone except him. And I do trust him. Do you think I should go after him? Or perhaps we all could? I am sure he would care for you as well. I don't feel happy about all this. . . .'

The Jacobis eyed each other. 'No, my dear, stay with us,' said Mrs Jacobi, putting her head on her arm, 'we're your own kind. You can't trust any Indians, you know, not really. Anyway, dear, your husband is gone. You know, it just would not *do*.'

And the subject wasn't mentioned again.

After a restless night and an early start in which all the baggage was loaded on to the carriage and the Jacobis and the baby went off to the entrenchment, Lizzie set out for the bungalow. The spare carriage had been stolen during the night, so she had to make her way on foot, but the

Jacobis insisted she take a bearer with her for safety.

'If you are not in the entrenchment in an hour we will come back for you,' promised Mr Jacobi. 'I shall wait in the gates for you. Make haste, you must promise me, and bring your sister-in-law, whatever you do.'

As Lizzie hurried along the winding streets round the edge of the bazaar, she was entirely unprepared for the scene that met her eyes — cartloads of Europeans filling the streets. Panic-stricken ladies shrieked out of the windows, the gharry bearers carried piles of suitcases on their heads, and odd sights were to be seen everywhere: a man who carried his Chippendale chair down the street, his wife's parasol clutched in his other hand, and an old lady in black, who clutched all her possessions in a small black carpet-bag and steadfastly refused all offers of help.

It was all chaos. Lizzie quickened her pace down the road as she approached the bungalow. But immediately she could sense something strange. The house had a strange look about it. The door was open, the blinds pulled up, a flowerpot overturned in the garden. Something was wrong.

Lizzie called out: 'Emily! Emily!' There was no answer. Cautiously she went inside. With horror she looked around her. The whole bungalow had been ransacked. The furniture had been strewn around the rooms and some of it smashed. The lamps were broken and the beds overturned. Crockery lay in shattered heaps, the food and rice had been spilled all over the floor. The settee was ripped and the cane furniture split and in fragments.

'Emily! Emily!' she called, panicking. She prayed desperately to hear her friend's voice but there was only silence.

Lizzie opened the door of her bedroom, and there sitting on her bed was her bearer, his wife and their children. His wife was trying on her clothes, and the bearer was weighing a string of pearls in his hand. When he saw her a look of fear passed over his face and he made as if to salaam her; then he put his hands to his sides and smiled.

'Is mine now, is not yours, is mine!' he said insolently,

laughing. 'All shall become red! Your rule is over, British people, it is written!'

'Where is my sister-in-law? Where is Emily?' Lizzie was too distracted with worry to care, for that moment.

The bearer pulled an envelope from his dhoti and flung it on to the floor. 'This is from Miss Whittle,' he said. 'You pick up. I am picking up no more, never I am picking up!'

Lizzie grabbed the envelope and pulled out the sheet of paper inside.

'Dear Elizabeth,' she read. The words were written in Emily's looped, childish hand.

I have gone to Azimullah. I doubt if you will even come back to find me anyway, since you have so little consideration for my feelings. We have planned this a long time. I shall be safe with him. I give you my good wishes, despite how you have behaved towards me.
Your friend, Emily.

Lizzie's head swam as she clutched at the piece of paper. It was as if she'd never really believed that Emily would actually go off with Azimullah. But now it was too late – and her friend was in the clutches of that slate-faced traitor. Lizzie felt bereft and frightened – frightened for her friend and frightened for herself, now completely alone. She looked up and flinched as she glanced into the bearer's eyes. All Indians seemed loathsome to her now. 'Keep them!' she said bitterly, gesturing to the pearls. 'Keep everything! Keep the house and the clothes! May they bring better fortune to you than they have to me!'

She left in a hurry. Now she and the servant had to get to the entrenchment. It was midday, the sun burned down and Lizzie had to draw her shawl over her face to prevent the dust getting into her throat. The traffic from the town to the barracks had got worse and after ten minutes Lizzie found she had hardly gone more than a couple of hundred yards. A monkey leapt suddenly upon her, using her head as a stepping stone in a scramble to pluck a mango from the hand of a woman in a carriage, and Lizzie couldn't help but cry out; the panic was infectious. Her stiff petticoats were stuck to her legs in the heat, the sun's glare made her head ache dismally. It was as if the sun were raining arrows of heat straight on to her head. She felt dizzy. She put up her shawl to cover her head and was almost knocked over by a cart rocketing in the direction of the entrenchment. She stumbled on a stone and pushed onwards but started to despair that she would ever get there.

The entrenchment was a small group of brick barrack-like buildings at the top of a gently sloping hill. There was a main gate, but it could not be seen at all now, so surrounded was it by crowds, horses, servants and a complete commotion of refugees from the town. And all the time there was the steady flow of carriages and gharries arriving at the gate to deposit more terrified British, the ladies sometimes bundled like peasant women in all their clothes, carrying clocks, jewellery and treasured knick-knacks. The Jacobis' servant went ahead, forcing his way through the crowds. 'Make way, make way,' he cried, until eventually they got to the large gates and found their way inside.

Lizzie felt utter relief when she saw Mr Jacobi's face in the gateway, scanning the crowds of Europeans that came pouring in, staring from time to time at his watch.

'Here! I'm here!' she cried. 'Mr Jacobi!'

He turned with relief, and took her hand. 'Thank heavens you're safe!' he cried. 'I was about to despair. But where's your sister-in-law?'

'She's gone to Azimullah,' said Lizzie. 'She left last night, I had no idea . . .'

Mr Jacobi shook his head. 'Dear, oh, dear, this is the last thing Whittle will stand. My God, my God . . . well, at least you're safe, we have quarters here, after a fashion, horribly uncomfortable, but Mrs Jacobi is trying to get things together to make it a bit more tolerable. Come with me.'

Lizzie was caught up in a maelstrom of panic inside the entrenchment. Everything was in disarray. Women huddled in corners clutching their children, soldiers squatted playing cards on the earth in the large compound that made the centre of the entrenchment, some drunk. One confused artillery man was in his pyjamas, lurching over a gun, and another soldier with a notebook was walking around trying to give everyone quarters and make some kind of sense out of the confusion. Mr Jacobi went up to him. 'I've brought Mrs Whittle – she'll be staying in our room,' he said, 'just for a while, with the baby. . . .'

The soldier turned to look at Lizzie and raised his pen, but just then a small gang of children raced by, shouting with laughter, and his pen dropped to the ground. When he picked it up it was so full of dust and sand it wouldn't work. 'Get on with it, then,' he shouted, marching off to organize some other part of the entrenchment. 'Yes, I see . . . now, the supplies . . .'

The Jacobis had established themselves in a small office-like room up some steep stone stairs in one of the buildings that lay along the side of the compound. It was hardly big enough for two, let alone three and a baby, but Mrs Jacobi as usual was being as good-natured as possible, and had pinned up some of her shawls on the grey walls 'to make it look more like home, my dear', she said. She had covered bales of straw with sheets brought from the house for beds, and opened up a folding table. Mr Jacobi opened a bottle of madeira, and Mrs Jacobi rummaged round in a case for a pack of cards. Lizzie felt a pang of gratitude to this kind and courageous couple who, against all odds, were still trying to make the best of things in the most British way they could. She picked up the baby from its cot of straw, and tears came into her eyes as she held Mrs Jacobi's hand, clasping it tightly.

'You are so good to us,' she said, 'I don't know what I would have done without . . .'

'Stuff and nonsense!' said Mrs Jacobi cheerfully. 'Now sit down, and let's have a round of rummy. We'll soon be out of here, you'll see. It's just an adventure, ain't it, my sweet?' And before she dealt the cards she leant over the battered table and chucked the baby under the chin.

But it wasn't an adventure for long. They had scarcely finished their evening meal and were thinking of settling down for the night when there was a terrible crack of gunfire from outside. 'What is that?' cried Mrs Jacobi, running to the window and looking out. The black sky was completely lit up by sparks, like fireworks. Each bright explosion threw the whole of Cawnpore into a sudden flash of light, and the roofs of the deserted bungalows shone like silver strips of metal for a brief second. Then in the ensuing darkness there was a shout from the ramparts above as Lizzie and Mrs Jacobi saw the first flame as one of the bungalows was set on fire. They could even hear the distant crackling of the dry thatch as it quickly caught, see the drift of smoke again caught in another flash of gunfire.

Outside the door was the sound of running feet, and Mr Jacobi, who had gone out to smoke a cheroot on the ramparts, burst in. 'The Nana's men are looting the Treasury and setting the town alight!' he cried. 'We are betrayed!'

11

That same night the 6th Native Infantry mutinied at Allahabad, a village some hundred miles from Cawnpore. Those families that had fled Cawnpore in boats to make for Allahabad had to disperse into the countryside on hearing the news; some were butchered by sepoys, others were hidden by sympathetic villagers, some simply died of disease and lack of nourishment on the roadside. In Oudh, the province which encompassed Cawnpore, Allahabad and Delhi, there seemed to the Europeans that there was nowhere to run.

Meanwhile the British army was making its slow but tortuous way from Calcutta. Colonel Neill, commanding the Madras Fusiliers, was first; and a week's march behind there followed Brigadier General Henry Havelock, who had orders from Canning to relieve Cawnpore and then to turn his attention to the siege at Lucknow.

Six hundred hot, dusty, dangerous miles had to be crossed by a thousand men and though a hundred miles of this could be crossed by train on newly laid track, most of the journey would be made in bumpy wagons pulled by bullocks. Other soldiers were waiting in readiness at Allahabad and further reserve troops were ready at Calcutta.

Serving as an officer in this column was Richard Applevale. At this moment he was resting, a hundred miles from Allahabad and at the end of another long day's journey, lying in a hammock that Arjun Gohar had rigged up for him outside the tent he shared with Patcham. Richard's face was white with the dust which hung like a cloud over the column as it marched along the road. He looked worn and weary, thinner now, his eyes lacking their usual sparkle. Anyone who had known him in England would have been shocked at the change. The sun had tanned his skin, and toughened it; his eyes had a bloodshot look, as if he had been drinking too much; his movements, once lively and sharp, had grown languid and weary; tension showed in the drawn lines of his face and the set of his eyes, which on the march were endlessly narrowed against the sun. He was still attractive – perhaps more attractive – than he had been; for as he had lost the bloom and the innocence that had been part of his charm, he had gained a wilder, tougher air, a restlessness that belongs to one who is permanently on guard.

Opening his eyes, he looked around at the desolate scene in the dark. Hundreds of soldiers lay stretched out, already nearly dead with exhaustion before they had even heard the sound of gunshot, parched and ill under the black silhouettes of the tamarind trees. Further down the road was camped the travelling bazaar which continued to trail the column despite Havelock's commands that it should return to Calcutta. It was there that the soldiers could buy tobacco, drink, girls, sweetmeats and any kind of pleasure that could be transported on the back of a bullock. Through the trees Richard could see the lights from the fires, hear the sounds of bells from the dancing girls, the shouts from the stray soldier who felt up to enjoying himself, and he could smell the smoke from the cooking fires and the sickening aroma of grilled chicken. The air was filled with the noises of a camp: billycans clanked, the soldiers coughed and swore, and the occasional hoarsely yelled song would carry across the night air interrupted only by the sudden screech of a parakeet.

Richard stretched; he could do with a drink. Every limb ached, every part of his body felt bruised and weary. Not that he wasn't glad to have left Calcutta at last. He had tired of the weeks of debauchery and drink that had followed the party at Government House when he was hardly to be seen without a girl on his arm and a drink in his hand, though by now it had become such a habit that he had nearly forgotten how to pass a night without either. He was secretly relieved that now he had escaped the city there was no chance of meeting Lizzie again; no risk of bumping into the unwelcome figure of George Whittle and his pallid sister. Now if he drank enough, numbed his senses with drink, he could spend a whole night without even thinking of Lizzie.

His behaviour during these weeks had brought him to the stern attention of the brigadier himself.

'Applevale, this is an army we are running, not a brothel,' Havelock had told him on the second night of the march, looking up from his Bible. A fly buzzed across the flimsy desk in his tent and rested on one of the pages. Havelock had been about to crush it, but, having second thoughts about staining his dearest book, he casually brushed it away.

'Yes, sir.'

'I had high hopes of you in Calcutta,' added Havelock, his white whiskers twitching with disapproval. 'You had the makings of a good officer. And then, just as we were needed, just as the Indians rose up, just at the *very moment* we needed excellent men, you disintegrated! That is the only word for it! You are frightened of fighting, perhaps?'

'Indeed not, sir.' Richard was not at all frightened of fighting, but he knew that he could do with a drink, particularly now. It was true; he felt uneasy in this particular division, 'Havelock's Saints' as they were known, compelled as they were to attend church services every day, and twice on Sundays.

Havelock's high-pitched voice continued, and the medals on Havelock's jacket jangled as the whole of his tiny five-foot frame shook with the intensity of his words. 'I am a man of God, Applevale, and I have asked God to give me the wisdom to fulfil the expectations of Government and to restore tranquility to these disturbed districts! I do not need drunkenness and debauchery to hinder me in my ambition!'

'No, sir.'

'Remember that.'

'Yes, sir.'

'Dismissed!' Havelock spat out the words and returned to his reading.

As Richard reached the door of the tent, he paused and turned back.

'Yes?' Havelock did not look up.

'Sir, you have not yet seen me fighting, sir. It's this waiting that makes me so impatient. I assure you that I shall give a different impression in action.'

Havelock had looked up and smiled, his whole face suddenly becoming charming. 'I am glad to hear of it, Applevale,' he had said. 'There is nothing like the love of God and one's country to give you courage to fight.'

'Sir.' Richard had left the tent.

Recalling the scene in the darkness, Richard spat on the ground. 'Love of God and one's country, indeed,' he muttered. 'Money is what makes men fight, not love. Money and hate. Hypocritical clap-trap!'

Then he stretched again and with one lithe movement sprang from the hammock to the ground, and sauntered into the tent.

Patcham sat on the edge of his roughly made-up bed, reading by candlelight, and looked up with pleasure as Richard came in, putting the book to one side. 'Have a drink, old chap,' he said, pulling a bottle from his knapsack. 'Not much choice, I'm afraid. Brandy, brandy or brandy. My God, I miss a game of billiards out here. They say pig-sticking's good fun, but nothing on a game of billiards, I'll bet. They say we might get a game of cricket at Allahabad, however.'

'I'll make it a brandy, please,' said Richard, sitting on the ground, and reaching for a pack of cards nearby, idly shuffled them with no particular purpose.

Patcham gave him a glass. 'I must say this is not my kind of do at all, Applevale,' he confided. 'I was far happier in Calcutta. Have you seen those niggers strung up on the trees on the wayside? They say that is Neill's doing – he just strings up any native he comes across. I think I'll lie pretty low in Allahabad when he's around.'

Richard made a face; he'd already been disgusted by the sights on the road. 'I hear Neill's got Allahabad pretty much under control now,' he said. 'He's a ruthless man.

They say he marched his men seventy miles in three days though every fourth man was down with sunstroke. And if anyone even threatens to delay him by a minute, he's hanged.'

'Then I shan't be here for long!' said Patcham. 'I still can't get the hang of these guns.'

'Lack of practice,' said Richard. 'We've not been fighting yet. A few sepoys after you and you'll soon get skilful. There's nothing like fear to give you talent!'

'D'you think we'll be fighting at Allahabad?'

'I hope so, by God, I hope so!' said Richard, surprising Patcham as he struck his fist on his knee.

'Watch out, old man,' Patcham said in a puzzled, soothing voice. 'Come on, snap out of it! This isn't like the Applevale I knew in Calcutta!' Richard drew a hand over his forehead and then smiled, apologizing.

'It's the heat. It makes me feel so pent-up . . . full of anger. Not against anyone in particular,' he added, 'but just . . . just . . .'

Patcham smiled knowingly. 'It's since that ball in Calcutta, isn't it? Something happened there that changed you, no? Tell me I'm right! I've got a wager on it with a couple of the boys!'

Richard looked away, 'That's nonsense, Patcham.'

But Patcham had started laughing. 'Don't say any more, Richard. Come on, I can see I'm right. I'll go and collect my money now and we'll go and get a couple of girls, how about it?'

But Richard shook his head. 'No, I'm going to get some sleep after this. I want to be ready for the fighting – whenever it comes.'

And so he got through another long evening, one of many, many more, when he became enraged with a mixture of boredom, frustration and the misery he refused to admit.

When Havelock's column finally arrived at Allahabad there was nothing to be done. The insurrection at this dusty outpost had indeed been successfully and brutally put down by Colonel Neill, who had instilled such complete reign of terror over the natives that all the villagers had fled to the hills with their animals, and Havelock found it almost impossible to get the livestock he needed to furnish the army on its last lap to Cawnpore. The two commanders, Havelock and Neill, hated one another on sight, Neill reluctant to allow Havelock any of his men as he had already sent Major Renaud on ahead to Cawnpore with 300, Havelock reluctant to move without more men and more provisions.

It was a pitiful message from General Wheeler from the Cawnpore entrenchment that had been sent to Lucknow that broke their deadlock.

We have been besieged since the sixth by the Nana Sahib joined by the whole of the native troops who broke out on the morning of the fourth. The enemy have two twenty-fours and several other guns. We have only eight nine-pounders . . . our defence has been noble and wonderful, our loss heavy and cruel. British spirit alone remains but it cannot last for ever. We have no instruments, no medicine, provision for ten days at farthest; and no possibility of getting any, as all communication with the town is cut off. We have all been cruelly deserted and left to our fate. We had above 220 soldiers of all arms at first; the casualties have been numerous. Railway gents and merchants have swollen our ranks to what they are – small as that is, they have done excellent service; but neither they nor I can last for ever. We wait aid, aid, aid! Surely we are not to die like rats in a cage?

Havelock and Neill now did their utmost to assemble the army, but they must, they felt, send some messenger ahead quickly, to encourage the garrison to hold on for as long as they could. They needed someone daring, cunning, brave, and someone impatient for action. Havelock had just the man. Richard Applevale.

General Wheeler may have been a broken man when he wrote that final message, but his description was no less than the truth; if anything, life in the entrenchment was far worse than he had described.

At first there had seemed quite an abundance of food – on the first day Lizzie had called the Jacobis to look at the ridiculous sight of a private trudging away from the main guard laden with champagne, a tin of preserved herring and a pot of jam; another was weighed down with salmon, rum and sweetmeats.

But, after only a week, rations were drastically cut. Now only a handful of split peas and a gill of flour a day was allowed, even for the soldiers who defended the sandbagged parapets which had been built shakily on the crumbling mud walls of the entrenchment.

And after a few days, the casualties started. First two or three a day, but after a week as many as four or five were dying every day from the heat alone; starvation and dehydration claimed more; cholera soon picked out its victims. Lizzie nursing the sick in a shady corridor below their room, soon learned to recognize the symptoms – the diarrhoea and vomiting, the muscle cramps followed by slow suffocation. There was little that any of the women could do for the wounded except comfort them. There were no medical supplies, and scarcely any water except the occasional blood-stained cup fetched by a soldier from the exposed well outside. The wounded were covered with flies, sometimes so thick on their faces their features were quite concealed.

When they died there was nowhere to put them. The ground was too hard to bury them, so the bodies were thrown out over the parapet where they swelled in the heat and burst before being finally eaten by vultures. The stench was intolerable.

Each evening Lizzie ate with the Jacobis, Mrs Jacobi preparing their wretched lentil supper as well as she could. She had never actually handled a saucepan before in her life – and she made up for her lack of skill in cooking with an admirable dignity in serving it. They would all sit on the floor around a sack that served as a table. Mr Jacobi would say the Lord's Prayer, then Mrs Jacobi would light a candle and spoon out the pitiful meal. Afterwards she would sing 'Home Sweet Home' and 'There is a Green Hill Far Away', temporarily drowning the sound of wailing women and children crying. The light of the candle was increased, too, by the glimmer of distant licking flames on the horizon that could be seen through the window; the Nana Sahib was looting and burning Cawnpore to the ground.

They soon learnt to drop the topic of escape from their talks in the evenings; each night Lizzie felt so eternally grateful that at least she, the Jacobis and the baby were actually still alive that she couldn't ever think further ahead than the next morning.

Sometimes Mrs Jacobi would tilt her head in the evening and say: 'Hush! I hear hooves! Perhaps it is help. . . .' Then, realizing she was wrong, she would say, 'Ah well, another time. Can't be long now,' and Mr Jacobi would change the subject.

Sometimes, as she nursed the sick, Lizzie would wonder what had happened to George and Emily. Emily, she hoped, was at least alive with Azimullah; it would be unlikely that George had escaped death on the roads. In many places Indians were killing Europeans on sight. She felt that were he alive he would have returned, even to protect Emily. She wished she had gone to Gupta Singh. She sometimes remembered his deep, black, calm eyes, his reassuring face, and almost physically longed for his protection. And where was Richard now? Gone on the march, perhaps, to Muttra or Lucknow, or perhaps he was storming Delhi. She had a picture of him in her mind, marching along the road, that same reproachful expression on his face. Sometimes she couldn't bear to think for whatever she thought of presented her with no solace, only doubt and fear. Several times during the day she would stop what she was doing, tempted to give up. The heat hammered down on her head as if trying to split it open; a deep breath would give no relief for it would simply be like breathing in the air from a furnace. Even a fan could hardly help, for the relief from the slightly cooler air was countered by the effort involved in waving the fan. The heat and the lack of food and drink made her permanently tired; sometimes she would find herself fast asleep in the middle of a job – like the others, she slept fitfully, twelve hours a night. Everyone had colds, Lizzie's throat was sore and it sometimes hurt her just to swallow the few spoonfuls of dhal they ate each night.

But at least the baby was all right. Both she and the Jacobis gave him any spare scraps that came their way, and despite the heat he seemed cheerful, growing and reasonably healthy. The other children had adapted well to start with, playing games with stones against the wall, pretending to be sepoys, or listening to the shot and running to collect it when it was still hot.

At the end of the second week, conditions were even worse. A quarter of the thousand-strong garrison were dead, and many of those still alive were severely wounded. Once Lizzie saw a round shot blow off an officer's head, while he was sitting on the verandah. To her horror he still sat there, motionless and headless, the blood spouting out and covering all those who vainly rushed to his aid; an ayah was only to last a few hours after her wounds – one morning she had been shot as she had crept to the well for a small dish of water for the baby; a railway-engineer, struck by a grape-shot in the spine, lay paralysed on his face outside the parapet walls, too near the enemy to risk rescuing in spite of his calls for help; one soldier had even discovered a woman lying on her back suckling her twin babies, both her arms broken and unable to rise. Babies were born in pain, and died in pain, sometimes of wounds, sometimes of disease or lack of water; General Wheeler saw his son Godfrey decapitated. It was this that broke the general, who from then on lay on his mattress, a crushed and broken man. He was not the only one. Even the clergyman had lost his mind and took to wandering around the ruined parapets naked, screaming obscenities at the enemy who, far better equipped with guns, kept up a constant and deadly attack, day and night.

By now their pathetic table had long since vanished, used along with skirts, petticoats, even pages from the New Testament, to ram the shot down in the guns; Mrs Jacobi gave her stockings to wrap up the grape shot for the guns; Lizzie gave her watch and necklace to be used as substitute for shot when it ran out.

114

Together she and Mrs Jacobi gathered stones for ammunition; they comforted the orphans, some so thirsty they could only suck on the leather straps of the water carriers for any relief. They were both so tired now, they would take it in turns to care for the baby while the other slept. Survival was the only important thing in their lives; all else was forgotten. And now it wasn't survival from day to day, but from hour to hour. The sound of wailing, the smell of the dead, the endless parched feeling in her mouth, the sights not only of the wounded and dead but of those remaining – once pretty women who in two weeks had become haggard and old, lined and mistrustful. All this made Lizzie sometimes wish she were dead, or could follow the crazed young woman who suddenly went mad and rushed out of the entrenchment, howling, straight into the eager bullets of the enemy.

Yet she still hung on, like the rest of them, clinging to the flimsiest pieces of hope, shreds of faith, hoping for a miracle. Each night she slept and dreamt of England, lost in a world of cool green fields, the chimes of distant church bells across the light drizzle of an English evening, the bark of sheep dogs and the glitter of dew-dropped buttercups at her feet – only to wake and find herself once again suffocated by the red dust, the heat, tormented by the gleeful shouts of the enemy as they hammered yet more shot into the garrison. And when she looked cautiously from the window to witness the destruction, she wondered, now, how she ever could have lived in that blackened wilderness that had once been a bustling town. Everything had been destroyed. The buildings were burnt: some of the roofs of the bazaar were still intact but she could see that most of the huts serving as shops had been torn apart; the steeple of the English church had been daubed with red signs and the cock on the steeple which Indians used as target practice was completely bent.

Lizzie was too tired to leave the room that day.

She stared out till nightfall, thankful that at least their room, uncomfortable as it was, had been spared from the cannons so far. It was as she looked at the last slanting strip of sun that streaked the black sky that she felt a tap on her shoulder.

'Lizzie?' It was Mr Jacobi. His face was smudged with dirt from being at the guns all afternoon, his trousers torn, his eyes hollow with exhaustion.

'Yes?'

'There's a messenger here, Lizzie. He came today, from Allahabad, from Havelock's army. Havelock will be coming, Lizzie, he says, but,' and he shook his head when he saw her face brightening, 'no, it will be too late, I fear. He won't be able to get here for two weeks. God knows what we'll do.' He sat down hopelessly on the floor. Lizzie's heart sank.

'Oh, the messenger asked to see you, Lizzie,' said Mr Jacobi, waking from a brief, dazed sleep. The sun was affecting him and his memory was going. He hardly knew where he was these days.

'To see me?' Lizzie shook her head disbelievingly.

'Yes,' said Mr Jacobi, summoning up all his strength to remember what he'd been talking about. 'He saw your name on the list. He's with Wheeler.'

Lizzie took the baby and left the room, slowly. What could this message mean? Perhaps it was someone who had met George – or had news of Emily? Stretching out a hand to support herself against the crumbling walls she quickened her pace slightly, through the labyrinthine corridors of the entrenchment, picking her way over heaps of rubble, sometimes dodging through exposed parts of the walls where the sepoys still amused themselves at night, taking pot-shots at anything that moved.

Wheeler's rooms were behind a large green wooden door, the paint now chipped with shot. Lizzie paused before knocking. Then she rapped on the wood.

A soldier opened the door and looked at her suspiciously; so many of the wretched group trapped in the entrenchment came and begged to talk to Wheeler that no one was allowed in except by appointment. And in the darkness Lizzie did indeed make an odd picture, dirty, drawn, skin peeling from the heat.

'Yes?'

'I'm Mrs Whittle,' Lizzie's voice was low, despairing. 'Mr Jacobi said a messenger wanted to see me. . . .'

The soldier nodded. 'Yes. Wait, please.' He left her in the ante-chamber, a room completely bare except for a chair, a cracked picture of a moustachioed army general, and a pair of boots that had been flung down in the corner. Lizzie put the baby down on the chair where he happily played with his toes. Time went by, and finally Lizzie heard Wheeler's voice.

'Mind how y'go, m'lad,' he was saying, 'you'll get your head blown off if you don't watch out, like m'son. Now hurry, hurry. . . .' The door of his room was opened and Lizzie couldn't help but be shocked to see the old man. His old sprightliness and dignity had left him, his eyes were clouded, his hair was completely white and his hands shook. He was stooped and bent – and finished.

'What are you doing here?' he asked Lizzie, noticing her.

'I'm Mrs Whittle,' said Lizzie, rising, 'Mr Jacobi said . . .'

Wheeler nodded. 'Yes, he wants words with you . . . here she is, I'll leave you, now hurry mind you. . . .' And he held the door open for Richard to go through.

Lizzie didn't recognize him at first. As everyone else in the entrenchment looked so bent and diminished, he looked like a giant. He was wearing a stained shirt and a turban, and his face was black with cork. Hours of hiding, running, crouching had all taken their toll; his hand was bandaged from a cut, his cheeks were scratched by prickly pear, his hair matted from sweat and dust, Lizzie shrank back.

Richard didn't say anything. He could hardly recognize Lizzie either. She was drawn and pale, her eyelids swollen with mosquito bites, her cheeks were sunk and her lips pale and cracked. She nervously put a hand through her hair as he stared at her, and when he saw the familiar gesture Richard couldn't help but approach.

'Lizzie,' he said, taking her by the shoulders and looking at her, shaking her slightly as if to jog her memory, 'Lizzie, it's me, Richard. What are you doing here? I thought you were in Calcutta . . . my God, poor Liz . . . where's George and Emily? Why aren't they here? I saw your name on the list of people, you see, I had to see you. . . .'

Lizzie stared at him. Then she sank down on to a chair to steady herself.

They were alone. The heat in the windowless room was unbearable. It felt as if they were being suffocated by invisible pillows, and the heat seemed to put up even more of a barrier between them, as if it were tangible.

'What are you doing here?' she asked, slowly. 'Oh, Richard, don't go . . . please, not this time!' Suddenly she was in his arms, sobbing desperately, the first time she had cried for weeks. The burst of emotion not only refreshed but released her features from their grim and desperate grip and as Richard looked at her he saw her blossom out, her eyes grow light, her mouth reddening, and underneath the torn, bloodstained bodice, he could feel her full breasts moving against him. 'Richard, why didn't you let me talk to you? If only you could have understood. . . .'

Richard pushed her from him gently, but shook his head. 'There's nothing to explain,' he said, 'it was all very silly. We were very foolish. You have married Whittle . . . well, I was stupid. Perhaps I shouldn't have gone to India. It was my selfishness that lost you for me.'

Lizzie shook her head. 'Is that all you can think? I was desperate. I went to your father, he was dreadfully ill, and they wouldn't let me see him, so I couldn't get any money. And on top of that, Richard, I was expecting your baby . . . this baby . . . he is yours, not George's! Anyway, I explained it all in a letter to you – and you did not care to reply. I *had* to marry him, there was nothing else I could do! You were gone . . . oh, God, I've never betrayed you or forgotten you! I love you!'

Richard shook his head, and his disbelieving smile was almost worse than any insult he could have hurled at her. 'You are very upset, Lizzie, you are weak and ill, you are confused. I received no such letter. . . .' He was doing all he could in his power to stop showing his emotions. His hands trembled as they gripped her shoulders. The sight of her, ill as she was, only served to open up barely healing wounds; it was all he could do to stop shouting or crying himself. He kept telling himself to keep calm, telling himself she was ill, possibly hallucinating with the conditions in the entrenchment. . . . 'Where's George, and Emily?' he asked in a controlled voice.

Lizzie stared at him. 'You don't believe me, do you?' she whispered. 'You think I've got sunstroke! Oh, you'd do anything not to believe me, wouldn't you! I trusted you, I believed you, and I loved you, and yet now I find I was right. For you it was nothing, just a cheap romance. Oh, God, to think I've fooled myself so utterly, I feel ashamed. . . .' She sat down again next to the baby, weeping, and the baby started to cry, too.

Richard could hardly take any more. He turned his back on her. 'Of course it wasn't a cheap romance,' he said, hoarsely, 'I was going to marry you. I loved you. I would have come back . . . then I find in Calcutta you arrive with George Whittle as your husband . . . flaunting him in my face. . . .'

'But you knew!' cried Lizzie, desperately. 'I wrote and the moment your father became so ill you must have known – there was no other course left to me. I had to marry. You would not return. And I had to marry someone with money to save us to keep father out of the courts!'

'I tell you, my father wasn't ill!' Richard turned, angrily. The room seemed to spin in front of him. He was so exhausted he could hardly follow what Lizzie was saying. 'He has been perfectly fit! I won't listen to any more of this nonsense! Don't you think I've been hurt enough? But this isn't going to help us, anyway. I must get back to Havelock before it is too late. No doubt your husband will take care of you and your baby while you are here,' he added, bitterly. As he turned to go, Lizzie put a hand on his arm. Her eyes blazed, and she looked at him fiercely. There were red spots of fever on her cheeks, her face shone and her hand shook.

'Richard, I'm not lying. I'm not ill, I swear to you, this is the truth.' Lizzie's hand tightened on his arm. 'George has

119

gone to Calcutta and left us here. He went to get more provisions. Emily has gone to Azimullah, poor girl. I am here, on my own, with your baby. George knows – he will tell you – God knows, I've suffered enough because of it! This is your child, Richard, our child, our baby!' And she pointed to the baby, with tears of rage and unhappiness pouring down her cheeks. Richard paused, his eyes flickering from the baby to Lizzie's face. Then he put his hand out and stroked the baby's soft head.

'Poor child,' he said, 'whoever you are.' He put his finger under the baby's chin and lifted its head up slightly. Then, his face full of puzzlement and unhappiness, he took Lizzie into his arms and kissed her, his whole body enveloping hers. He still felt faint from the heat. He also felt out of control. Lizzie's story had enough truth in it for him to feel waves of doubt about his feelings. Had he been anywhere but on his mission, he could have allowed his thoughts to wander, and to question her. But he had to get back to Havelock. He gripped her tightly, and looked down at her. 'I'll bring help as soon as I can,' he said. 'I've been told so many times – never trust a woman. I would give anything to believe you, Lizzie, anything. Escape with me now . . .' His cheek against hers was warm, gentle. For a moment Lizzie clung to him, the flickerings of desire lapping at her, longing winding itself around her. . . . Then, his words sinking in, she felt herself grow cold. He didn't believe her. He didn't trust her. It was hopeless.

She drew away coldly. 'It's too late,' she said, bitterly. 'Too late. Whether you believe me or not, it's too late. Now go – go away, get help. Leave here!' she added, turning away to hide the pain that must show in her face. 'Go away and get help!'

Richard walked to the door. His hand on the latch, he turned and looked at Lizzie's forlorn figure, her ragged clothes, her lank brown hair hanging like a gypsy's down her back; he looked at the baby, into its eyes, framed by dark lashes, its small dimpled cheeks, its tiny fingers. As he left he felt, despite himself, suddenly torn by a baffling feeling of pity, anguish and, above all, terrible unhappiness.

12

The monsoons had not yet come. They were late that year, as if, sympathetic to the Indians, they were holding off, determined to make the British even more harassed by the weather. The ground was hard and cracked and outside the entrenchment it was as if nature was holding still; everything, the trees, the plants, the flowers were all held in suspension by the heat.

Richard had managed to smuggle himself out of the entrenchment walls under cover of darkness; the problem was how to slither through the enemy lines and on to the road to Allahabad without being killed. Even at night, every move he made prompted a cry from a sepoy; every crackle provoked spasmodic gunshot. Inch by inch he made his slow and painful way, crawling through bushes, running swiftly for cover under a tree, sometimes simply lying flat on the ground, palms outstretched on the parched earth, trying not to breathe for fear of attracting attention.

By dawn he had made it. Not that his troubles ended there. Once on the open road, other problems faced him; he knew he could just pass for a Eurasian if he spoke as little Hindu as possible, as the sun had tanned him deep brown and he had dyed his hair glossy black. Some villagers might help him and shelter him, some out of loyalty and friendship, others out of fear, villagers who would make him sign a chit saying they had helped him so that they could be assured of mercy if the British descended on their village. But there were also the Nana Sahib's sepoys who would kill him on the spot if they discovered who he was.

The important thing now was time. He had to get a horse. The journey back on foot would take him two or three days; on a horse he could probably get back to

121

Allahabad in twenty-four hours. It was the thought of Lizzie that spurred him on; even if he didn't trust her now, he had loved her once, and the last image he carried of her would cause him to forge ahead faster, more to obliterate the memory of that wretched scene than anything else.

At midday he rested under a huge banyan tree, the leafy shade a luxury. Nearby a holy man with limbs thin and brittle as twigs squatted by the roadside, impassive eyes staring straight ahead. For him there was no mutiny; whoever won in India, he would still be sitting there, gazing into eternity, waiting for the chink of a rupee or the brush of a handful of rice thrown into his begging bowl.

From the tree, the country swept away, dusty white and parched, in front of him. Somewhere beyond a small grove of neem trees and beyond the fields was the river Ganges, 'mother' Ganges as the Indians always called it, the holy river of healing water, the place to pray and die. Richard, squatting, his hands on his knees, could see far away the faint but elegant curves of the horns of the water buffalo, standing patiently in the shallow mud that lined the river. The sun burnt overhead, glaring, a scalding white light that, shaded by the fronded leaves of the tree, seemed even brighter than usual.

His head fell slowly over his knees; his eyes closed and he slept.

It was an hour later when he woke, stiff and uncomfortable. He stretched, and blinked at the view in front of him.

It had changed, very slightly. The sun had moved a few degrees to the west, but also in the grove of neem trees Richard could make out a small group of men standing around some horses. He squinted to see them more clearly. Something about their appearance reassured him. They were a sober group of six men, talking. He guessed they must be servants of a rajah, for they were all dressed in the same uniform, dark blue coats and dazzling white silk turbans; they had the well-rounded faces of those used to regular and substantial meals. The horses, too, looked well cared for.

Before he had time to consider further, one of them

noticed him and beckoned him over with a shout. He had no choice. He went over to them. At least he had money on him; perhaps one might be bribed to accompany him and take the horse back if they would not agree to sell one. They said nothing when he approached, and he could tell nothing of their reactions from their faces. He knew they must know he was not Indian, but he could not gather whether they were hostile to him or not. They stood around him, staring at him, chattering to themselves.

Richard reached into the folds of his shirt and pulled out a wallet. He pointed to a horse and coughed, 'I will buy a horse from you, or rent one,' he said in Hindustani, 'How much?'

He was met with the same impassive reaction. He was used to this by now but it still irritated him. Slowly he pulled the money from the wallet, letting the coins jangle enticingly into his hand. They looked more interested but still said nothing.

'British,' one of them said at last, spitting a jet of red betel juice from his mouth on to the ground. There was no note of criticism in his voice, just the odd flatness of a statement. They then started chattering among themselves. Richard watched them warily. The tide could turn either way with them. Maybe they would help him. He turned from face to face, smiling, offering them the money, each in turn.

They seemed about to resolve something, when their chattering was stopped by the appearance of another man, a tall, fine-looking young man, his figure emphasized by the soaking tunic which covered his body. This was the owner of these horses, Richard realized. A servant dried him, another rushed up to him with a long, clean, white shirt and another slipped his jewellery on to his fingers. Richard decided he must have been taking his daily immersion in the Ganges at a special spot. This changed things. Should he now stay? Or should he run? He stayed. It was worth the risk. And there was nowhere to go.

'I would like to buy a horse, sir,' he said, in Hindustani, looking the stranger in the eye. 'I am on urgent business.'

123

The servants chattered around the young man, each giving their view of Richard, some of which was too quickly spoken for Richard to understand.

The stranger, now completely dressed, put out a hand to hush them and walked slowly towards Richard, a half smile crossing his face.

'So you are British. You have urgent business. You want a horse. You have big problem!'

'Richard nodded.

'Where are you going? To Allahabad? You are a soldier?'

Richard said nothing. His spine prickled as he felt the gaze of the young man upon him.

'I have money,' he said, showing it. 'I need a horse.'

The stranger paused, stroking the silk of his jacket with his brown bejewelled hand thoughtfully.

'I think you need rest, *firinghi*,' he said, suddenly decisive. 'You need a meal, a bath. We will take you with us. I am Rajah Meera. I will consider your offer.'

Richard's immediate instinct was to run, but as he tensed his muscles the servants surrounded him. He was trapped.

'I will talk to you later,' said the stranger. 'You will not be being afraid. Perhaps I will consider your proposals. Perhaps I will not. Maybe I will take a little time in thinking about it.'

He smiled courteously at Richard, then snapped a word of command at the servants who immediately came up to him and removed his possessions, money and pistol, and handed them to the stranger.

'This is for your safety,' he said. 'I am keeping these for you, so you will be being protected. There are many robbers on the road, and I am afraid to say even my servants are not entirely trustworthy. So all this will be better with me, sir. Safer. Come with us, and we will see if we can help you. Come.'

Still entirely uncertain what his fate was to be, and cursing himself for a fool, not knowing whether this man was friend or foe, Richard joined a servant on a horse and

124

followed the rajah across the dry, caked land. There was nothing else he could do, anyway. He would certainly be safer and more likely to get help if he continued to behave politely and unprovocatively. He looked back briefly. The whole scene he had left had vanished into a huge cloud of white dust set up by the horses' hooves.

At the entrenchment, the hours of unremitting horror continued, only after Richard's message there was perhaps an even greater feeling of pessimism about the place than before. Before there were at least some who had clung to the idea that Havelock's army might arrive any day; now they knew for certain that there was no chance of his arriving for at least ten days. They could not possibly hold out for even half that time. There was talk of surrender, some people just lying down and refusing to eat from despair and exhaustion.

As there was no ammunition even the guns lay nearly silent now, and apart from the odd brick hurled feebly over the entrenchment walls by a soldier whenever a sepoy approached, the growing silence hung over the entrench-ment like a shroud. All vestiges of life had simply been beaten out of them. Something had to happen.

The following afternoon Mr Jacobi came half running to their room. 'Come up to the ramparts! Mrs Greenway is here! Come and look!'

Lizzie and Mrs Jacobi hurried up, and shading their eyes saw what was indeed the figure of Mrs Greenway, ragged, without shoes, holding a baby on one arm and carrying a stick with a white rag tied to the top.

'She's gone mad, poor soul!' said Mrs Jacobi, squinting out. 'I thought the Nana would have killed her. He must have been keeping her prisoner! Why look, poor dear, her ears, so bloody, my goodness they have torn her earrings from her. . . .'

'She's carrying a note – a message.' Lizzie screwed up her eyes against the sun. 'Perhaps we have a chance. . . .'

Mrs Jacobi put her arm around her and squeezed her hand. 'Oh, I hope so, I hope so,' she said, tears coming to her eyes at the idea. 'For we cannot go on like this, indeed we can't.'

Mrs Greenway had brought hope. While her children were being kept hostage by the Nana Sahib she had been sent to General Wheeler with a note from Azimullah Khan, offering terms of peace. 'All those who are in no way connected with the acts of Lord Dalhousie and are willing to lay down their arms shall receive a safe passage to Allahabad.' That was the message, and the tension in the entrenchment was so explosive, everyone's emotions were so tautly strung, that some could swear they could almost hear the conversation in Wheeler's room in the silence. There was argument about whether to give in or not, of course. Some officers insisted it was a trap because the Nana Sahib knew that relief was coming from Havelock and wanted to avoid a confrontation; others argued that, trap or no trap, everyone was certainly done for if they stayed in the entrenchment. The rains would be coming soon, the rations had quite run out and Wheeler argued there was no reason for the Nana Sahib to break his word now. After all, there were only the wounded, the women and children and old men left.

That evening when Mr Jacobi announced that Wheeler had accepted the rebel's terms, both Lizzie and Mrs Jacobi broke down and cried. Even Mr Jacobi's mind had been cleared by the news; he held his wife, clasped Lizzie's hand. 'We will be free, at last,' he cried. 'We will be out of here. Back to Bombay, or Calcutta or even England, away from here . . .'

The relief of knowing it was over was overwhelming. Wheeler had insisted that the British be allowed some ammunition and that someone should be shown the boats to take them to Allahabad to prove that it was not a trap, and had insisted that the garrison be given one night's sleep before the journey the following day. But few could sleep that night. Soldiers who had previously been unable to rise from their sick-beds got up and hobbled about beating old tins with sticks to entertain the children; the children whose eyes had been empty with despair even started to dance as well as their rickety legs could manage; mothers rocked babies in their arms moaning: 'Heaven be praised, the Lord be praised. . . .'

The more practical and realistic of the group, like Mr Jacobi, sewed bullets into their uniforms and clothes until they were walking armouries, and Mrs Jacobi took Lizzie to show her where she had hidden her jewels, on a far edge of the compound. 'I buried these when I arrived,' she said, with a grin on her face, as she unearthed a little tin casket full of turquoise, silver and gold spoons. 'I wasn't going to let those rebels have them, even from the barrel of a gun. I must sew them into my skirts!'

Everywhere people were collecting their pitiful belongings, Bibles, stained photographs of loved ones, locks of hair, coins slipped into any secret pocket they could find. Hidden stores of lentils and dhal were delivered up. Mrs Jacobi prepared a last supper for them in their room, and, drunk on one precious glass of brandy that had been found, Mr Jacobi started to dance in the middle of the room while Mrs Jacobi clapped her hands and sprinkled him with water now freely available from the well.

Even Lizzie could hardly restrain herself, despite her misgivings. The relief made her heady, and she ran around the ramparts in full view of the sepoys, revelling in the freedom, drinking in the night air that, now purged of the acrid smell of gunfire, smelt pure and sweet. The guns at last were silent; instead the sound of wild rejoicing took their place, yells, songs, screams, whoops, tears and laughter as, merry with the prospect of freedom, the British enjoyed their last night in the entrenchment.

The night slowly turned to day and by then the British were prepared to evacuate the entrenchment. Huddled by the gate, this mere handful of 500 survivors were a sorry sight, ragged, many men shirtless and some of the women with bandages instead of shoes. Now it actually came to leaving a few became frightened. The entrenchment had been a living hell – one last backward glance at it showed the dusty compound, now deserted except for a few broken pieces of china, torn pages from books, a bent fork, a few bones; above, the vultures circled waiting to descend on the unburied bodies that still scattered the ground, black shapes in the hazy blue sky. But at least it was familiar; now the group faced the unknown, a journey with no guaranteed protection, dependent only on the word of a man who had already betrayed them. The doors opened slowly, creaking painfully, and the group made its straggling way on to the plain. After the line had hobbled a short way, it was met by the cavalcade provided by the Nana – sixteen painted elephants and eighty palanquins for the wounded.

'I don't like the look of this,' said Mr Jacobi, keeping the two women close to him. Nearby rebellious sepoys clustered round the group of Europeans, some bursting into tears on hearing the death of a beloved officer, some greeting their former masters with heart-felt salaams, others spitting disdainfully on the ground. The elephants still stood, the mahouts looking scornfully down at the bedraggled group.

'Why the hell didn't they make the elephants kneel?" asked Mr Jacobi. "Come on, boy, put the elephant down! We can't get up!"

The mahout pointed in a surly way to the animal's tail, and by that they gathered they would simply have to haul themselves up as best they could. No one was going to trouble for them. Another officer followed them. Lizzie turned to him when they were on top, suddenly stricken by panic. 'Do you think it will be all right?' she asked, desperately. 'Will they really allow us to go to Allahabad in safety? I'm so worried – they wouldn't kill women and children, surely?' The officer said nothing, just put his arm around her and hugged her tightly, looking at the baby, and as he did so Lizzie wished she hadn't asked him the question. Only two days ago his wife and two children had been shot to pieces in front of him.

From the top of their elephant they could see the other Europeans getting up on to the other animals. One woman of about sixty fell from the tail of the elephant into the dust, and several of the Indians hooted with laughter, then pushed her back up with their hands uncaringly shoving her up by her bottom, provoking even more mirth. Finally all the wounded were in the palanquins, and the rest of the refugees on the elephants. The sorry procession moved off to make the mile-long journey to the river. The sun was only just starting to rise up into the sky, and the heat and the silence was putting everyone into unbearable suspense. The knuckles on Mr Jacobi's hands as he clutched his Bible, Lizzie noticed, were white with tension. The faint whispering Lizzie heard was Mrs Jacobi, muttering the Lord's prayer. Lizzie's mouth was set; something was wrong, terribly wrong.

Finally they came to the sandy gorge where the river turned. It was a bleak, sheltered spot with nothing but prickly pear and fronded trees on either side. On the banks of the river, where the boats waited, stood crowds of Indians staring in silent amazement at their former rulers, half clothed, bedraggled, wounded, starving, clutching each other with fear. As the elephants stopped there was a sudden shriek as a parakeet flapped noisily into the air; for an instant everyone turned in panic. Then, in their fright, they dismounted, with no assistance from the Indians, and brushed themselves down as they stood in a group on the shore.

The next move was to the boats. There were no planks or boarding gangways provided so the men had to wade out thigh-deep to carry the women and wounded into the boats as the Hindu boatmen stood immobile on the boats which were anchored midstream. The officer who had sat next to Lizzie carried her and the baby out, and her torn and dirty skirts pulled at the water as they fell over his arm. Looking around her fearfully she could only see the crowds, and above them, the empty sides of the gaping gorge. A stone rattled down one side, making everyone jump; then there was silence except for the rustle of water as the Europeans waded to the boats. On the boats a small ten-year-old boy suddenly burst into tears. 'I want mama,' he sobbed, suddenly. 'Where is mama?'

Mrs Jacobi put her arm around him. 'Mama is with

129

God,' she said. 'There, there, we'll take care of you, we'll be fine, just fine, you wait and see. Look – the boatmen are preparing the oars, see the ropes being loosened. . . .' She tried to distract him, but nothing assuaged his grief and in the end she could only hold him, rocking gently, soothing him.

The water splashed on the sides of the boats, lapping in sinister peace as the Europeans continued to embark. A man near death at the other end of the boat gave a sudden and alarming sigh as if he had expired. His brow was cooled with water, and his breath still came, only very shallow now. A squirrel chirruped as it dashed from tree to tree on the bank. Now the boats were nearly full. They were so loaded up that the water was only a foot from the top and they rocked precariously, as the Europeans jostled for the most shady sides of the boats where the thatched roofs offered some protection from the sun. The embarkation was now over. The shore was bare of Europeans now, and the Indians pushed down to the shore to fill their places, to get a better view. It was, felt Lizzie as a prickling feeling went down her spine, as if they were waiting for something. . . .

Then there was a bugle call. Searing into the silence it was almost like a scream; birds rose fluttering from the trees and there was a gasp from the watching crowd on shore. The Europeans stared around them, wondering what it meant. Then they realized. For, as if obeying a secret command, all the boatmen leapt out of the boats and swam for the shore; at the same time hundreds of sepoys, hidden in the trees, suddenly appeared from their leafy camouflage and, taking aim, opened fire on the boats. At the same moment, the thatched roofs of the boats burst into flames, sparked by burning charcoal left by the boatmen. A piece fell on Lizzie's skirt and, screaming, she jumped up. The officer beside her pushed her down to avoid the bullets and as he did so he was hit. Clutching his chest he reeled off the side of the boat and into the water, leaving a bloody trail behind him.

Everywhere was chaos and uproar. Screams of horror

and panic mingled with the crack of gunshot as the Europeans opened fire back at the sepoys, bullets spraying into the river and throwing up fountains of blood. Men and women leapt from the boats into the river and started wading, panic-stricken to the shore, but here they were shot down, too, and soon the river was churning and there were bodies everywhere.

The air resounded with the shrieks of women and children, screaming out for mercy in agonized prayer. Lizzie kept down in the boat, frozen with terror, witnessing the scene of horror through a chink in the boat. The water was red with blood and the smoke from the heavy firing of the cannon and muskets, and the fire from the burning boats lay like dense clouds all around them. Mrs Jacobi had jumped out of the boat, clutching the boy in her charge, and stood screaming with pain as pools of blood billowed around her. Mr Jacobi's body floated in the water beside her, his eyes open and gazing sightlessly at the sky. Thankfully another sepoy's bullet hit her straight in the heart and she slumped forward with a dreadful splash, dead, into the water.

Nearby the chaplain opened his prayer book and began to read from it in the middle of the water; he had not got beyond one verse before he, too, was killed. The sepoys waded in from the shore with cutlasses, slashing at the men, spearing the children in front of their mother's eyes, and everywhere were the signs of dreadful carnage, the whole place now stinking with fresh blood and gunpowder.

Eventually the firing ceased. There was calm again, interrupted only by the odd splashing of a dying man in the water, the sound of the unscathed people who were now helping each other up the river bank. From all the boats appeared a few survivors from the charred remains, and they slowly disembarked, making their way to the bank. Lizzie followed suit, clutching the baby. On the bank she stood with the rest, shivering uncontrollably, so shaken with terror and rage that she felt she could break into a thousand pieces, like a shattered ornament. She thought she had witnessed horror at the entrenchment, she thought she knew what betrayal was like when she had seen her bearer dancing on her bed, clutching her pearls; but torment and betrayal were nothing like this scene she had just witnessed and, miraculously, escaped from.

A sepoy jabbed at her at the hip to keep her pushed into the group, and as she looked at him she felt a great shot of hatred inside her.

'I hate you!' she hissed. 'You are all treacherous! Look what you've done!' she gestured to the river, and for one moment remembered the eyes of Mrs Jacobi as she fell into the river. . . . Tears came to her eyes. 'My friends . . . you have killed my friends . . . you are wicked, wicked . . .' and she began to weep, overcome with grief and horror.

The sepoy looked at her dumbly. 'But memsahib, I am not killing your friends, this killing is not my doing, it is another group, I am not understanding. I am saving you. . . . Here.' He pulled a piece of chapatti from his tunic and gave it to the baby. 'Here, stop your crying, be assured of my friendship.'

Lizzie took the chapatti from him and threw it to the ground. 'I'd rather starve than eat your food!' she said, between tears. 'I wish you had killed us, too. . . .'

The sepoy turned away contemptuously. A woman next to Lizzie whispered: 'Don't antagonize them, my dear, they really will kill us if you do.'

'They'll kill us anyway,' said Lizzie. 'Don't fool yourself they'll save us. Not now.' The woman next to her gave a small scream, put her hands over her ears and shuddered, moving away from her. 'See,' said Lizzie, not noticing the effect she was having, 'they are starting already.' The few men left had been picked out from the survivors and were briskly shot. This time there was no reaction from the hundred or so remaining women or the crowd of Indians. They had all seen too much killing to be moved one way or the other by the death of a few more.

Then the crowd was cleared, a path was made, and the

surviving women and children were pushed up the banks and on to the road, where they were pushed and prodded into a line of dirty bullock carts. Sullen with rage, Lizzie waited until the last cart and, ripping her skirts, got up at the very back. The eyes of the other women were dead with fear. Few could speak. Lizzie stood crammed against them waiting for the bullocks to move off.

'Oh, surely they won't harm us, not now, not after all this,' moaned a woman near her. 'They must intend to save us, at least.'

'Of course they will,' snapped another, a sturdy old lady of seventy with a brown face wrinkled like a walnut. 'They'll keep us as hostages. They would have killed us back there if they'd wanted us dead. The Nana wants to keep us alive for some reason. Probably to bargain with Havelock.'

Lizzie stared at the woman who had just spoken, a bitter smile of cynicism crossing her face. 'You can only be certain of one thing with these people,' she said. 'None of us is safe. We are all as likely to be killed as saved! There's only one way out – escape!'

'Escape?' said the old lady. 'We've got no chance of that. They are putting us all in the Ladies House.'

Lizzie looked down at the road. The cart was not going fast. She craned forward to look ahead. There was a clump of bushes on the side of the road that would offer some kind of protection. Without waiting to think, she pulled up her skirts, wrapped the baby up in them tightly and then jumped. She ran for the bushes. She fell, she rose and stumbled further and finally collapsed on her face in the bushy undergrowth. Not daring to look behind her now, she heard the rumble of the cart passing by, and then the crunch of gravel as a man leapt off and she heard his footsteps heading towards her. She covered the baby completely, then, biting her lip as hard as she could to make it bleed, she sucked at the wound, getting as much blood as possible into her mouth. She turned over, protectively covering the baby, her eyes open to the sun. As the footsteps approached she released the blood in a trickle from the side

133

of her mouth. She willed herself not to blink and yet could still see the face of the sepoy looking down at her, sword in hand. He thought she was dead, she knew that. But would he make sure? She would have to blink, soon. He seemed to stand there an age. She was holding her breath until she was sure he must be able to see her heart, thumping through her shawl; or she must be turning red. Still she lay, immobile. If she didn't blink in a second, she thought, her eyes would dry up. After an eternity he finally gave her the most enormous kick in her ribs, spat on her face and ran back down the road where the sound of the cartwheels were getting fainter in the distance. Sobbing with relief she rolled over and the baby, faint and red with suffocation, started screaming while she held him, rocked him and soothed him, clasping him tightly to her.

When they arrived at the palace, Rajah Meera disappeared into his own quarters, leaving orders for Richard to be entertained and refreshed until the evening meal. The palace was set in the middle of a forest and the first view was of its bright white marble walls sparkling through the trees. Then the forest cleared, and there was the palace, turreted at each corner, its domed roof set all over with pieces of mirror that sparkled in the sun, and reflected the sky and the greenery of the forest in a kaleidoscope of colour and brightness. He was shown down deliciously cool marble corridors to a room where a nautch girl immediately appeared, towel in hand, to give him a bath.

Richard sank into the bath with relief, and later the girl led him to a heap of cushions and massaged him with sweet-smelling oils. He was lulled by the swift strong strokes of her small hands, heady with the cool perfumes from the garden that wafted in through the windows of this marble room, made comfortable by yellow and purple cushions scattered everywhere, great tapestries of carpets hanging on the walls. He was nearly asleep by the time she'd finished, but when he heard the light step as she tiptoed away, he opened his eyes, turned his head and looked at her. She moved closer, smiling knowingly. He reached out his hand and took her arm and pulled her down on top of him. Finally exhausted he slept, and was woken by a bearer who handed him his freshly laundered clothes.

'I will take you to the rajah,' he said in perfect English and, bowing, waited until Richard had dressed before he led the way to the rajah's reception hall. It was a magnificent room, covered with mirrors, each studded with pearls. In the centre was an enormous fountain which played endlessly, cooling the air, spouting from golden fish. Pebbles lay at the bottom of the pool, their dull brown and grey colours glowing and shapes moving as the water played over them. Sitting on a marble step covered with piles of silk cushions decorated with embroidered roses, the rajah lay smoking a hookah, one elbow resting on the seat of an enormous gold-wrought throne.

'Sir,' Richard clicked his bare heels under his long shirt and bowed slightly.

Rajah Meera waved a jewelled hand at him to be seated on a long low couch in front of him. A servant appeared and offered him a hookah which he accepted. Behind Rajah Meera's head was a dazzling curtain of cut gems that shimmered in the light, making it almost impossible for Richard to look at him.

'You are British soldier?' the voice that came, eventually, was as impassive as stone.

Richard nodded. But why ask questions? The rajah had all his papers so he must know everything about him.

'The British are not so popular as they used to be,' said Rajah Meera ambiguously, taking a short pull at the hookah and letting the smoke gently out of his mouth in slow puffs.

'No, that is true,' Richard could be ambiguous, too. He stared coolly into the rajah's eyes. Whose side was he on, anyway? What game was he playing? The next question came after another silence.

'When were you born?'

Richard told him. This was common practice in India;

135

every rajah had his astrologer who he would consult before making any move. The rajah sat for a long time absorbing the information, deep in thought as if he were working on astrological charts in his head. Eventually he seemed satisfied.

'You will be wondering,' he said, picking his words carefully, 'whether I will be killing you or not killing you.'

Richard was not expecting such a direct approach, but he showed no sign of surprise or horror. He said nothing. Then he leant back on the headrest of the couch. 'I am sure you do not kill your guests,' he said, coolly.

Rajah Meera laughed. 'Indeed? This is – what is it called in your country – etiquette? I think it is also etiquette there not to kill your host, too?'

Richard had a sudden flash of the bodies of the Indians he had seen along the road, decayed, blackened, sickening objects, their heads hanging down, black tongues sticking out, legs eaten away up to the knees by the wild pigs.

'That is so,' he replied.

'Myself, I am thinking that the hosts in this country are getting a little tired of the guests. We do not like guests who come and take everything from us, kill our people, who take advantage . . .' He waved his hand, leaving the rest of the sentence to Richard's imagination.

'I agree,' Richard's face gave nothing away. 'I believe the British have in many cases taken too much advantage – and not given enough in return.'

Rajah Meera smiled again, showing his white teeth. He clapped his hands. 'Good,' he said, 'I shall enjoy discussing with you. We will continue this talk another day. We will dine first and then play polo.'

The phrase 'another day' struck Richard like a prison sentence. He realized he was not expected to leave soon. He would have to find a way to escape – and quickly.

'Isn't it a bit dark for polo?' he said, keeping his thoughts to himself. Three servants came in, each bearing an enormous round tray of beaten gold covered with curries, chicken, pappadams, dhal, sweetmeats. . . . They put them down between the rajah and Richard.

136

'We have a special polo here. We play with balls of smouldering wood so you can see the ball in the dark. And the field is lit with a thousand candles. It is very pretty,' said the rajah, leaning forward and helping himself delicately to a piece of chicken with his fingers. 'You will like it. Now go ahead – you must be hungry.'

Richard ate, but as hungry as he was his mind was working fast. He was trying to remember how they had reached the palace, trying to reconstruct from memory how the grounds were laid out, trying to imagine where walls led to, where bushes formed barriers, trying, on the basis of a short trip from the forest to the palace, to imagine the boundaries of the place in his head.

He must have been unnaturally silent for the rajah was eyeing him suspiciously, and he forced himself to make a few polite comments about the meal. Afterwards a nautch girl danced, and Richard found himself tense with the frustration of his position. His dark eyes narrowed as he sank more and more into his own thoughts; his mouth was set in grim concentration. A small vein on his neck contracted and expanded, the only sign of his anxiety as he assessed the situation.

Finally the rajah clapped his hands. The nautch girl curtsied. The rajah rose, brushing the crumbs from the skirt of his coat. 'Come,' he said. 'Polo.'

Richard followed him into the darkness and round to the other side of the palace. The sight took his breath away. A large field was lit by thousands of candles, round the outside and hanging on the trees; men carrying large torches stood at each corner to illuminate the field, and to the head of each horse a small flaming dish was attached, lighting each one up. It was a fine team of horses. They were glossy Arabs, well-fed, muscular beasts, pawing at the ground in anticipation of the game, and they stood at the side of the field, held by about a dozen men.

'We will have a practice run,' said the rajah, as he was helped on to his horse. 'It is not easy the first time.' Then, with a sweeping gesture he snapped his fingers at one of his men. 'Light the ball!' he commanded, and immediately a

137

burning orb appeared in the middle of the field. It was glowing orange and yellow, blue flames leaping from it, reminding Richard, like a bizarre joke, of an English plum pudding at Christmas. A faint smile crossed his face as he mounted the horse he was given. His hands gripped the reins tightly. Now he was on a horse he felt more secure; just the feeling of that sturdy muscular back beneath him, the feeling of power in his hands as he expertly twitched the reins this way and that, the whole feel of the horse as it cantered to the middle of the field, all that made him confident. He straightened his back and made for the orb. He galloped past, missing it as the horse swerved at the flames. The rajah followed him, hitting it far across the field where it was struck back by another on his side. Everywhere was the smell of scorched grass as the ball soared across the field. Richard forced his horse on to intercept it, and now he was beginning to get the feel of the game, he swept it across again to the rajah's posts.

'Now we will begin!' The rajah's voice carried over the field. 'Enough practice. You are a good horseman, Mr Applevale!'

Richard wheeled his horse back to the side of the field, screwing up his eyes to try to assess what lay beyond the field. A wall? A bush? A trench? It was too dark to see.

He deliberately hit the ball in the direction of the side of the field as an excuse to check out the terrain, but he could still see nothing except a patch of scrub, and then complete darkness. Above him the moon lay icy silver in the sky, but only a slither of itself, and not enough to light up more than the tops of the trees. Across the field the fiery globe skidded through the hooves of the horses, and he cantered back. The rajah galloped by, aiming low, and the ball raced across again to the other corner; Richard reined his horse in and assessed the situation. Then, taking up the reins and whispering in his horse's ear, he spurred him over; he got the ball and paddled it up the field, pursued by the rest of the players, the sounds of their hooves pounding behind him; then suddenly he wheeled round and, scooping up the ball with his stick, he whirled it backwards into the air,

138

right into the centre of the group. Sparks flew, the horses reared and whinnied, and for a moment there was chaos, shouts from the men, curses, panicking horses. . . . At this moment Richard leant forward and extinguished the flame on the head of his horse. Kicking into the sides of the horse, spurring it on, he galloped to the other side of the field, knocking over one of the men who held the candles, and leapt off into the darkness. He couldn't see where he was going, and the horse, too, was frightened. But he simply put his head down, charging ahead, regardless. He would have to trust to luck. Crashing forward they went on and on until the lights of the palace were far behind them, and they were successfully hidden in the forest. By now Richard had got accustomed to the darkness and began to see where he was. He pulled a hand across his forehead. It was covered with sweat. He rested for a moment, panting deeply. Then he jerked the reins and silently made his way through the forest and back on to the road.

13

The road that joined Cawnpore to Allahabad was the Great Trunk Road which weaved along the banks of the Ganges. This road, one of 'John Company's' contributions to the alteration of the Indian landscape, was, in the summer, a wide, dusty but well-maintained track. Journeying along it, the traveller was struck by the beauty of the fronded neem trees, the glimpse of the broad, grey-brown river, where camels loitered and watered, the wayside temples built precariously into the trunks of the holy banyan trees where a wandering holy man might be sitting, naked except for a loin-cloth, his alms-pot by his side. Across the flat and dusty fields he would see the elephants toiling by the farmers, the flash of a sari as a child played by its mother, perhaps an elegant line of women, silent, straight, and poised, baskets on their heads, the blues and yellows of their saris only occasionally showing through the tall grasses.

But the Great Trunk Road was changed the day that Richard galloped towards Allahabad. The rains had come. The hard surface had become sloppy and muddy, making the going hard; the skies were covered with vast clouds racing across the blue; the farmers and women were no longer in the fields and the only people to be seen were refugees – Europeans from Cawnpore and other stations up the Ganges in vast boats on the river, huddling together, a stray sepoy on a horse, Indian families pushing their entire possessions in carts, presumably fleeing from Allahabad or nearby villages where the British under Neill had instituted a reign of terror. No longer was the road a place to linger, to smile and salaam and say hello; now strangers passed hurriedly on their business, hiding their faces, none knowing who was friend or foe.

Richard galloped on. On the sides of the road now were toads and frogs, croaking in the dank pools that had formed since the last rains; vapour hung near the ground, rising up like strange misty vegetation; everything was soggy, the ground, sated with water, could absorb no more that day, and the steam that rose from it was like the gasps from the thirsty earth, exhausted with drinking.

Later that day, through the mist, Richard saw a British officer on a horse; he must be nearing the town. He spurred his horse on and soon shouted to the soldier who, at the sound of Richard's voice, smiled and saluted back. As Richard drew up, the man pointed across the road. There was a dull red glow in a field beyond and, listening, Richard could hear the wails of Indian women.

'Another village burnt to the ground,' said the officer with some satisfaction, rolling some tobacco surreptitiously and pulling a pipe from his uniform. 'That's the sixth so far and we're still a hundred miles from Cawnpore.'

Richard guessed this officer must be part of Major Renaud's army, sent on ahead to clear the road before Havelock set out. His eyes narrowed.

'You're wasting time, man,' he said, angrily. 'I've come from Cawnpore, from the entrenchment – while you're lagging behind burning innocent villages! Get on, for God's sake!'

The officer sighed as he took the pipe from his mouth. 'Tell that to Major Renaud, not me, old chap,' he said, wearily. 'He's got a thing about this. You'll see some nasty sights on your way to Allahabad if that's where you're headed.'

Richard nodded. 'It is indeed,' he said, wheeling his horse round. He stared once more at the pathetic wisps of smoke that rose up from the blackened earth that could be seen occasionally when the vapour shifted. It made him uncomfortable, sad, angry. He nodded curtly at the officer and rode on.

The officer had been right. There was not a single tree on the road to Allahabad now that did not bear witness to

Major Renaud's cruelty. From every branch an Indian hung, tongue blackened, legs eaten away, some still wriggling feebly on their ropes, their eyes bulging. Although Richard cut down the few that he could save, as he got nearer Allahabad the bodies were all still, though the widows sat below them, mourning their husbands, some making pitiful attempts to drag the bodies down to give them proper funerals. Richard deliberately kept his eyes on the road. Pity and compassion were right, but they should not be indulged in at a time like this. They would help no one. And yet anger was one feeling that he could not hold back. These punishments were only acts of utter stupidities that would infuriate the Nana, acts of revenge that would reap revenge as a reward.

Richard galloped into Allahabad late that night, exhausted. The windows in the tiny streets were all shuttered, or, if unshuttered, opened on to empty rooms that stared down like blind eyes into the alleys below. There was utter silence; it was after the hour of curfew. Allahabad had indeed been brought to heel by General Neill; it was not just tamed, it was utterly cowed. Even the birds seemed silent, and animals woken by the sound of the hooves of Richard's horse did not spring up with characteristic squawks and flutters, but slunk, as if afraid, into the darkness.

There was still a light in Havelock's quarters in the cantonment area of the town, and Richard went straight into his room to make his report. Havelock was sitting as usual at his desk, his Bible in front of him, an old map of Oudh territory on one side, a glass of iced soda by his hand. He looked fresh and quick, as usual, even at one in the morning, and greeted Richard warmly.

'I haven't got good news, sir,' said Richard, sitting down at Havelock's request. 'It is hell there. Wheeler is utterly broken. I can't imagine they have lasted out even until now as they had no more supplies. . . .'

Havelock paced the room as Richard continued, his small frame erect and alive, his eyes bright and interested.

'We must leave at once,' he said, decisively. 'I will give

the command. We are ready to go, but I had thought we might leave the day after tomorrow. In view of what you tell me, Applevale, we will leave at dawn. Now – you need sleep, refreshment. I will arrange it. You can sleep here for the night. I shall talk to General Neill.'

Richard, now he had delivered his message, felt his limbs heavy with exhaustion. He longed to rest, but he forced himself awake.

'One last point,' he said. 'I can't help feeling that Major Renaud is behaving very provocatively ahead of us. Is there no way to stop him? His actions will not help the situation in Cawnpore.'

Havelock shut his eyes and shook his head furiously, clasping his hands intensely in front of him. 'Applevale, Applevale, don't tell me, I know it, too well I know it. I am not for showing mercy to these devils, not one inch, but Renaud is not helping our cause. Justice – that is what God put us here to administer – justice, not slaughter and unnecessary cruelty! Canning is right. He has said he will not govern in anger. He said that he will deal out justice and that as stern and inflexible as law and might can make it. But he will never allow anger to proceed from the government of India. And everyone jeers at him for this!' He shook his head again in exasperation. 'But you tell one man out there your opinion, Applevale, and you'll be strung up yourself more than likely. Yet it is this hatred that makes them good fighting men, and God knows this army is pitiful enough. We need every strength we can get.' He paused as if exhausted, then lay his hands out, palms up. 'No matter. We'll be at Cawnpore in three days now, if we march quick enough. We will catch up Renaud before we reach Cawnpore and before news of his actions have reached the Nana Sahib, I trust. I am glad to see you, Applevale, and I admire your courage. I also admire your convictions. But we have fighting to do. We have to face the Nana Sahib. And win.'

The straggling line of soldiers that made its way out of Allahabad the following dawn was pitiful to see. There were barely over a thousand men, followed as usual by the camp followers, natives, wagons and supplies. There were the 78th Highlanders, sweltering still in their heavy red woollen tunics, Neill's 'Blue Caps', a motley selection of rogues who preferred to join this regiment than go to prison or face dishonour for various misdeeds – these were the black sheep of the army, an ill-assorted bunch of drunkards or thieves, hard-drinking, hard-swearing and some called 'the cohort of the damned'. Then there were the volunteers, all amateurs, mostly gentlemen. There were 160 Sikhs who wore their whiskers tied on top of their heads over their turbans and who seemed happy most of the time to be paid rations of drink; and finally there were the young Eurasians from the Madras Military Orphanage who scarcely knew how to fire a gun let alone the new Enfield rifle that had been issued to a few of the troops. However, Havelock, with his iron discipline, had somehow managed to forge an army out of this ill-suited bunch and though the progress was slow and the Highlanders dropped out quickly under the sun, sweltering in their heavy clothes, they marched ahead bravely.

On the second day they caught up with Renaud's 200 men and continued on and on, through the mud, slipping sometimes in the wet, through the same deadly flat landscape, the land the colour of straw pitted with great pools of grey water where buffalo wallowed luxuriously, the only creatures except for the mosquitoes, the frogs and toads, to revel in the rains. Every building on the way had been destroyed – the Indian villages by Renaud's army, the British buildings by rebellious sepoys; the milestones lay smashed at the sides of the road, the telegraph poles toppled precariously, their wires hanging torn and wild in the hot, damp air. Steam rose from the fields in the distance and Bibles rotted in the soldier's bags in the wet.

It was just outside Cawnpore, on the afternoon of the ninth day, that their main battle was to be fought. They had a couple of skirmishes, with no casualties, but the spies had reported that the Nana's men were assembling; this was the time this tiny, peculiar army would be tested as never before.

The site was bleak. It could have been any other spot anywhere in that part of the country. For there is a sameness about the countryside in Oudh – a monotony, an endless deadly repetitiveness of view: flat, grey, hot and never-ending, except for the odd grove of trees that breaks up the landscape.

Now the army collected itself under an enormous banyan tree to listen to Havelock, who was standing on two boxes in order to make himself seen and heard above the men. The hanging roots of the tree seemed to be reaching down to grab him from his perch; from nowhere there came a hot, dusty wind, the sign of more rain. Like a blast from a great furnace it swept through the crowd of soldiers so they sweated; the leaves on the trees rustled dryly and beyond, the light topsoil danced as it swirled in the wind's wake.

'By God's help, men, we shall save our people at Cawnpore,' said Havelock, his voice shrill to make himself heard. 'Or every man of us die in the attempt. I am trying you sorely, men, but I know the stuff you are made of. Think of our women and the tender infants in the power of those devils incarnate!'

Patcham, who was standing at Richard's side, whispered:

'It's all very well, but the Nana Sahib's got five thousand chaps waiting for us out there and we've only got a fifth of that. We haven't a chance.'

'But we must try,' said Richard, turning passionately to his friend. 'Patcham, if you'd seen what I'd seen you wouldn't talk like a coward!'

Patcham bristled slightly, and twirled his moustache nervously. 'A coward! I'm no coward! It's you who are the nigger-lover, Richard, with all your talk of cruelty! I've heard you . . . I don't understand you, I'm sure. Why, you know they roast our babes alive, or kill them and make their parents eat them! Our women are raped in front of their husbands and sold at market places! Children are forced to eat their mother's eyes. And you talk of cruelty to these fiends!'

'I don't believe it,' said Richard flatly. 'I've not yet seen anything like that. It's a lot of gossip, that's all. But what I do know is that we've got to win this battle whether we face five thousand, ten thousand or ten million. And I've got no time for talk of our not having a chance. Of course we have a chance!'

'Of course we have a chance!' Patcham, always good-natured, slapped Richard on the back cheerfully. 'I'm proud to be your friend! We'll kill everyone of 'em.'

'Aye, that we will!' A voice behind them made them start. Richard looked around and saw the back of a man sitting behind them who had overheard their conversation. '*And* we'll string them up so they don't know their hands from their toes!'

He started slightly, for the voice sounded slightly familiar, though he couldn't instantly place it. He looked questioningly at Patcham, raising his eyebrows and jerking a thumb at the man, 'Who's he?'

Patcham sighed, then leant closer to Richard and whispered. 'Poor devil, his wife's at Cawnpore, shouldn't think she's still alive myself. He's a boxwallah chap – didn't we meet him in Calcutta? I seem to remember his sister, a sweet girl. Anyway, the big fool left his family in Cawnpore to come to Allahabad on his way back to Calcutta, and then he heard the news. Joined up straight away, of course. He'll be in the front line, I can tell you. I've never seen a man so pitiful, nor a man so ready to do battle, either.'

'Don't you call me pitiful.' The man now stood up and faced them. 'I'm not so daft as I can't hear people whispering about me. I'm no fool, either. I've got ears and I hear everything around me. If I didn't want every man in this army to be fighting fit I'd knock you down, Mr Patcham!'

There was no mistaking the man now he'd got up. Even though his face was now burning red with the sun, even though his eyes were sore and swollen with grief, even though he hadn't shaved for days and his once smart frock coat was now dusty and torn, the rings were still intact on his fingers and the gleam of ambition still fresh in his eye. It was George Whittle.

For a moment the two men stared viciously at each other. Richard found his hand reaching automatically for his gun and at the same time Whittle's fist clenched as he recognized Applevale, and he drew back his arm to give weight to the blow; then a loud 'Hurrah!' from the soldiers threw them off guard. Havelock had finished his speech and the soldiers turned to busy themselves with preparations.

'I say, you chaps,' Patcham chipped in, 'You met before? Come on, give over, shake hands, we're on the same side now . . . or has the sun got to the two of you?'

Richard shook his head slowly, 'I can't shake hands with him,' he said hoarsely. 'I'll never shake hands with a man like that.'

Whittle said nothing, but stared at him as if he hadn't heard what he'd said. 'I didn't know you were on this column, Applevale,' he said slowly. 'I'd no idea it was you. Then you must have been the Applevale who was sent on ahead to the entrenchment. . . .' A light seemed to dawn on his face and he became more animated.

Richard swallowed. 'Yes, yes.' He nodded. Again that image of Lizzie kept returning to him, that image he was trying to beat out of his brain, that image that refused to leave him. 'I saw her, Whittle. I saw Lizzie and your son. They are alive.'

Whittle said nothing but then he turned and buried his face in his hands. 'Thank God,' he said. 'Thank God.'

Richard forgot his animosity in this one moment they shared together. He put his hand on his shoulder and turned him round gently. 'They are alive. If we fight hard we might get them. They might still be alive. There *is* hope.'

'My sister? She's died? You didn't mention Emily.'

Richard shook his head. 'She is with Azimullah Khan. Lizzie told me. She will be safe.'

Whittle nodded slowly, recovering. Then he held out his hand to Richard, and Richard, not knowing why, took it and they shook hands with each other solemnly.

147

'That's better!' said Patcham cheerfully. 'Now you're friends!'

Whittle looked at Patcham and smiled rather cynically. 'No lad, we're not friends, we're enemies. But even enemies can be comrades sometimes, eh, Applevale? And today we're comrades, no one can part us today.' He chuckled, recovering his spirits. He put his fingers into his cummerbund and loosened it, then pulled down his purple coat – a garment that was once garish but now was torn and stained with mud and sweat. 'Applevale and I are together,' he muttered to himself, amused at the remark. 'Who'd have thought we'd ever be equals. And yet we are equals, aren't we now, Applevale. War does funny things to men, I'll say. Eh . . . *my* baby you say? *My* son is alive?' he chuckled even more, and Richard felt a strange uneasiness as if these words held some significance for him.

'What do you mean?' he asked, brusquely.

'Oh, nothing, nothing,' said Whittle still laughing. 'Nothing to tell. And now, comrade, we'll go into battle together, and we'll get them out alive, eh? I've got a small supply of champagne back there and a few oat-cakes, come on, you too, Patcham, let's share them, we need the strength for this. . . . You've given me good news, Applevale, good, good news, so now you can come and have a free taste of the last of Whittle's stores!' And laughing roughly he led them to his small tent. Richard lagged behind momentarily. He was thinking of Lizzie's baby – the ruddy cheeks, the dimpled chin, the thin, fine hair on his head, his tiny hands and nails. . . . Then he pushed the thought from his mind. He followed briskly and joined in with the others as they had their last good meal before the fight.

It was the 78th Highlanders who were the heroes of the day. Despite the constant pounding of the Nana Sahib's guns, the 78th moved relentlessly forward, their heavy red tunics making bloody silhouettes against the white-grey of the dusty ground. The air resounded with the sound of shots, howls and the mocking sound of 'Auld Lang Syne' played by the rebel trumpets. Richard, Patcham and George were all equipped with Enfields, and swiftly followed the Highlanders to complete the slaughter. For a moment there might be a pause, always shaken by the sound of Havelock's voice: 'Charge! The longer you look at 'em the less you'll like 'em! Rise up! The brigade will advance!'

On and on they went, hiding, crouching, running, killing; the infantry crept forward with deadly accuracy, bayoneting the shrieking sepoys who fell, their white tunics covered with blood; in other parts of the field the only noise was the relentless 'Fire! Load! Rod! Home! Return! Cap! Fire a volley at one hundred yards only! Present! Fire! Load! Rod! Home! Return! . . .'

At one moment, faced by the appearance of a mighty howitzer, Havelock's army looked as if it might hesitate. Then with a great crash it exploded into action, and as Richard struggled to his feet to his horror he saw Patcham lying, one arm torn off beside him. He was stopped from thinking any more by Whittle's hand on his arm. 'Come on, Applevale, think of Lizzie . . .' and with a chilling howl they both rushed on the enemy, redoubled in their frenzy of hate and determination to win. To the left the Blue Caps lunged forward and to the right the 64th, the volunteer regiment, attacked on horseback, their broad hats and frockcoats silhouetted in the sun. Again and again they attacked, until finally, after three hours, the battle was over. The surviving sepoys scrambled away and there was no sign of the Nana Sahib. Cawnpore was theirs.

And yet it was a hollow victory. When they marched into the town the following morning, a ragged procession of soldiers, some using rifles as crutches, others, more seriously wounded, being carried on stretchers, the news came filtering down the column, and the gasps of the soldiers could be heard as the news was absorbed. The entrenchment was empty. The women and children had all been slain, butchered and all the men were dead. Not one European survived.

The feeling in the army was one of complete despair, frustration and futility.

They had marched for days and days in the most appalling condition; they had fought bravely, using the men as cannon-fodder; they had starved, sickened, fought and some had died — and for nothing. As retribution for Renaud's cruel devastation on the road, the Nana Sahib had slaughtered all the women and children. Worse than that, it was said, he had kept them for days, with no food or exercise in a cramped room in the Bibighar, or 'Ladies House', as it was known. On hearing of Havelock's arrival he had ordered the sepoys to shoot all of them dead; when they refused, out of compassion, he had summoned the butchers from Cawnpore who had committed the slaughter with hatchets and knives.

Whittle had ridden up ahead of the column as Richard and Patcham wandered through the alleys in the town in search of quarters. Patcham was still alive but very weak and was unable to keep from fainting. Richard, filled with despair, kept his arm round his friend's waist, helping him as best he could. Arjun Gohar, still faithful, ran ahead darting into buildings, prying, looking. Finally he found a deserted house near the bazaar and helped Richard carry Patcham into a dirty downstairs room where they collected boxes and rags and made them into a makeshift bed. An Indian shop owner peered nervously round the door when they were settled and crept in, offering sweetmeats as a peace offering. Tired, wretched and despairing, they simply accepted them gratefully. They were too exhausted to do anything else. Patcham slept for a while and Richard watched over him, mopping his brow with a dampened rag. Richard tried to focus his attentions on Patcham, to think of the living, not the dead, but from time to time he found a great pain welling up in his chest and enveloping his whole brain and he realized the implications of what had happened. Lizzie was dead. He would never see her again. He felt totally alone, bereaved. True, it was ridiculous, for she was married to another man. But while she was married he could still love her, still hate her through love; indeed, when he looked back on it, his entire behaviour over the last few weeks had been in response to her, his debauchery and anger had been a reaction to her marriage — and now there was nothing, nothing even to react to, nothing to feel betrayed by. She was dead. Pictures kept coming into his mind, pictures of her at Penworth Court on that last night, her glossy hair piled high on her head, her white teeth flashing him a smile across the table, the chance brush of her hand against his — he could even smell the stale woodsmoke in the drawing room as if he were there, himself. Then he had a picture of her face as he said good-bye, her eyes so troubled, her hand on the mantelpiece . . . and then her hand on his shoulder, her mouth against his, her warm moist lips. . . . And yet still, all the time, as a kind of background, there was the last picture he carried of her, tattered, despairing, the baby next to her, her eyes sunken but still flashing, her lips cracked but still red, her body drawn and hair matted, but still a body enclosing a life and a spirit. The pain rose within him again and he turned away from Patcham, the room spinning around him as he tried to contain the pain he felt.

Later Arjun Gohar, who had gone out to look for Whittle, returned with him. He seemed dazed and broken, his face collapsed and his eyes glazed. He staggered into the room almost as if he were drunk. Arjun Gohar dragged a box over from the side of the room and Whittle sat down heavily on it. His pallid face was covered with sweat, and as he searched through his baggage for a bottle of brandy, Richard noticed his hand shook like an old man's. He was trembling all over.

'Have you got a fever?' Richard enquired. That was the last thing they wanted, to be enclosed in a room with an infectious man. 'You must go to the hospital.'

Whittle poured a glass of brandy slowly. He tossed it back and poured himself another. Then he shook his head slowly. 'No, I haven't a fever,' he said, and his voice was shaky and uncontrolled, his words coming out in a kind of jumble.

'Then what is it?' Richard tried to sound kinder than he

felt. He turned to Patcham who groaned, then fell back into sleep again.

'I've seen it,' said Whittle, staring into space as if blind. 'I've seen it. It's like looking into hell, it truly is. I wish I'd not gone. Oh, God!'

'Seen?'

'Havelock showed me. The 'Ladies House'. And I've seen the well where the bodies were dragged and thrown in, great bloody stripes along the grass and inside the well a pile — a pile of severed heads, the raw stumps of limbs, sightless eyes, all pressed together. . . . I have faced death in many forms, but I could not look down that well again, Applevale. It was full right up to the top. There must have been near two hundred women there.' He turned to Richard and stared at him and now his eyes were almost mad with shock, grief and hate. They were bright white, bloodshot round the edges, pupils like pin-pricks as if he were trying to blot out every bit of the horror he had witnessed.

'The blood is still on the bushes around, limbs lie like branches on the ground. . . .'

Richard rose up, immediately, to see for himself, but before he could get to the door Whittle shouted, 'You'll not go and see that!' He rose from the box and grabbed Richard's arm. 'I'll knock you down before you do that! It makes men mad, that sight. For God's sake, don't go!'

Richard whirled round. 'I loved her too, you know! I have a right to see her grave!'

But Whittle had seized his rifle and lunged across the room. For a moment they were locked, fighting. Then Whittle pulled away and swung the rifle butt at Richard's head, and he slumped senseless to the floor.

He stood over him, this fat, gross man, and spat on the floor next to him. 'You'll not see what I saw,' he said, muttering. 'It's not fit for any man, it's hell. And she was my wife. Lizzie was *my* wife! I'm the only one to see her grave!'

He kicked at Richard's body, then went over to the other side of the room, dragged his coat from his bag and, huddling in the corner with his bottle, he drank himself into a stupor in order to sleep. Arjun Gohar crept into the room. He looked quietly at Whittle snoring in the corner. He quietly padded over to Richard, gently examining his head. Then he sighed with relief, moved him slightly and covered him with a blanket.

He went over to Patcham. 'Sahib?' he said 'sahib? I am here.'

Patcham opened his eyes. 'Gohar, good man,' he said, giving a weak smile. 'Get me some water, there's a good chap, and tell me – did we win?'

Arjun Gohar smiled slightly as he poured a glass from a hip flask, and handed it to him. 'Yes, we won, sahib,' he said, 'we won.'

It was well into the next day when Richard woke. Fatigue had worn him out so that even when he had recovered from being knocked out he had continued to sleep, and no one had thought to wake him. His head throbbed agonizingly and it hurt him to move. He groaned and opened his eyes. On the other side of the room Whittle had got up, and was sitting by Patcham's side feeding dhal into his mouth like a nanny. Patcham smiled slightly when Richard moved and got up from the floor.

'You've had a long sleep, old chap?' he said. 'This is a terrible do, isn't it? Whittle's been telling me about it. You'll think differently about the niggers after this, I'll bet!'

Richard stared at Whittle who stared back. 'Well?' said Whittle gruffly. 'I thought you wanted to go to see the sights, eh? Go on then. They'll have dug the graves by now, or at least covered up the well. Go along. See purgatory. But at least I've spared you hell.'

Without a word Richard turned to the door and left, making his way through the narrow streets of the bazaar to the 'Ladies House'. On his way natives stole out of their houses to press gifts on him, which he dismissed with a wave of his hand and a muttered Hindu curse. Here and

153

there was the old soldier, looking stunned and disgusted, and when he finally got out of the bazaar and into the gardens where the 'Ladies House' was set, he was struck by the pools of vomit among the grass where men had simply been unable to control themselves on witnessing the sight.

Richard paused. A Scotsman sat on the lawn, a bottle of whisky in his hand. 'Want to see the sights, sir?' he asked, drunkenly. 'Through there. Though I'd advise against it. That's where they were killed, sir. The bodies are in the well over there, but there's nothing to see now, they've covered it all over with earth, thank God. Made you sick to look it did. But the 'Ladies House' is not pretty. Go on, go and look for yourself.'

Richard looked across at the building. The sun danced on the orange tiles, glancing off the windows, and a slight breeze made the leaves of the mango trees behind quiver in the heat. He hesitated. On a thorn bush a piece of blood-stained lace fluttered tauntingly at him; below it was a pool of blood, drying on the grass.

He walked forward across the lawn, holding his breath. A soldier guarded the door and saluted when he arrived. 'In there, sir,' he said. He was holding a handkerchief to his nose. 'You'll excuse this, sir. It's the smell of blood. It makes me feel sick. . . .'

'Then go outside and breathe some fresh air,' said Richard. 'This is no place to hang around.'

'Thank you, sir.' The soldier retreated to the lawn.

Richard stepped into the room, and as he did so he felt the colour drain from his face. It was large and pillared, but not large enough to contain 150 women and children. And now it was inches thick in blood; there were cuts on the wall where the butchers had missed their victims, getting lower and lower as if the victims had crouched in terror to avoid the blows; there were Bibles on the floor, stained with blood, bits of hair torn from women's scalps, pieces of clothing, children's shoes. Looking up to take his eyes from the scene Richard saw a hook on the wall, surrounded by the small and bloody handprints of a child. He felt his whole frame seizing up. Choking, trying to stifle the vomit

154

that rose into his throat, he ran outside on to the lawn where he stood, gasping and horrified.

The Scotsman looked up, amused. 'I warned you, sir,' he said. 'Drives men mad, that does, sir! And you didn't see the pit yesterday. I'll tell you exactly what I saw. . . .'

But Richard walked on, dazed with horror. He reeled into the bazaar, hardly able to focus on the buildings, gaining self-control only after taking deep breaths and stopping every few minutes. He stopped by one shop and leant against a wall to control himself. A fellow officer he recognized who was walking down the street stopped and saluted him.

'Disgusting business, isn't it?' he said, his eyes glittering wildly. 'We'll be staying here a fortnight. Every native you see we have orders to shoot on the spot. Neill has got everything under control here, you see. He's going to force every native or sepoy he can find to lick the Ladies House clean with his tongue, then to be stuffed with pork or cow, whichever is most distasteful to his religion or caste, then shot from guns. I can't wait to see it, there'll not be an Indian left! My God, I used to trust them, the devils! If you'd seen what I'd seen – you missed the well. What a sight!'

Richard stared him in the eye. 'If I'd seen what you've seen I'd be mad like you,' he said, dully. 'What atrocity are you going to think of next? The Nana would never have done this had it not been for Major Renaud! Now we are preparing a retribution even more disgusting than the one we have witnessed! Not all Indians are like this. My God, I'd like to see the Indians wiped out, but at least I can keep a cool head against my feelings. My bearer's a good man, for one.'

'Huh! They all say that! He'll be murdering you in your bed tomorrow,' said the officer, snorting with cynical laughter. 'I'll come with you and we'll get him. He'll be on his knees licking the blood of our women and children till he's sick on it! And he'll be shot to a thousand fragments. Where are you billeted? I shall follow you! I can't see an Indian without killing! My mother was in there, you know? Killed by the people you trust!'

The officer was now beside himself, his eyes crazy with hatred and his cheeks red with mad fervour. Richard pushed him roughly to one side and started to run back to the house. He passed troops of Sikhs looting shops, while the shopkeepers were dragged off, tied and humiliated; sacks of rice and grain were spilled from the shops on to the streets and stray dogs charged in for a free meal; saris, blankets, sandals, potions, the contents of every shop lay smashed and trampled in the streets while the windows were broken with yelps of glee by the marauding British. A small Indian baby girl came running barefoot from one shop, crying. A soldier immediately lunged at her with a bayonet shouting: 'This is for your father! I'll kill a hundred Indians for every woman and child slaughtered in that place!'

Before he knew what he was doing and before the bayonet touched the child's skin, Richard shot the soldier dead on the spot. A few of the Sikhs looked up in surprise for a moment, then continued plundering the market place, as if nothing had happened.

Finally Richard reached the quarters; Patcham lay still on the bed; Arjun Gohar now was by his side, feeding him. Whittle sat at the end of the bed.

'You must go,' said Richard to Gohar. 'All the British soldiers here have gone mad. You'll not be safe for one moment, even with me.'

Arjun Gohar looked astonished for a moment, then his face relapsed into its usual impassive stare. He shook his head. 'I stay with you. You are my master. I will stay with you.' For one moment Richard looked at him and felt a terrible pang at the idea of parting with such a good friend; then he remembered what the British soldier had threatened.

'If you want it like that, very well. I am your master. I am ordering you to go. I am ordering you to go now!'

'I am not going,' replied Arjun Gohar, his features set into the resigned pose of Indian obstinacy.

'If you don't go you'll lose your caste and maybe get shot

from a gun. There's nothing I can do about it. Maybe you'll be lucky but there are crazy people out there, people who will kill every Indian on sight. Now go, for the last time, and never let me see you again!'

He heard a pounding on the door outside. It was the British officer who had tracked him down. 'Hide in the back,' he hissed, hurrying Gohar out.

Whittle opened the door to the officer.

'Come to visit the bearer, old man. Like to use him as a translator in the court we've set up.' The officer was still crazed. He walked forward, his gun at the ready. 'Come along, where is he now? Or has he fled already?'

'He was killed,' Whittle spoke sharply. 'I killed him.'

The British officer looked taken aback by this cool, terse remark; then he smiled jovially, his eyes still staring with madness. 'Oh well, one down, ten million to go,' he said cheerfully, and went back into the street to continue hunting.

There was a silence in the room. Then the inevitable question from Whittle.

'Did you see it?'

Richard paused as he went to give Gohar the all-clear. Then he shook his head. 'No, I didn't see the grave. I saw enough, though. I saw the 'Ladies House'. That was bad enough, Whittle.'

'I'm glad you missed the grave,' Whittle stared at Richard suspiciously. 'When I said I'd killed Gohar I was near speaking the truth, you know. I can't see an Indian now without a killing feeling coming over me, not even a loyal sepoy. I'm done for now. Or rather,' he added, with a new gleam in his eyes, 'not completely done for. For there's still Emily. I want your help, Applevale.'

Richard said nothing. He wanted to be alone, to be rid of George Whittle for ever.

'I've got to get to Azimullah. I've been thinking. Azimullah and I were good friends. I think I'll go along to the Nana Sahib and offer myself as a spy, eh? Not a true spy, of course, I can feed him some wrong information here and there but I'll be able to see Emily – and if I'm lucky I'll be able to get her out. Look after Patcham, Applevale. He's a good man,' he added, patting his hand. 'Just the sort of man I'd like to have married my sister. Ah well.'

'Why don't you take Arjun Gohar?' said Richard as he opened the back door and let him in. 'You don't speak a word of the language. It would be better for Gohar to be away from here. And he can help you.'

'Very well,' Whittle nodded. 'I'll take him.' He gathered up his belongings and tied them with a rope, heaving the bundle over his shoulder. Gohar quickly collected a small bundle of food and a prayer wheel and was ready to accompany Whittle.

'Good-bye Applevale,' said Whittle. He stood, this big bulky man, with a curious smile on his face. He didn't now offer a hand for Applevale to shake; now Lizzie was dead their brief comradeship was over.

'Good-bye.' Richard stood opposite him, staring at him coldly. Each knew what the other must be thinking, each hating the other in his heart, unable to bridge the gap of jealousy that parted them.

Whittle made for the door. His hands started trembling again and he paused. He turned before he left. 'One last thing, Applevale, you might like to know. Now it's too late, anyway.' He gave a rather cruel laugh. 'That baby. It wasn't mine, you know. It was yours. Bonny lad. However, too late now.' With that he turned and left, followed by Gohar.

Richard stood broken in the middle of the room. Whittle had finally got his revenge. What had only been suspicion had been verified. Lizzie had been telling the truth. He hadn't believed her. She had remained faithful to him, in her way. Now, he thought, perhaps his father *had* been ill – perhaps his family had not wanted to worry him in a letter. Perhaps she had written. He sat down by the window. Perhaps . . . perhaps anything now. He felt useless regret stab at him, regret that he knew he would have to live with every day of his life. She had tried to explain, after all. And he had been so blind in his jealousy that he had doubted her. His eye strayed to his gun in the corner, but then he turned away. That was no answer. He paced the floor, his mind racing with thoughts of the past. He still couldn't really grasp that she was dead. In one way he felt she must still be in England, waiting for him. Perhaps all this was only some dreadful nightmare. But the noise outside brought him back to reality – screams of plundering and looting, howls of terror. How he hated the Indians! How he hated India! He looked back into the dark room where poor maimed Patcham lay mumbling on his bed. Outside, the vultures wheeled in the sky in anticipation of the carrion; they could already feel it in the air. A British soldier noticed Richard's face at the window and called to him. 'Come on and help us! We're off to the court to do justice, justice our way!'

For a moment Richard hesitated. The reason that had prevailed until now lingered for a moment longer. Then he looked again at the wretched sight that presented itself in the street, the ruined market, the skinny, fawning Indians, the treachery, the brutality of it all came home to him. And finally he remembered again the last picture of Lizzie, but this time he particularly remembered the baby, *his* baby, the hope in his great dark eyes despite the surroundings . . . his baby, his and Lizzie's child that had been killed by the Indians, probably slaughtered with a sabre-thrust. . . .

He leant out of the window and called after the soldier. 'Wait for me! I'll bring some rope and a knife!' And he ran out of the door, blood-lust in his veins, tears suddenly pouring relentlessly down his cheeks, and yet knowing, deep down, even then, that no amount of revenge and slaughter could ever compensate his loss.

14

Although she had survived at the hands of the sepoy, Lizzie's troubles were only just beginning. She got up from the ground, picked up the baby and dusted her skirt down, still surprised at the feel of her bones which now jutted out from her thin hips. Even her hands were worn and bony, nails torn and ragged from work, dust engrained into the skin.

The baby started to cry once more. Wearily Lizzie put him to her breast and he was comforted. At least, however weak she was, she could still support the suckling baby, and as she looked at his firm flesh, his healthy skin, she felt grateful. She must survive if only for his sake. She had to get to Allahabad. George, if he were still alive, must be there. Having heard the news of Cawnpore he would have broken his journey: he surely wouldn't have continued on to Calcutta. Richard, too, would certainly be at Allahabad, if not already on his way to Cawnpore. The British would be at Allahabad – she must reach it. But could she make the journey? It meant travelling hundreds of miles on foot, without any money or food, relying for charity to support her on the way, charity of which she could by no means be sure even though she was a woman with a child.

Wearily she set off. For the next three days Lizzie trudged along the Great Trunk Road, another traveller on this great highway that now teemed with people. Some spat at her, some followed jeering, but some smiled and offered the baby a small portion of dhal which she accepted gratefully. Most of them wanted nothing to do with her. Wisely they wanted to take no side. Their eyes stared at her vacantly, uncomprehendingly, as if she were not there; for however much they might hate the *firinghis* few Indians would want to harm a woman and her baby.

160

The landscape was bleak and flat, the only beauty in the occasional grove of mango trees, or the dappled shadows cast by the banyan trees, their snaky roots falling from the tops of the trees like muddy fountains. A squirrel might scamper up a tree as she approached, or a wild pig might snuffle aimlessly along the road. A monkey might follow her, with a baby clinging to its fur, as it jumped with bright-eyed interest from tree to tree staring at the lonely, parched-lipped woman who walked the road, steps firm and sure but gradually getting slower and slower.

True, she could find water, dirty as it was, from the pools by the roadside that had gathered since the monsoons, but as she started feeling dizzy she knew she must be becoming faint with the heat, even delirious. The sun beat down on the back of her neck as if it were trying to burn through it. Occasionally everything would become blurred and she would have to sit by the wayside, sometimes so confused when she got up that she had forgotten in which direction she was travelling.

Sometimes when she slept she would dream of Whittle and wake in a rage, pushing his imaginary figure away from her body screaming: 'Go away! Get off! I hate you!' Then she would find herself alone, at dawn, with not a soul in sight, the pink sun just kissing the tops of the trees with a gold-pink glow, the sky a pale, duck-egg blue behind it. Or she would dream of Richard, dream that they were together again, that he was lying by her side, pressing against her on a mound of satin cushions, feeding her fruit and nuts and kissing her all over, and she would wake with her face still burning from his kisses, and her eyes bright with delight – then she would look around and once again see nothing but the hazy dawn as the sun started to quiver through the mist. And then the sun would become so hot that everything seemed to tremble in a heat haze.

Rubbing her eyes, Lizzie could not now be sure of anything. Perhaps it was her own weakness that seemed to make the landscape slip, slide and never be still; perhaps she was growing fainter than she thought. She would rise and splash herself with water, drink again, and continue her journey, though by this time she was almost unaware of where she was going. She had thought she was on the Great Trunk Road to Allahabad, but surely this small track could not be that great highway? Or was it a small track? Was it her eyes playing tricks again? If only she could get something to eat; if only she could lie down and sleep and sleep and be fed, she might get some more strength.

The baby was starting to cry more now, so she was sure that at last her weakness was having an effect on her milk. She fell more often than before, waking later after her morning nap, sometimes not until night had fallen, as if she were in a coma.

She *had* to get to Allahabad . . . but as she made the final effort to press herself on she stumbled again and as she tripped she felt her ankle twist in agony underneath her and she knew she would not be able to get up again. It was no good. She stared up at the hot blue sky and saw the vultures already circling above her, and she thought of their eager anticipation of the meal they would get before nightfall. She was too tired to care any more. Everything around her started to turn black, and she felt as if she were falling backwards, head first, into a dark pit.

'Memsahib! Memsahib!'

It was much later when she regained consciousness, and now she was no longer on the road, but in a small room. The brown face of a man looked down at her, a gold tooth flashed and a whiff of foul breath passed over her face. 'Memsahib, memsahib, you are living, you will give me chit, you will sign. . . .'

Lizzie had no idea what he was talking about, and was far too faint to do more than simply keep her eyes open, which was effort enough. She groaned slightly, closed her eyes and fell asleep again.

Later she was woken once more, aware of lentils being spooned down her throat, aware that she had hardly the strength to eat them as she felt the trickle of dhal running down her dress. However, she managed a small amount, managed to ask about the baby and when she was re-assured that he was 'happy, happy', she sank back into sleep again.

It was a woman who woke her next, darker than the man, with a small jewel set in her nose. Lizzie could only see her silhouette except for the sparkle of the jewel, and as she woke, the woman, who had kinder hands than the man's, hands more skilled at nursing, leant over her.

'Memsahib is better now,' she said, comfortingly, help-ing Lizzie to sit up slightly on the coarse charpoy, and putting pillows at her back. 'Memsahib will eat more now. Then memsahib will sign.'

Lizzie looked around her. She was in a small room, with no furniture except a worn rug on the floor. Three Indian children with dirty faces and no clothes on sat mutely on the floor, scraping lethargically at the earth. One of them urinated, an acid yellow trickle that ran in a dismal line across the room and under the bed. There was a small window through which she could see another glaring Indian sky, grilling the earth outside. Next to her was a makeshift cot of boxes, and inside it the baby slept. She put out her hand to touch him and could feel, by his heavy response, that he was satisfied.

'Who are you?' she managed to whisper, though her voice sounded strange to her, as she had hardly spoken for a week, and her throat had been dry with the dust and hunger. She looked at the Indian woman questioningly and spread out her hands.

'I am Vani,' said the woman. 'You have been near death – near *death*!' Her voice became quite piercing as she leant closer. 'My husband and I have save you from death! You will sign!'

Lizzie stared back at her. She didn't know what she was talking about. The woman had a manic look in her eye, a coarse twist of the lip that Lizzie found unattractive and ugly; but she had saved her.

'I will do anything I can for you,' she said hoarsely, but when the woman thrust a pen into her hand with a piece of

163

paper, she found she was too weak to hold it. However, her statement had relieved the woman, who put it aside when she saw how weak Lizzie still was.

'When you are strong, you sign,' she said, comfortingly, and Lizzie saw she looked more pleasant as she bustled around the bed, fanning Lizzie, wiping her brow. 'You get good sleep now, you eat lots of good rice and dhal, then you sign.'

Lizzie nodded, 'Yes, I'll sign.' And she fell back to sleep again.

It took a long time to get her back to health. It was days before Lizzie was able to walk about the room and feed the baby. Vani had taken her clothes away to wash by the river, and they had come back clean but different. The carefully stitched tucks were all ripped by Vani's persistent beating, the sleeves distorted by being stretched in the sun on the earth to dry. But Lizzie couldn't care less. The feeling of those fresh clothes was so good that she could have worn a Highland uniform had it been clean.

'And now,' said Vani, the first evening she was well enough to get up to eat, 'you will sign.' They ate around a fire outside the hut, and in the candlelight Lizzie read a bizarre note.

This is saying that I am being kind for the Ram family, are good people to me, Mustapha Ram and Vani Ram is saving my life from death, I sign by the Queen Victoria in Christ, God Save the Queen, and the Holy Ghost . . .

And then there was a blank. She smiled as she put it down and shook her head.

'You want me to sign this? Why?' she asked. Suddenly the Ram family looked threatening, and in the darkness Lizzie noticed Mustapha's grip tighten on the knife with which he was eating.

'We save your life. You sign. We friends of the British. We don't want to be strung up like pigs on the trees . . . we are not wanting to be shot from guns, lose our caste, our blood all over the land like a shower of rain. . . .' Mustapha was getting angry and threatening, while Vani

164

had thrown herself on the ground at Lizzie's feet pleading, screaming and begging so piteously that Lizzie had to reach forward and help her up.

'Please don't distress yourself, I'm so sorry,' she said quietly, 'I will sign anything to help you of course.' Vani's sobbing quietened down. 'Look, let me write this again for you, because it is not quite right, so you can be sure. . . .' A look of suspicion passed over Mustapha's face, and Lizzie hastily added, 'I'll sign this anyway . . .' and taking up the pen she signed. Before the ink was dry Mustapha had snatched it out of her hands and was examining it by the light of the flames, greedily tracing over every letter of her name. The atmosphere had changed completely.

'But I will write you another, all the same,' said Lizzie. 'You have been so good to me, then you will have two, one for each of you.' Mustapha thought this such an excellent idea that he rose and came over to clasp her by the hand. 'Good memsahib, you are good, you are very good to us, Vani say you will not be signing, but I am always knowing you will be signing. . . .'

'Why, of course!' said Lizzie. She found the Ram family difficult to understand. However, she realized she had performed something crucial for them, and was relieved to find the tension over. Mustapha produced another piece of paper and Lizzie wrote, in copperplate:

This is to certify that I, Elizabeth Whittle, married to George Whittle of Whittle Stores, Cawnpore, once of Penworth Court, Nr Barnstaple, England, owe my life to Mustapha and Vani Ram, who saved me and my baby from death by starvation. Please treat them kindly and well. They are friends of the British, and by their generous actions my life has been saved. Elizabeth Whittle, July 1857.

This pleased Mustapha even more as even though he was not well read in English, he could understand that this was a more authentic document than his own. He pointed to the date, smiling: 'I miss that. The date. That is very good. But where is your God?' he added, disappointed to find no reference to it. Lizzie leant over and took it, adding,

'By the grace of God,' at the bottom.

Mustapha burst into smiles and nodded to himself. 'By the grace of God, by the grace of God, that is being *very* good, Mrs Whittle, memsahib, *very* good. Now we will be having some more to eat, and we will be giving you some provisions tomorrow morning and you can go.'

'Go?' Lizzie looked startled. She hadn't been planning to stay long, but she certainly wasn't expecting to be told to go the following morning. 'Why, of course. I . . .'

'You are *firinghi*,' said Mustapha darkly. 'If the sepoys find you here they will kill us. We are doing very bad thing, but now we have this —' and he tapped the piece of paper. 'Now we are safe with everyone.'

Lizzie felt shocked. The only reason they had saved her was to get a signature out of her! They were guided by no feelings of loyalty to the British — far from it. And now she had served her purpose she must move on lest she become an embarrassment to them! However, she reflected, there was no need for them to give her another night or provisions the next morning, so she should feel grateful. She accepted another bowl of rice and curry and relaxed a little.

'Tell me, what did you mean about losing your caste,' she asked. 'Why are you so frightened of the British? They are good, they wouldn't hurt you.'

Mustapha spat on the ground, then apologized with a salaam. 'Oh, memsahib, if you only were knowing how your countrymen are being now. You will never be saying they are good.' He leant over the fire, the gold in his tooth glinting as he spoke. 'They murder our women and babies, they eat the children for breakfast, they cut the breasts of our women and disgrace them in the market-place. Every man they hang, they are so vengeful, and they will make the Hindus eat the sacred cow, and they will not let their bodies be burnt, so they will never rest in peace, and they force the Muslims to eat pig, and they burn them instead of bury them so their souls will wander forever abroad, they are being cruel, memsahib. Vani and I, with our children, we hear they are coming and we are afraid.'

'I simply can't believe it!' said Lizzie, contemptuously. 'British soldiers would never do anything like that!'

Mustapha shook his head. 'It is after Cawnpore, after what the Nana did . . .'

There was a pause when there was no sound but the crackle of the fire. Wood smoke, bitter and sharp, got into Lizzie's eyes, and she blinked.

'Yes?' she said cautiously, questioningly.

Mustapha looked down. 'They are all dead,' he said. 'It is being very bad. The Nana then, he is saying all his sepoys must kill the women and children, but they are not able to, so the Nana has ordered the butchers of the town to cut them to pieces. It is terrible, terrible.'

For a moment Lizzie had a terrible, vivid memory of the sight of the carts full of the European women . . . she could even remember the sound of the cartwheels getting even fainter as she held her breath in the bushes . . . then suddenly a parrot gave a screaming squawk from above her and she was startled.

'I must go to sleep,' she said, getting up. 'I am grateful to you. I . . .' But she could say no more. Her feelings were so confused that she longed to get away from the house and Mustapha and Vani and their peculiar loyalties.

Vani had made up her provisions in a coarse bag, left by the bed, and Lizzie was all prepared to go, early the following morning. She knew she needed the rest, but that night she could not sleep. Perhaps it was the thought of what Mustapha had told her that kept her awake – the awful vision of those women and children all horribly slaughtered. Whenever she closed her eyes she imagined the carts going off in the distance, she imagined the fate that befell them and she found the pain of even thinking about it too hard to bear.

She tossed and turned on the charpoy, rose and looked out of the window, forced herself to return to rest and found herself, half an hour later, still tense, gripping the coarse strings of the bed. She listened. Perhaps it was because there was a difference in the sounds outside that made her restless? Perhaps a slight rustling; perhaps it was the absence of Mustapha's heavy snoring that made her full of fear? Something was making her anxious, and after a few moments of indecision she decided to attend to her intuition, however foolish she might appear. She wrote a note to Mustapha and Vani, thanking them, which she left on her pillow, gathered up the baby and the provisions and slunk stealthily from the room into the compound outside. There she waited, in the shadows, looking back for a moment at the house where her life had been saved – and noticed a movement of leaves in the moonlight. She huddled into the shadows of the trees and watched. The shape of Mustapha appeared, holding a glinting knife in his hand, creeping along the side of the hut, then tiptoeing inside. A candle was lit in the room she had been in; then she heard a muttered curse, a curious laugh, and he came out shaking his head, holding her note. 'By the grace of God!' he was saying. 'By the grace of God! Well, her God is having something after all, maybe!' And he sauntered back to his own quarters.

Lizzie stood trembling in the darkness. He had planned to save her, get the signed note from her, so that he would be in favour with the British, then kill her and perhaps give her body to the Nana, to gain favour from him! Turning on her heel she ran wildly down the road, thanking God for her narrow escape.

Gupta Singh was not feeling well. As he lay inside the howdah on top of his elephant he had to admit that if anything he had been feeling worse than usual, despite his son's medicine. He lay back on his cushions shutting his eyes. But then, it had been a long day, and they had shot two tigers which was exceptional. Also his astrologer had told him it was a lucky day for him, so perhaps he would be feeling better by the evening. It was now four o'clock, his retinue had passed down the Great Trunk Road on its way back to his palace, and was now turning off on the familiar path, through the small village that lay on his land. The tiger had indeed been courageous, he thought, courageous

168

and beautiful as it had leapt right at them from the bushes and then, stung by a bullet in its heart, had stopped almost still in mid-air before crashing to the ground, blood trickling across the beautiful yellow and black stripes of its body, that even in death still held grace and power.

He wondered, as he lay back on the cushions, what would happen in India. They were so alike, the Indians and the British – brave, cruel and foolish. What a mess their country was in! Before the British arrived everything was backward, everything was slow, but everything had worked in its own way, everyone understood everything, the justice was swift and simple, not long-winded and read out of books. In his day a thief would be taken to the head of the village and made to swear on Krishna's foot if he were innocent. To swear a lie on Krishna's foot meant eternal damnation, so anyone who could not do that was guilty. It was very simple. These British, they got witnesses, law books, evidence – and in the end they never got the right man.

Then there were the taxes. They used to be simple and just, in their way; now they all had to be written down, land was taken from those who had much and given to the poor whether they knew how to farm it or not. It seemed to Gupta Singh that the country had got poorer and more wretched since the British came, despite what everyone said to the contrary. Who needed telegraphs in a country where people could walk with their messages? Who needed forms and documents when words had done just as well before?

He was disturbed from his thoughts by shouting outside. '*Firinghi*! *Firinghi*!' The word was being screamed with a mixture of hate and wonder.

There could hardly be any *firinghis* left around these parts, thought Gupta Singh – not after what the Nana had done at Cawnpore. And his dark black eyes flinched slightly in pain as he remembered the bodies in the well that he had been shown by the Nana. No, however much his son wanted to join forces he could never now go with the Nana. Not after that.

He left the curtains on his howdah closed. He wanted no more problems with *firinghis*. They had brought enough trouble. He would do no more for anyone, he would just continue his own life, going on as if nothing had happened. And nothing would happen. Someone would win the war. But Gupta Singh would still be in his palace, still smoking his hookah and taking his powdered rubies; he would still be looking at his miniatures, picking which nautch girl to sleep with that night, still polishing his diamonds, reading his poetry and consulting the stars. But that day there seemed no peace for him.

There was a banging on one of the posts of the howdah from his mahout.

'Sahib, sahib! Please see!' he shouted in Hindi at Gupta Singh, 'It is a *firinghi* – a woman! Have a look!'

Gupta Singh paused; then with a wince of pain he lifted himself from his cushions and twitched open the curtain so slightly that no one could see his eye peering through the slit.

On the ground he could see the tops of heads. A group of men and women were clustering round a woman who was holding a bundle. One of the men was holding a handful of stones, while another was arguing with him to put them down. One woman spat at the European, and another slapped her and told her to behave herself, that you should never spit at a woman. No one knew what to do with this lost European – and finally Gupta Singh called down. 'Leave her! Let me talk to her! Who is she? What is she doing?'

The crowd immediately dispelled and the woman in the middle turned to the curtained howdah and said: 'Please, I only want to be left in peace. I am trying to find my way to Allahabad to join my husband. I wish no one any harm. Please do not harm me or my baby, please I beg you, let me be!'

With growing astonishment Gupta Singh recognized the woman in the road. He flung open the curtains in amazement. It was Mrs Whittle with the baby! How could it be? He was sure that they had all been killed!

'Mrs Whittle it is I, your friend! Come with us! Let me look after you! What great luck this is!' As he saw her face, bursting into a tearful smile of hope, he suddenly felt better. His cramps left him. Despite the ravages of starvation and poverty, Elizabeth Whittle still possessed a beauty that exhilarated him. He felt his heart leap slightly.

He gave orders for the mahout to force the elephant to kneel and, swaying from side to side as the elephant bent its great legs to the ground, the howdah soon was low enough to allow Lizzie to step in. Gupta Singh drew the golden curtains and put out his hand to assist her. She surely would not have been at Cawnpore, he felt, for despite her exhausted condition, she looked well. Her hair shone, her skin was smooth and glowing from the heat, her mouth red as a rose which bloomed as she smiled at him; but there was something wrong with her eyes – there was an emptiness in them which he had never seen before, an emptiness which was a shield against great pain.

He saw that she was properly seated and then gave orders for the elephant to rise again.

'Mrs Whittle, how did you escape? Why did you not come and stay with me as you agreed? I was sure you were at Cawnpore, but you can't have been . . . why are you travelling on your own? Where is Mr Whittle? Surely he has not abandoned you . . .' There were so many questions she could not reply at once, but explained the situation as best she could. When Gupta Singh heard of the Rams he made a mental note to have them dealt with according to his own laws; they would suffer for such behaviour.

'Well, you will be coming to my palace now, I am hoping,' he said, taking her hand and holding it as if it were a treasure. 'You need rest, food and friends, too. You shall have them all, you shall have anything you want. You must stay for a long time.'

And as he said it he decided that indeed she would stay for a long time. A very long time.

15

Lizzie did indeed feel withdrawn. It was perhaps a build up of the experiences of the last few weeks that had reduced her, lowered her trust, fired the deep look of near-Indian fatalism into the centre of her black eyes. Whittle's departure in the face of imminent danger had begun the pattern; then there was Richard's message at the entrenchment that Havelock would not be with them for ten days; then Nana Sahib's betrayal, the experience with the Ram family, the news, too terrible even to think about, of the massacre of the women and children at Cawnpore.

Nothing could reassure her now, not even the warm presence of Gupta Singh, nor his promises, nor his hospitality. Lizzie felt as if something inside her had died; it showed in a suspicion in her eyes, a caution that could be heard in her voice, a tension around her shoulders. She experienced a kind of deadening of the senses, as if numbed against good and bad alike.

Even when they dismounted from the elephant and Gupta Singh threw his hand out, pointing across a silver lake to his white palace, glimmering in the sunlight, Lizzie felt as if it were not real, as if it were only a picture in a book and that she and the baby and Gupta Singh were all only figures drawn into the landscape.

'It's lovely,' she said, staring into the distance, her voice betraying the deadness of her feelings. She gave Gupta Singh a vague smile that never reached her eyes. She couldn't even think properly. Her mind was a petrified blank, as if all memories and thoughts had been erased to enable her to put just one foot in front of the other. She stumbled slightly as she got into the boat that was to take them across, and she realized that even her limbs were affected by this paralysis that had overtaken her.

At the palace she disembarked, automatically and un-smiling, and allowed herself to be led down an arched marble corridor to a room where the doors opened on to a marble balcony that overlooked the lake, and the luxurious garden that lay in the very centre of the palace. The room was hung with glittering canopies stitched with red and green jewels, gleaming brass gods stood guarding the door and the walls of the room were studded with a thousand fragments of inlaid mirrors – which served only to reflect her own shattered feelings.

She sat, fatigued, on the edge of the bed. Another room, another view, another friend. When would she be free of this dreadful journey? Was there no peace for her, no rest?

A light tap on the door prompted her to speak. 'Come in,' she said, wearily.

The door opened and a beautiful girl entered. She had a kind, lively face with even features and eyes like black violets that stood out strikingly against the earthy brown of her skin. She smiled, revealing her sparkling white teeth.

'I am Sushma,' she said, in hesitant English, pressing her hands together in a salaam. 'I am here to be your servant, memsahib. I will do whatever you are wanting. I will see to the baby and attend your every need.'

Lizzie looked up and smiled feebly. 'Thank you,' she said, 'but all I want to do is sleep.'

Sushma clapped her hands and three other girls appeared with a tray of sweetmeats.

'First you may like something to eat. Then you will be having a bath, for you are bruised and dusty and this will be making you feel not happy.'

One of the girls approached and took the baby from Lizzie's arms. He immediately began to scream, tugging viciously at Lizzie's hair to hang on to his mother. His face contorted into sobs and she came towards the girl to take him back.

Sushma put her hand gently on her arm. 'He will be all right, memsahib. This is very good girl with babies, she is liking babies. Kitmutghar, he is having some little toys, the

173

baby will be very happy. You must be having some rest. . . .'

And true enough, the baby's screams slowly subsided as he was carried down the corridor, and to Lizzie's relief she could hear him gurgling and cooing as his new ayah sang to him.

After her bath, her skin was massaged with milk and healing oils; Sushma pulled down the dampened blinds in the room and sat by her on the bed, her very presence soothing Lizzie as she sank into sleep. The sun filtered round the corner of the blinds, casting straight rays beside her, and softly lighting her face, highlighting the strong cheekbones, the dark lashes, the smooth contours of her arms, stretched out as if in supplication, on the pillow. Finally her breathing became slow, deep and regular, and there was no sound to be heard except for her slow breaths mingling with the lapping of the lake's water against the palace walls and the distant, monotonous 'thwack thwack' of the dhobis as they beat their washing by the shore.

When she woke in the late afternoon she felt refreshed, but still as though in near shock. Sushma slowly rubbed perfumed oil into her back; then the servants dressed her, and she stood doll-like as Sushma's skilled hands folded a lilac-coloured silk sari into a thousand intricate folds around her waist and silver slippers were put on her feet. Another servant put bangles on her hands, and another combed her hair till it shone. A mirror was brought and the servants bobbed before her saying: 'Pretty memsahib, pretty, pretty!'

When they had finished, Lizzie walked over to the window feeling strange in these foreign clothes. She looked through the carved stone lattice-work to the garden and breathed deeply. It was indeed beautiful, even if it did not have the power to move her. She could smell the heavy scent of lilies from the garden and make out the shapes of the fronded trees surrounding the small pool. Reflected in the water was a sky of blues and pinks, streaked with hints of grey cloud, as if a storm had passed leaving only ragged pieces behind. Dusk was falling. The sky was becoming greyer and greyer, hazier and hazier, as the sun fell with extraordinary speed. Each second it grew darker; but occasionally light would flare up again as the sun's rays came out from behind a cloud. Finally it became impossible to distinguish the horizon from the sky, even the pool had vanished in the dark and there was nothing left but the heavy smell of lilies; no sound except the light rustle of grass.

Lizzie turned away. Sushma was still there, watching her. She beckoned, and Lizzie followed her passively down the corridors until she came to the main banqueting hall. There, sitting under an awning at the far end, surrounded only by arches and columns that led into the garden, was Gupta Singh.

The room was lit by dim oil-lamps which let out a heavy smell of their own and in the half light she could see the splendour with which Gupta Singh was dressed.

He lay on a pile of cushions woven through with gold and silver silk, and in his bright blue turban gleamed a single pearl, of a beautifully distorted, natural shape. His thin black moustache was curled slightly under his nose, and his lips were pale. He wore a tight jacket of pale blue, buttoned down one side, a scarf of red and gold around his neck, and his trousers were tight, wrinkled cotton. But it was his eyes that were most impressive – so white against his skin, with centres so dark and mysterious that it seemed that to stare into them was to see into another world.

He gestured her to sit down, with a hand glittering with rings.

'I am sorry not to have seen you before,' he said, quietly, 'but I have been feeling particularly unwell. I am afraid my illness is not getting better yet. But,' and here his eyes sparkled slightly, 'I always feel better to see you, Mrs Whittle, though I must admit you look as if things have not gone well with you since I was seeing you.'

Lizzie shook her head, staring at the ground. 'I have seen a lot of trouble,' she said slowly. 'I have seen too many things. I am afraid, Rajah, I am much changed.' She tried to smile but the smile didn't seem to reach her mouth.

'I understand,' said Gupta Singh quietly. 'But you must not let life change you like this. It is for you to stay still while life goes on around you, whatever things you are seeing.'

Lizzie sighed. 'I am still,' she said slowly, 'too still.'

Gupta Singh spat out a piece of betal juice on to the stone slabs beside him. 'Yes, indeed, Mrs Whittle, too still. You are nearly dead! You must return to life, Mrs Whittle.'

Lizzie looked up at him. 'I don't think I shall ever be able to do that,' she said. 'Too much has happened ... too many things. ...'

'Then tell me,' said Gupta Singh commandingly, 'tell me everything.' He clapped his hands and soon a huge tray arrived, with pappadams, chapattis, curries, sweetmeats small pieces of grilled meat, crisp fruits, all carefully arranged. ...

'Eat, Mrs Whittle, and tell me!' he said, reaching forward a glittering hand and pulling himself into a cross-legged position on his cushion.

And so she did. She started at the beginning, with her life in Devon, she told him of her mother, her life with her father, and George Whittle and his gambling. She even told him of Richard, how good he was, how much she loved him – but she was careful to leave out certain parts of her story – and as she spoke she found her hands moving expressively to describe him, and her voice becoming warmer and more enthusiastic.

'But then he came to India. My father's gambling debts were such that I had to marry George Whittle and I came over here with his sister Emily, who, as you know, had met Azimullah. Oh, how I wish we had never come here! My husband is gone, almost certainly killed on the way to Allahabad, Emily must be dead by now, for I'm sure no foreigner would survive long in the Nana's court,' she said bitterly. She got up, unable to bear the memory of what Mustapha Ram had told her, and walked to one of the archways overlooking the garden, putting her hand on one of the columns, and leaning her head against it to cool it.

Against the guttering candles that stood on long iron

poles, her figure was a sharp black silhouette, her black hair tumbled down with stray locks moving slightly in the hot night wind. Gupta Singh could see the curve of her hip, and almost sense the outline of her legs under the sari. He watched her, drinking her in with his eyes.

'Gupta Singh, will you tell me the truth?' Lizzie's voice was low and trembling.

'Of course,' Gupta Singh replied evenly and quietly. He could not take his eyes off the beautiful English woman who stood before him.

'Is it true what I was told? What the Nana did to the women and children at Cawnpore?' she asked, turning round. 'I was told . . . it's since then that I have been so . . . so unlike myself. I can't bear to think of it. I was *there*, you see! I saw them go!' She was leaning forward to Gupta Singh now, her arms outstretched, pleading with him to contradict the story. 'I was in the cart, and the other women and children were there, and they all thought they would be safe . . . but I had a feeling. Do you know what I mean? Do you get that sort of feeling, Rajah? When every ounce of your blood tells you "No!", when you can sense things that your mind cannot tell you about, when you simply know fear, and know there's nothing to do but run?'

Gupta Singh nodded, slowly.

'I jumped off the cart, I pretended to be dead, I escaped.' Her voice was trembling now, the memory was so painful, 'and I heard the carts rumble off, with the women, my friends, with their children, and now they are all butchered, murdered – *that* is what I was told! It could have been me! Why did it have to happen? Oh, tell me, please, is there anything, can you help me. . . ?' Tears were now coursing down her face, 'I have my religion, and I've thought sometimes about why God allows bad things to happen, but why this? Oh, God, why this? Was this why I nursed the children and the sick? So they could be massacred?' And then, overcome with pain at the memory that she had been hiding from herself for so many days, she broke down into long, deep sobs.

Gupta Singh got up from his cushions and walked over

to her. He put his arms around her and led her back to where she had been sitting.

'My dear Elizabeth,' he said slowly, stroking her hair, 'you are safe. That is what your God has chosen, that you should be safe, you and your baby. This is what fate has decided for you, and none of us know why these things are done, not Christians, not Hindus, not Muslims. But we Hindus know they are done for a reason. You said you had a sense of danger. . . . I, too, have a sense about these dreadful events. I do not understand them, but I understand that I will never understand, and this comforts me. Dear Elizabeth, you have been saved, and that is what matters.'

She turned her face up to his, still questioning.

He nodded, and as he did so his eyes filled with tears. 'Yes, my dear, it is true. I saw it myself. The Nana showed me, trying to persuade me to join him. But after seeing that I will never join the Nana. It was terrible, truly terrible. But they are not suffering now, my dear. Your soldiers will give them Christian burials. They will be safe. And now my dear, you must sleep some more. You have exhausted yourself this evening. But you, too, will be safe here. Do not forget that. You can begin your life again here, Elizabeth.'

And as he said this he took her by the shoulders and looked directly into her eyes, coming so close to her face that she could feel the heat from his mouth near hers.

'You can begin here, Elizabeth, you can start again. You and the baby. No harm will come to you. I can help you. We are destined – we must be destined. My astrologer has told me things. . . . There is only one way I can get back to health. It is with a European woman – *you*. . . .'

Lizzie looked back at him boldly. He was offering her the security of his palace, perhaps even more; but he wanted something from her in return. Just as she drew back to ask him what he meant, they were interrupted by a sudden, mocking laugh at the door, and Gupta Singh turned sharply.

'So, father, making love with a *firinghi*!' The figure at the door was taller than Gupta Singh, stronger, full of tension and fire where his father had quiet, inner strength. His white teeth flashed as he smiled; then he spat insolently on the floor.

'And who is this?' he asked, approaching with long strides, and taking in Lizzie in a single glance. 'My goodness, it is one of the Cawnpore ladies – where did you find her, father, at the bottom of the pit? Did you rescue her from the massacre? Well, I admire your choice,' he added, mockingly, sitting down and helping himself to the remains of the meal, 'but it's a pity she's so fair-skinned, eh? Aaagh!' he added, suddenly roaring with laughter and tugging at his father's coat in an affectionate way, 'I'm sorry, I'm spoiling your evening! She's a lovely girl! Tell me her name! Madam, I apologize, my father will tell you I'm a hot-tempered devil, but it's not true, just sometimes, I have to admit I am *not* too friendly with the British, unlike my father, but I am my father's son, so we must live as he wants. Too bad. What is her name, father? Father, don't look at me like that! Forgive me, I beg you, and let us be friends. I am Jamira.' And he put out his hand, English-style, to shake Lizzie's.

As she shook his hand, she assessed him. He was insolent but not unattractive. Lizzie remembered Gupta Singh telling her that it was his son who had recommended the powdered rubies for his illness, and instinctively, Lizzie disliked him. His smile was too quick, it came too fast after the insults, and his cold eyes belied his cheerful grin.

When she dropped his hand, Gupta Singh nodded his head apologetically in her direction. 'I will see you tomorrow, Mrs Whittle. I am sorry for the intrusion. Tomorrow we will dine alone. Completely alone. Tonight I have some business to discuss with my son. But remember –' he smiled at her, 'there is a reason for everything. There is a reason for all bad things, too. So sleep well. Be not being troubled.'

Lizzie nodded good-night to Jamira and left to go to her room. So, there was a reason for everything, was there, she thought, as she walked down the cool corridors. Perhaps there was a reason why Jamira had appeared at that moment? Perhaps there was a reason he was administering such strange medicine to his father? There were too many reasons to think about at once, however. And too many reasons she did not want to think about.

The following day Lizzie sat in the garden on a seat by the pond with the baby. The ayah had made him a small white tunic, the kitmutghar had provided bricks and beads, and he played at her feet, occasionally tugging at her sari, and attempting to stand up on his own, usually falling happily on to the path only to try again. Nearby groups of women squatted, cropping the grass with small scythes. In the pond Lizzie could see her reflection in the glassy water, a portrait occasionally ruffled by a fish that would dart out from the lily leaves and back again. Then the water would become calm again and she could see her face, fuller now, more rounded and relaxed. She could see the sun reflecting off her hair and mirroring in the pool and she felt a rare glimmer of happiness. But as she stared she became suddenly aware of another shape beside her reflection and with a splash her image was broken by a stone thrown violently into the pool. She started and looked up. It was Jamira, who stood by the bench where she sat, hands on his hips and a cold, hostile smile on his face.

'Well! Admiring yourself?' he said, curtly. 'Do you admire yourself as much as my father admires you? It looks like it, doesn't it?'

'Why, I've not seen myself for some weeks,' said Lizzie with as polite a smile as she could muster. 'It's hard to see how I look in the chink of mirrors in the walls of my room. I've been half starved and really it's not so much vanity as hope that I'm not the skeleton I was a month ago.'

'At Cawnpore?' said Jamira, knowingly. 'Come, let me sit by you. . . .' He moved round and settled himself at the other end of the bench, one leg jauntily crossed. 'We must talk, I think. We must get to know each other's plans, no?'

'Plans?' Lizzie brushed a strand of her hair from her

180

eyes, she looked at him in surprise. 'I have no plans.'

'Huh!' Jamira scoffed, and tossed another stone into the pool sulkily. 'Don't you pretend with me! Of course you have plans! All women have plans! Yours are clear as your reflection in that water . . . until I come into the picture,' he added, menacingly. He gave a low, soft laugh that made Lizzie's skin grow cold.

'Come, let's not pretend. You're a pretty woman. My father is a rich man. He is also a very sick man, eh?'

Lizzie interrupted, 'Indeed he is. I am worried about him, and I must say I feel sure that your medicine is not the right—'

'Be quiet! I know what is best for my father!' snapped Jamira. 'He is not only a sick man but a dying man. You are trying to marry him so that you can have his wealth. So that your white-faced baby can be rich.'

Lizzie looked so genuinely startled that even Jamira noticed and the hatred in his face relaxed. 'Maybe, maybe not. Anyway, that will be the outcome,' he added, darkly. 'Whether you want it or not, that is what my father wants. I know it. Ever since he had a dream about you after the Nana's banquet, he has been interested in you. And now his astrologer tells him that if he marries you he will be cured! That astrologer! He is simply in the pay of the British. They tell him they will reward him well if he can persuade my father to marry a European woman, for then he will be less likely to take up arms against them! My father's astrologer shall pay dearly when the day comes, that I know. And that day may not be far off!'

Lizzie looked him straight in the eyes. 'Does your father like the British?'

Jamira turned up the palms of his hands and shrugged. 'Who knows what my father likes? He likes what the astrologer says he must like. But he does not like the Nana who is the only person in these parts to be gathering an army around him to beat the British, so my father, like a coward, is keeping out of the war; like so many of us, he just wants to eat and sleep and read his poems and shoot his tigers and forget about the war.'

'I can't marry him,' said Lizzie, angrily. 'I have a husband. He knows that.'

'A husband? What white woman has a husband these days?' Jamira's voice was softly scoffing. 'Come on, you know he's dead. There's not a man left from Cawnpore who's alive.'

'But he wasn't at Cawnpore. He went ahead of us to Calcutta . . . before the mutiny. . . .'

Jamira laughed outright. 'And you think he'd last more than a few days on the road? You are living in – how is you are saying – a fool's paradise. All the *firinghis* were slaughtered by the Nana's men. Even the ones in the boats. I will be betting you are a widow now, Mrs Whittle. And widow or not, that will not be stopping my father, I am telling you. In India life is cheap. Children die, men die, women die, as you have seen. Wives die when their husbands die. They burn themselves rather than live on alone. And if they will not burn themselves they are made to burn themselves. But though we die, we live again. Unlike you, you Christians, we live again. When you die – poof! You are gone, like a candle. But we are born again, many, many times.'

Lizzie got up. She walked a few paces to get the baby who had crawled dangerously near the pond, brought him back on her hip, and stared angrily down at Jamira.

'You don't like me, Jamira, and I don't like you,' she said, frankly. 'You think I want to marry your father. It's not true. I don't. I am already married. And I have no intention of marrying again. Jamira . . .' She looked down at him earnestly, 'give me safe passage to Allahabad, I beg you, and I shall leave! Then we shall both be happy!'

'Good idea,' said Jamira, idly throwing stones into the water. His eyes had narrowed thoughtfully. 'But I am changing my views all the time with talking with you, Mrs Whittle. It is so stimulating talking with the British. Their minds are so active, they have such original ideas. And in talking to you, now I come to think of it closer, I think it might be better if you stayed. I have suddenly had an idea. It was when I was talking about life being cheap. Yes, I am sure you would make a good wife for my father, Mrs Whittle. A loyal wife, too, who would follow him any-where!' Here he laughed unpleasantly. 'Yes, marry my father with my blessing! Why, you don't want to go on the road again, you might meet the Thugs! You are our guest, Mrs Whittle. We must be protecting you!'

'The Thugs! They've been wiped from the roads,' snapped Lizzie. 'The British have seen to that! You may not like us but we have stopped a great many cruelties! We have stopped widow-burning, and we have stopped men marry-ing young children, girls so small they are torn apart and die when they give birth, and we have stopped Thugs, that is for certain. Any woman is safe on the roads in India, even now, and I should know.'

Jamira gave a particularly nasty snort of a laugh. 'You *think* they have stopped it, and they think so, too, but you haven't. Not everywhere! Your Colonel Sleeman thought he had got rid of the Thugs but still on a dark night they will accost a traveller on the road at night, still they will entertain him with food and songs . . . and then,' his voice became still and quiet, 'one of the party will notice, perhaps, that some of the gang have disappeared. They have gone up the road, to dig the graves . . . and later on, they will move camp, the group will move up the road and they will build a fire around the graves, lightly filled in, and invite the guests to sing. And as the guests put their throats back to sing, the Thugs will get out the yellow scarf, pull it around their necks, while others tug at their feet and – snap! Then they will bury them! And all for the goddess Kali, the great goddess Kali!'

'Rubbish,' said Lizzie, her heart pounding. 'You're trying to frighten me! You're talking nonsense! There are none left! And I would rather face them than be married to your father! Let me leave – give me a boat at least to get away. I'll make my own way then. . . .'

Jamira got up, brushed down his dark velvet coat, and reached out a long, thin brown hand to touch the baby's cheek. A long hard nail slowly dented the baby's skin and he smiled as the baby tried to push his hand away. Then he clapped his hands, startling the child and laughed as he cried.

'No, no, I shall hear of no such thing, Mrs Whittle. I have wedding plans for you! I am anxious for your safety. I shall have a servant put on your door at night to stop marauders getting in to you. I shall want my father's bride to be kept very safe, from now on. A happy life, I am wishing you!' he added, as he turned on his heel. 'A happy life, if a short one!'

16

Sushma noticed how tense Lizzie looked when she returned to her room. She salaamed nervously, then said: 'Memsahib is not pleased with Sushma! I am not making happy. I shall get some music for you? I will summon the tailor and he will make you some clothes, beautiful clothes like the British ladies . . . perhaps some flowers in the room, some jasmine . . . is it too hot? I will be taking the baby now?'

Lizzie put her hand reassuringly on her arm and smiled at her. 'I am all right, Sushma. Don't worry yourself. I am just tired. It is so hot. I feel – restless. There is nothing that can be done for me.'

Sushma looked anxiously at her. 'My master will not be being pleased with me. You must be happy! British people are never being sad, it is said, they are happy, they have locked away their devils.'

'Oh yes?' Lizzie gratefully received the cool moistened flannel that Sushma handed her and sat down on the bed with an amused smile. 'And where are our devils? I only wish we could lock them up, Sushma, but we are just like you – they live here. . . .' And she lightly tapped her own breast.

Sushma shook her head vehemently. 'Oh, no, is wrong you are being, memsahib. The Brahmin he has told us you lock your devils in the engines of your trains and that is how they go so fast, and you can hear them shrieking and crying to get out, and the smoke, that is their hot breath. . . .'

Lizzie laughed. 'No, it's not true, Sushma, I promise you. We don't have magic like that! If only we did!'

Sushma, relieved at having made Lizzie smile, did not pursue the subject, but glided round the room straightening things here, polishing bits of the mirror, finally leaving quietly with the baby while Lizzie slept, or pretended to sleep.

It was utterly impossible that she could marry Gupta Singh! One part of her kept arguing that the idea was a lie dreamt up by Jamira, another felt there might be some truth in it. But whatever the truth, she felt trapped, trapped and duped. Had she dreamt of this possibility she would never have accepted Gupta Singh's invitation – she would rather have taken her chances on the road with the other Europeans. She tossed and turned, the bright sunlight from the window now moving straight into her eyes, the lapping of the water outside now sounding threatening rather than soothing.

A light tap on the door from Sushma broke the monotony. Gupta Singh would not, after all, be dining with her that night. But he would like to talk to her for a moment. Slipping from the bed and following Sushma, Lizzie met Gupta Singh in the garden. He smiled at her when she arrived, then turned back to a great red rhododendron that lay cupped in his hand, delicately examining the petals.

'Is it not beautiful?' he said. 'It is very rare. Like some other guests in my lake palace,' he smiled, turning to her. 'I am sorry, Mrs Whittle, but I am not able to dine with you tonight. I was so hoping. . . . But tomorrow we will talk.'

Lizzie looked at him questioningly. 'May I ask why?' she said.

'My son has guests,' said Gupta Singh letting the bloom drop roughly from his hand. Lizzie thought he was going to stop there, but he continued. 'I am afraid, Elizabeth, that my son is not liking the British. More and more he is trying to persuade me to join with the Nana.'

'But after what you have seen him do . . . you couldn't!'

He shook his head, the big jewel on his turban glittering as he moved. 'No, indeed, but he is talking to me about it every day, every day he comes into my room and says "Father, will you not talk, at least, with the Nana?" "Father, please come and meet him again." "Father, it was not on his order that this massacre was carried out . . ." I

186

am getting weary. And yesterday he came to me and said he had asked Azimullah here to talk to me, and so I must entertain him, devil as he is.'

'Azimullah? Here?' For a moment the bed of rhododendrons that bordered the garden seemed all one ghastly colour, a sea of blood-red, and Lizzie had a sudden vivid memory of Mrs Jacobi screaming before she fell into the bloody river. She steadied herself by putting her hand on Gupta Singh's arm. 'But you must not tell him. . . .'

Gupta Singh put his hand over hers, smiling and looking into her eyes. 'That is why we must not dine tonight,' he said, gently. 'I have told my son, too, that he is not to say you are living here. I am sure that Azimullah is not liking you, after you have tried to stop him seeing your sister-in-law, and I know what happens to people who Azimullah is not liking. I have seen. And nothing must happen to you, my dear.' He gazed at her too intensely for Lizzie's comfort and she drew her eyes away. 'You are dear to me. You are very lucky and auspicious for me. My health has improved since you are being here. The sun that used to beat down so oppressively now warms my soul. The water that lay stagnant in the pool now sparkles. . . .'

'What about your son?' Lizzie looked him boldly in the eye. 'He doesn't like my being here. He's told me.'

Gupta Singh stared at his hands and twisted a large ruby ring around a brown finger. 'My son is very dear to me. My son is only confused about our country, he is young. He sees you as British and he cannot see through the British to the soul. He will learn, however.' And he took her hand and slowly lifted it to his mouth, kissing it. 'We will dine tomorrow, my dear,' he said, 'and we shall have a special meal. I have something very important I want to ask you.' He raised his eyes, looked deep into Lizzie's and turned away.

Lizzie turned, too; a feeling of dread rose up in her.

In her room that evening she picked dully at her meal. She sat on the edge of her bed, her mind whirling with thoughts. She couldn't marry Gupta Singh! It was out of the question. A dark shadow fell on the floor from outside her room and she started momentarily. She called out: 'Who's there?' and a figure entered.

'Do not be frightened,' he said, 'I am to be guarding your room. Jamira sent me.'

Lizzie nodded, and he took up his post again. This did not help her, either. Was he there to protect her – or to keep her there? If only she could fathom Jamira's motives. Perhaps she had only to say to Gupta Singh, 'No, I cannot marry you', and he would allow her safe passage to Allahabad. But she felt he would not say that. And perhaps he would not even ask her to marry him? After all, George was surely still alive.

She paced the floor, the cool marble soothing her bare feet. The sun had long since set and her room was lit with candles. She had started work on a tapestry and she tried to settle down to it, but she couldn't.

Lap, lap, lap – outside the water still slapped endlessly against the walls; a breeze whispered across the lake and she could hear the rippling noise as the water moved; the dhobis had finished their work and apart from the water there was silence. Azimullah would probably be here, now. She looked involuntarily at the door. It was strange to think that in another part of this palace that lean, grey-brown figure was sitting, chattering to Gupta Singh, without any knowledge of her presence. She shivered slightly. She remembered Emily with a sudden affection, and hoped desperately that she, at least, was safe. The thought made her yet more restless. It was so frustrating to think that Azimullah was here and that she couldn't ask him about her, that she'd never get any news. . . . On a sudden impulse she snapped her fingers and the servant came into her room.

'Let's play cards,' she said, smiling at him. 'Go and get some. And . . .' She lowered her voice to a slightly naughty tone, 'get some *bhang* as well. I would like some. I am sure you would, too, no?'

The servant bowed knowingly and returned with a

hookah, a pack of cards, and a small earthenware pot filled with the brown, crushed leaves and seeds of the *bhang* — the drug that was used by so many Indians to dream and forget.

Silently the servant packed the *bhang* into the hookah and, with the flare of a match, warmed it up, sucking evenly and happily while Lizzie dealt the cards. She dealt them slowly, and handed a pile to the servant. He handed her the hookah, and she refused, as if suddenly changing her mind, and then handed it back to him with a conspiratorial look. 'For you . . .' she said. 'It is good — for you.'

The servant started to play, but whenever he offered Lizzie the hookah she pushed it back to him. Sometimes he would refuse, and she would have to urge him to take another puff to show that she, too, was enjoying it. She started to feel slightly dizzy, being unused to the smoke, but continued to play. Now the servant was feeling the effects. The cards started to slip from his hands and he picked them up slowly, deliberately, and continued. Lizzie got up and placed the candles in the room behind a gauzy screen; then she lit some incense. The atmosphere got more and more soporific.

She took the cards out of the servant's hand and shuffled, encouraging him to take more *bhang* while she did so. He shook his head, but she snapped at him. 'More! Smoke more!'

She dealt out the cards as he reached for another puff. As he did so his cards slipped from his hands, scattering on the floor. Eventually, to Lizzie's immense relief, the servant slumped forward and, with a groaning yawn, fell fast asleep.

Lizzie sprang up, covering herself with a dark cloak so that she would be less likely to be seen, and tiptoed swiftly and silently down the corridors until she could see the lights of the covered courtyard where Gupta Singh was entertaining his guests. There was the sound of laughter, the hot smell of curry, mixed with incense, the jangle of bells from a nautch girl's wrists.

Stealing forward, Lizzie hid herself behind a pillar and watched.

The nautch girl was still dancing. By her, on the ground, a man sat cross-legged beating drums; another scraped at a violin-like instrument; another blew down a long hollow pipe. The girl was startlingly beautiful, with a diamond in her nose, spangled glass bracelets up her arms, tiny brown bare feet. Her fingers were long and smooth and curved as she stretched them out in the movement of dance, and she wore a gold and green dress, pleated, and pleated again, so that as she danced the folds of her dress fell in accompaniment to her movement. At every pose she looked like a statue, beautifully designed.

To Lizzie, frozen behind the pillar, the dance seemed to go on for ever. Each time one was finished Jamira, Gupta Singh and Azimullah would clap and clap until she started again; but finally, with a flash of her dark eyes, a smile from her bright red lips, and a sparkle of her long earrings, the nautch girl vanished into the night, and the men started talking.

Lizzie hadn't seen Azimullah for many weeks, but he seemed unchanged by the terrible events he had set in motion. In the darkness the candle lit up his features which looked cruel rather than noble.

Lizzie's Hindustani, though not fluent, was adequate enough to follow the men's conversation.

'I am very glad you have asked me here,' Azimullah said to Gupta Singh. 'We have much to discuss.'

Gupta Singh leant back and stared at him, distinterestedly, a chicken bone in one hand. 'Yes? I think we have discussed a lot of things. I think I have made my feelings clear to you and the Nana. I do not want to join forces with you. I am not joining forces with anyone.'

Azimullah laughed. 'You will have to join forces with someone soon,' he said. 'The war is getting worse. It needs more Indians to tip the balance. Delhi has nearly fallen to the British, but there are still chances that we could recapture it. All is not lost – if only we can get more help!'

'I cannot help a man who slaughters women and children,' said Gupta Singh. 'You know – I like the Nana, he is an educated man. But I am not for killing.'

'Cawnpore, Cawnpore! You sound like a British man, Gupta Singh! That is all they can say! Remember Cawnpore! Cawnpore had nothing to do with the Nana! He was going to give Wheeler and the people in the entrenchment free passage – but some mad sepoy started to open fire, then the British fired back – and there you are! As for the women and children, the Nana looked after them well, very well. Again, there was some mistake – they were killed. The Nana – he cried when he saw what had happened there, he cried, I saw him!'

'You say you hate the British,' said Gupta Singh, thoughtfully, 'but yet I hear you have a British wife . . . how is that?'

Lizzie's heart beat with panic. She only hoped he wouldn't tell Azimullah how he had heard.

Azimullah leant forward, a snakelike look around his eyes. 'And where did you hear that, Gupta Singh?' he asked, slyly. 'I would be interested to hear. Very interested.'

'Why, from Mrs Whittle, whom I met when she was fleeing to the entrenchment,' said Gupta Singh casually. 'She said that Emily had gone off with you – but of course that cannot be so, can it be, for you hate the British so much!'

Azimullah spat on the floor. 'No, it is not true! I have never married her. Anyway, she is no use to me, and I have orders to get rid of her. The Nana will not stand a British woman in the palace. So – she will be killed. I am tired of her anyway. And would you believe? Her brother, do you remember Mr Whittle, the trader in Cawnpore? He has come crawling to us, asking to spy for us! Those British will do anything for money. Who knows whether we can trust a man like that? Maybe he is being a counter spy, who is knowing? If so, we are feeding him false information, while he, poor fool, tells us all about the British. Whatever happens we are using him, and he too will be killed when

191

the time comes. What a man—first he tries to buy marriage for his whey-faced sister from me, then he turns coward when he runs out of money, now he is back crawling like a cockroach – huh! They are both trapped now, though I am sure they would happily leave if they could.'

There was a laugh which Lizzie recognized as Jamira's. 'These Whittles! They are clever enough to survive, at least, a strange family!'

Azimullah turned slowly, the moonlight glinting on his steely eyes. 'What do you know about them, Jamira? What happened to Mrs Whittle? Did you ever find out? Now there was a beauty. I'd have had her any day – Mr Whittle would not have had to part with a penny for me to take his wife; indeed if he had played his cards right then he might have become rich!'

'She was killed at Cawnpore like the rest of the people your master killed,' said Gupta Singh abruptly, throwing down a chicken bone and taking another. 'That is what happened to her. She was murdered with her baby!'

Azimullah looked thoughtfully at Gupta Singh. 'No, I don't think she was slaughtered. I looked at all those bodies and I didn't find her. Perhaps she died in the entrenchment, for how anyone survived those conditions I shall never know. Emily is always wailing for her – oh, women's tears! They drive me mad! And the tears from this pale spinster – sometimes I cannot help laughing! She is so silly she is giving me much sport!'

'My father is fond of women's tears, I think,' said Jamira slyly, 'I think I am right, no, father? Any woman cries and my father is in love with her!'

'And which woman is this?' asked Azimullah, curiously. There was no question, thought Lizzie, Azimullah was like a hound with the scent of a fox. He already suspected.

But Gupta Singh changed the subject. 'Come, eat. Let us be friends, I have told you I will not join you, and I will not. Eat your supper, my friend. Have you brought those poems you promised me?'

Azimullah shook his head. 'We cannot be friends if you do not join us,' he said. 'We will not bother with you now, but when we win the war we will remember who helped us and who did not. Gupta Singh, Rajah of the Lake, did not help us. He will be punished after the war. His palace will be taken away, his poetry burned, his nautch girls given to the Nana, his miniatures thrown on the fire. Only his son will be spared, for he is doing everything in his power to stop you, you foolish old man, from your obstinate ways. You just look at the stars, play chess, meditate and pray. Have you learned nothing from the British?'

'It is because of what you have learned from the British that you want to fight them,' said Gupta Singh. 'It is because they ruin our way of life.'

Azimullah clapped his hands contemptuously. 'You learn and discard, my friend, you take what is good and throw away what is bad . . . however, there is no convincing you, I can see. I am sorry to see you throw your life away like this, for there are many good years left in you – or would be, if you joined us – but now . . . everything will be over for you in a few weeks. Are you all right?'

Gupta Singh was holding his chest, painfully. His mouth was deathly pale, and his hands trembled. He lay back on the cushions, almost fainting. His son looked on contemptuously. Then Lizzie saw a look pass between Azimullah and Jamira that made her blood run cold. They smiled at each other and nodded. Then Azimullah produced a phial from his coat and handed it slyly to Jamira. 'It is working,' he whispered. 'It will not be long now.'

When his father started to recover, Jamira's expression changed and he went over to him, his face now full of concern. 'Father, this conversation is making you ill. Please, go and lie down. I will talk to Azimullah, I will entertain him. Please go to bed. Don't worry. You need sleep and rest. I should not have asked Azimullah here – how can you forgive me, dear father. It was too much for you. . . .' He clapped his hands, and two servants helped Gupta Singh to his feet.

He was breathless, but determined. 'I shall not go until Azimullah goes,' he said, firmly. 'I do not trust him.'

Azimullah rose to his feet with a knowing smile. 'As you

are ill, Gupta Singh, I will not argue with you. I am wishing you will get much better, very soon. Also that you will change your mind. And you will help us, and live a happy life, rich, healthy and prosperous, in an independent India!' They both salaamed each other, and Azimullah left, a blue-black shadow in the night.

Shuddering with fear, Lizzie ran back to her room. The servant was still asleep, the candles had burnt down so low that they just guttered now, sending odd shadows around the room. Cautiously, Lizzie replaced them, then sat down where she had been sitting before. She took the cards in her hands again, then gently tapped the servant on the shoulder. He yawned and stretched, and then, sensing where he was, sat up with a start.

'You fell asleep for a few minutes,' said Lizzie, smiling at him reassuringly. 'Don't worry, too much *bhang*. But I am tired, too, now, so we will leave the cards and go to sleep. Please clear this away —' and she gestured towards the hookah. The servant, relieved not to be rebuked for his behaviour, sprang into action and resumed his post at the door. Lizzie slept, though it was a fitful, miserable sleep, mixed with nightmares of George Whittle, Emily crying, and the constant sight of Azimullah's cruel face.

Lizzie's meeting with Gupta Singh the following day came sooner than she had expected. She was summoned at mid-day to the marble quay where the boats floated, tethered to the palace. Above, the sky was clear blue, except for a few white clouds that never seemed to cross the sun. The far shore of the shimmering lake was shrouded in haze, and the sounds of bells and chanting could be heard across the water. Overhead a bird keeled, bright white against the sky, and the air rising from the water was fresh and cool. A shoal of fish disturbed the surface of the lake, and then disappeared under the blossoming water tulips that grew by the marble steps, leading down to the boats.

Gupta Singh was dressed in white silk with white slippers embroidered with diamonds. His narrow wrinkled trousers were the only plain garment he wore, for his coat was patterned with silver thread, and his turban was crowned with a single pearl. He sat cross-legged on a cushion of duck-egg blue, staring at a marble chessboard in front of him on which he was playing a game with himself.

When Lizzie coughed, he turned and rose, kissing her hand and then gesturing her to sit opposite him. A servant cleared the chess pieces and a glass was placed in front of each of them.

'I have had a special drink made for you,' said Gupta Singh, gesturing to a glass of white liquid on the table. 'It is of buttermilk and nuts, with rose water and the petals of lotus. It is for an important occasion.'

Lizzie sat down apprehensively.

'It is only drunk very rarely,' he said, rubbing his hands together, slightly nervously. 'It is a special drink.'

Lizzie leant forward to taste it, but Gupta Singh stopped her. 'No, you cannot drink it yet. We must talk.'

Lizzie withdrew her hands and rested them on her lap. 'Is it about last night?' she asked, after a silence.

Gupta Singh slowly shook his head. 'I am not thinking of them. Fools. They have forgotten about India. They think they are fighting for India but no, they too have been corrupted. I remember the Nana's father – his adoptive father. Very good man, wise man; how he would cry to see his son now.'

There was another silence. The servants stood around them, motionless, white serving cloths over their arms. They stared impassively into space. But Gupta Singh continued as if they were not there.

'Elizabeth, I have a question to ask you,' said Gupta Singh finally, staring out over the lake. 'It is a difficult question, so you will be being patient with me.'

Lizzie nodded. She clenched her hands together, as if trying to ward off the inevitable question, but tried to keep her face as still and quiet as she could.

'You must also sometimes be asking yourself, Gupta

Singh, is he like ordinary men? Why does he not have a wife? Who is Jamira's mother? Does he have many wives? Where are they? You have asked yourself these questions, have you not?' Gupta Singh rose up and paced around her.

Lizzie nodded. 'Yes. Indeed I have. What normal woman would not?'

'And what have you concluded?' Gupta Singh smiled.

Lizzie hesitated. 'I concluded that you were married once, to Jamira's mother, that she died, that you then did not take another wife. I don't think you do have other wives, or I should have seen them. And I have thought you have not married again – because you are happy on your own.'

Gupta Singh smiled. 'How well you are reading my nature, Elizabeth. Indeed I am happy on my own. There is nothing I like more than my poetry, my meditation, my prayer and my solitude. But I am not well. At least, I have not been being well until you have been sent into my life.'

Lizzie smiled slightly and politely. 'I am glad,' she said.

'My astrologer has told me many things.' Gupta Singh became more agitated. 'He has told me of your arrival into my life, and of our lives together – yes, Elizabeth, our lives together. For that is what I am trying to tell you – without you I am having no life. I will die. He is telling me, Gupta Singh, marry this woman and you will live, a long and happy life, and he is telling me it is written in the stars. . . .'

Lizzie rose, her cheeks flushed. 'I cannot possibly marry you!' she said, firmly, 'I am married already. I have a husband!'

Gupta Singh stared at her. Then he looked down at his white slippers and in a low voice he said: 'That is some bad news I have to tell you, Elizabeth. Azimullah has told me – your husband is dead. You will never see him again. He has been killed.'

'But that's not true!' Involuntarily Lizzie spoke to deny his lie. 'I know . . .' Then her voice dwindled away. She could hardly tell him she had been listening to his conversations the night before.

'You know . . . ? What is it?'

'Nothing,' Lizzie became subdued.

Gupta Singh came up to her and put his arm around her. 'I am sorry,' he said. 'You will be sad, of course, but it is sensible for you to take another husband, quickly, so as to replace him. I am here. I will marry you.'

Lizzie pulled herself away. 'No, you will not!' she said. 'I will never marry again! It is impossible. I am your friend, but I do not love you!'

'Love!' Gupta Singh laughed slightly. 'Now you are talking like a British lady! Ah, well, if you won't agree – I will have to wait. But you cannot cross the stars, Elizabeth.'

'Wait?'

Far away a monkey shrieked across the still lake, shattering the quietness. Gupta Singh was looking at her evenly, determined and resolute.

For one moment Lizzie glanced at the boats by the side of the palace. But she could never escape, and never would without the baby.

'Yes, wait,' said Gupta Singh. 'Maybe is not auspicious time. I will be consulting my astrologer and he will be telling me you will be changing your mind. We will wait till then.'

'And if I do not?'

'He is always right. But if he is not right, then we must wait again.'

Lizzie shivered. There seemed to be no escape. She could be here for ever. She must play for time. She moved towards the table where the glasses of buttermilk stood.

She spoke slowly. 'I will only consider marrying you, Gupta Singh, on one condition.'

'Yes?'

'You must rescue my sister-in-law from Azimullah.'

'But she is also . . .'

'I have a feeling – I get these feelings as you know – I have this feeling she is alive, that she is not well and that you know something. She is not dead.'

Gupta Singh paused. 'No, she is not dead,' he admitted.

Lizzie sighed with relief. At least he admitted the truth.

'You must rescue her and bring her here and then I will consider marrying you. I am not saying what my answer will be, but I will give it some thought.'

Gupta Singh approached, a warm smile opening up on his face. He took her two hands and held them in his. 'Yes, indeed, Elizabeth, I will send – I will send two messengers. One I will ask to say to Azimullah I am reconsidering his offer, while the other will bring Emily to us. Yes, I will promise you that.'

He clapped his hands and gave orders to two men who appeared from the palace. Together he and Lizzie waited while the two talked among themselves. Then they climbed into one of the boats, unleashing the rope from the chain and making off into the mist to the shore.

'It will be done,' he said, triumphantly. 'Now – drink.'

And Lizzie leant forward to the table, took the glass in her hand, and drank. At least she had given herself a little more time. And when Emily arrived they could make plans to escape together. It was no good refusing Gupta Singh outright for he would simply prevent her from leaving. But to feign interest in his offer, to appear to consider it – that way she would get freedom of movement. She, too, could reach the shore. She looked out into the mist. There was no sound except of the oars dipping into the water, getting fainter and fainter.

17

When she returned to her room later, Sushma stopped her before her door, with a frightened look on her face, one finger on her lips, pointing inside with the other hand. Thinking Jamira was waiting for her, Lizzie stepped into the shadows where Sushma beckoned.

'There is astrologer to see you, memsahib, he has been listening, I think. . . .He wishes to talk with you. But beware. He is a dangerous man, Jamira tells us, I am being frightened for you.'

Any man who Jamira described as dangerous could only interest Lizzie. She turned her eyes to the door thoughtfully. She had only seen him in the corridors before, and then rarely – a very tall, lean man clad simply in a white dhoti, a man with a worn face, but a face you could trust, etched with lines of experience. She wondered what he wanted.

'And what do you think?' she asked Sushma, who was half hiding her face with her sari in fear. 'Do you think what Jamira thinks?'

Sushma cast her eyes to the ground. 'I am thinking he is a good man, he has been very good to my family,' she said, apologetically, 'but he is – is –' she hesitated, unable to find the word, then gestured with her hand, curving it through the air like a snake.

'Devious? Too interested in the affairs of your master?'

Sushma nodded. 'Yes, yes, he is not just interested in the stars, he is being interested in everything.'

Lizzie nodded. She pulled her sari around her head and went into her room.

The astrologer was standing there, quietly. He had nothing with him except a small book tucked under his arm, a book engraved with a golden triangle. When Lizzie entered he bowed deeply and salaamed.

'I feel we must talk,' he said, unhesitatingly. 'We have not met properly, but now we must discuss.'

Lizzie gestured to a cushion and he sat down, cross-legged, and she sat opposite him. 'What can I do for you?' she asked.

'I am finding it difficult to tell you, but I can only hope that what I say will be in confidence,' he said, slowly. 'It must be a secret. I do not know if I can trust you, but I must risk it.'

Lizzie smiled and pointed to his book. 'Why, surely that will tell you whether you can trust me or not,' she said. 'It seems to tell you so much, at least so I hear.'

The astrologer took it from under his arm and placed it on the marble floor, patting it with his hand. 'It tells me much, but not everything,' he said. 'It gives me ideas, but not the small things. . . . For instance,' he continued, 'it tells me that the British will win the war very soon.'

'Really?' Lizzie raised her eyebrows, incredulously. 'Well, I certainly hope so.'

The astrologer shook his head. 'There is no hoping, that *is* so,' he said. 'But knowing it, it is my duty to protect my master in every way. From his enemies.' Here he looked sharply at Lizzie.

'I'm not his enemy,' said Lizzie, frankly. 'Though I must admit I'm starting to find it very upsetting that I seem to be a prisoner here. And that, as far as I can gather, has something to do with you.'

'Indeed,' said the astrologer. 'I have long been recommending my master if he will not join the British he must marry a European, so that he will be protected if the British take revenge on all the Indian rulers. But he must also marry someone who will protect him from the enemies within, someone who cares for him. And, above all, some-one he trusts. You are that person, Mrs Whittle.'

'I'm married!' said Lizzie. 'And I could not possibly marry him even were I free!'

'So I have heard today,' said the astrologer. 'That is why we must talk.'

200

Lizzie said nothing but her silence encouraged him to continue.

'You have only to marry him, Mrs Whittle, nothing more. That is all I ask. You must stay a few days, then you are free to leave. This will be only ceremony, nothing else.'

'Why?'

'One thing is because I have told him you will marry him; I thought you would accept his proposal this morning, but now I consult my book I see I have not taken into account the fact that there is someone else dear to your heart. I suppose this is your husband, but watching you in Cawnpore I felt you did not love him. But there is someone you love.'

Lizzie looked at the ground.

'Yes, I am right,' said the astrologer, coolly, observing her reactions. 'I did make a mistake. But you care for Gupta Singh, do you not? You would not like him to die?'

'No, indeed, he has been very good to me. But I am worried about his health, yes. I feel that powdered rubies are doing him no good.' Lizzie said this hesitantly, for she had no idea of what properties they were supposed to have.

The astrologer allowed a thin smile to cross his face. 'Exactly, no good. Not good, but bad. For they have poison in them, too. For a year now his son Jamira and I have been at war. He wants his father to join forces with the Nana. If he won't he will rather his father dies quickly so he can control the men and ally with the Nana himself. But I know the British will win, and Gupta Singh must live, and ally himself to the British, by marriage if not by other means. And so Jamira tries to kill him, I try to save him. But Mrs Whittle, if you were to marry him so much could be done! He would believe what I say so much more! He would listen to me even more! And if he were married to you and you, his wife, said, 'No powdered rubies', he would stop. He would no longer listen to Jamira, he would listen to his wife, most dear to him!'

Lizzie stared at him. He knew so much more than she did. For a moment the idea of marrying Gupta Singh crossed her mind as a possibility. She closed her eyes and briefly imagined his soft brown hands caressing her, his black eyes staring into hers, and his sweet, scented breath hot on her cheek. She felt a small rush of desire . . . and then realized it was out of the question. She was British. If she ever survived she would return to England. She could not afford to have children here, with Gupta Singh, for she would be imprisoned, then, for ever. She shook her head.

'No, I could never carry out my duties as a wife with him,' she said. 'And how would I know you would let me escape? How could I trust you? And if I did, would your word then not be doubted, again?'

'It is all planned,' said the astrologer. 'You will marry him. I will predict that you will be taken from him if he does not ally with the British. He will never do this. You and Miss Whittle, if she escapes, will take a trip to the land and disappear and my predictions will come true. And as for your . . . being a wife . . . I can arrange that. Gupta Singh is most superstitious. I can say, for instance, that if you lie in his bed on the night of the first full moon after the British victory and not before, you will give birth to a poet. I can arrange things. Do not be frightened. But all I am saying is . . .' and his voice gained urgency as he leaned forward, 'it must be soon. Jamira's plan will work very soon. My master is getting weaker and weaker. Please agree to marry him soon – in a few day.'

Lizzie got up and turned to the window. She stared out over the lake and shaded her eyes. What was the alternative? If she didn't marry him she would be kept prisoner on this island for weeks, perhaps years, and if Gupta Singh died then Jamira would see that she was killed.

The astrologer still sat. 'Take time, Mrs Whittle, to think. I will sit here consulting my book. But I promise you – this way you will be out of here quicker, off to Allahabad to join the British, safe with your own people. And Gupta Singh will be safe, too. It is good thing you will be doing, good for you and for the British people.'

It was a matter of whether she could trust the astrologer or not. The Indians were so difficult to understand. What would happen if he were to keep her prisoner after they married? But then, she argued, why should he do that? Even if the astrologer didn't fulfil his promise, as Gupta Singh's wife she would almost certainly be free to come and go as she pleased, and after a few trips to the shore and back to reassure him, one day she would be able to go off and not return. If she married him, went through this one ceremony, she would, paradoxically, be freer to go than if she were to hesitate. She turned. The room seemed black in contrast to the glaring of the sun on the water outside. Gradually it became lighter as her eyes accustomed themselves to the room, and finally she could make out the astrologer still sitting, impassively, on the floor.

'Very well,' she said, slowly, 'I will do as you say. But I will have to trust you to carry out your promises or I will betray your schemes to Gupta Singh. I must have nothing more to do than perform the ceremony – then I must be allowed safe passage as soon as possible.'

The astrologer rose and gave a smile of relief. He salaamed again. 'I never break my word,' he said, calmly. 'I tell you with my hand on my book that I will do everything you ask. Do not be worrying, memsahib. And may I say, thank you. You are a very good lady.'

Lizzie salaamed back and the astrologer left the room, his bare brown feet making no sound on the marble floor.

The news of the impending marriage spread swiftly through the palace. Garlands were made and festooned from arch to arch of the colonnades, bright marigolds against the grey marble. Musicians started practising their pieces on the quay at dawn. The cooks went ashore to buy boatfuls of food which they unloaded in great baskets by the kitchens. Tailors arrived to measure Lizzie for a wedding dress, and even the baby merited a special costume. Women sat grinding spices and flowers to make perfumes, great bells were lowered and polished and hauled up again, the brass dishes in the kitchens were got out and cleaned, and all over the palace there was a hum of activity as the hasty preparations got under way. Lizzie could go nowhere for peace — even the garden was full of servants trimming the bushes, or men cleaning out the pond, making everything special for the occasion.

Lizzie did not actually see Gupta Singh — and she would not, she was told, until the wedding day which would be at the end of the week. She now spent most of her time in her room, keeping away from the bustle of the palace and playing with the baby who, in the few days she had been there, had already started to thrive on the attention and good food he was being given, even starting to make his first tottering steps towards her and calling her 'mama'.

The day before the wedding a knock on her door made her jump. Before she had said anything it opened and there was the figure of a large man in blue who stood watching her jauntily and mockingly as he leant casually against the door-post. It was Jamira.

'Let me congratulate you,' he said. Lizzie had not seen him since their meeting in the garden and she faced him with challenging eyes.

'Thank you,' she said, coolly. 'I might add that I am only marrying your father as he wishes it. . . .'

'And you are a little bit frightened, even of him, no?' said Jamira, laughingly, coming further into the room. 'And what about your husband? Does he know of this new plan his wife is carrying out?'

'Why, you yourself told me it was impossible that he should be alive. And your father told me he knew for certain he was dead!' said Lizzie, feeling ashamed even as she repeated the lie.

'So that's what he told you, is it? Very interesting,' said Jamira. 'I hear otherwise. I hear he is alive and well and working for the Nana. A pleasant man, is he not, your husband? A man who works against his own country. Well, he suits us well enough. He is very useful to us at the moment, too. I am sure he will be interested to know what his wife is getting up to, no?'

Lizzie said nothing. She just wanted to get the wedding over and get away as soon as she could.

'And your sister-in-law, she is there, too, with him. Not

looking as pretty as she used to, which isn't saying much, is it, as she was never a good-looking girl. She won't last long, I'm afraid.'

Lizzie again said nothing lest she betray Gupta Singh's plans. She moved over to the other side of the room and turned when she got to the window, her figure silhouetted against the sunlight.

'Well, is that all you came for? To congratulate me? I thought you wanted this wedding, anyway, or perhaps you have changed your mind?'

Jamira looked at her through narrow eyes. She saw hatred in them and in the cruel twist of his mouth as he spoke. 'I think we both understand each other, Mrs Whittle,' he said. 'I can feel your suspicions in my bones. And you can feel mine. But time will reveal whether you are making the right decision or not. Anyway – a very happy wedding night, I am wishing you! My father is *very* excited at the prospect!'

As Lizzie blushed, so Jamira suddenly laughed again, but this time by accident. It was as if a wild giggle of a child had escaped his lips and he ran out of the room.

As he left, Sushma, who had been waiting outside, came in with some necklaces to show her. As she fastened them round her neck she suddenly said: 'Will you have children, memsahib?'

Lizzie looked at her strangely. She wondered if she knew something. 'Why do you ask?' she said rather brusquely and suspiciously.

'I am thinking it is not possible because you are British,' replied Sushma.

'British women have children like Indian women,' said Lizzie, puzzled.

But Sushma shook her head authoritatively. 'Oh no, is not possible. My grandmother told me that the British ladies are born in big eggs that grow off trees in a far-away land, and your God had brought these eggs over here and they have cracked and you have come out like that.'

Lizzie laughed. 'Do you think my baby came out of an egg, Sushma?' she said. 'You must think we are strange.

No, we are ordinary people, ordinary people like you!'

Sushma smiled. 'Ordinary?' she looked at Lizzie. 'No one in India is ordinary. You are not ordinary like me, I mean. We are a different caste.'

'In England we don't believe in caste. . . .' Lizzie tried to explain.

But Sushma simply looked at her in disbelief. 'You must be mad in England then,' she said. 'Not to believe in caste. Caste is true.'

'Caste is as much of a myth as your eggs,' said Lizzie, exasperated. 'It need not be true. In England we have no caste.'

Sushma thought. 'Caste is true in India, anyway, even if it is not true in England,' she said, thoughtfully. And Lizzie could not help but agree. And that was the whole problem. What was true in India was not true in England. What worked in England did not work in India. Nothing worked – new laws, new ideas, new methods of agriculture – everything imported to India seemed to be turned back on England, distorted, made bad, inefficient, bizarre, disrupting. Even the guns that the sepoys used were British guns, and now they were turned on their inventors.

By the morning of the wedding, Lizzie was increasingly anxious about Emily. Surely she should have arrived by now if she had escaped? The Nana's palace was not many miles away and Lizzie only realized how very much she had looked forward to Emily's arrival when, with each hour, she did not appear. Perhaps it had been thought unwise to bring her to Gupta Singh's palace in the circumstances; perhaps it had been arranged that she should go straight to Allahabad. Whatever had happened, Lizzie had not had an opportunity to ask Gupta Singh and could scarcely do so on the wedding day.

The day's celebrations started at dawn when Lizzie had been led, wearing a gay sari embroidered with pearls and a scented veil, to the boats on the quay. The bride's boat had been decorated all over with white flowers, and fine white silk curtains hid her from view as the boat slowly moved to the shore. But from inside, on her golden cushions, Lizzie could hear the light patter as the servants sprinkled the boat with pink rose petals from the shore.

When she reached the far bank, with Sushma still faithfully by her side, she was carried in a palankeen to the temple. She knew there was a crowd inside, but they watched in silence, saving their cheers for later. All she could feel was the oppressive presence of many people outside, the mysterious shuffling of their feet, coughing, even hoarse breathing and gasping, and the shadowy shapes she could just make out through the curtains of the palanquin that shielded her from public gaze.

Already the bells of the temple were tinkling, the Brahmins wailing their endless prayers again and again, and they grew louder as she grew nearer. At the steps of the temple the palankeen was set down, and servants helped her alight on to the marble steps. Before she entered she looked up. The great marble towers stretched to the bright blue sky, the pink arcades leading to many chapels reached down from her left and right into the distance, and she could just smell the first faint whiff of incense.

Inside it was cool. She could not begin to understand the ceremony, simply doing as Sushma told her, sitting on a red cushion at the feet of the Brahmin who was to marry them. Turning slightly she found Gupta Singh already there, head bent in prayer, beside her.

The prayers seemed endless. She sat for hour after hour as the orange-clad Brahmin spoke, and she understood none of it, except that she felt she might go to sleep at one point as his low murmuring voice continued on and on. Occasionally he would rise and pray himself, lift a handful of lentils to give them both to eat, or scatter them with rosewater. The Brahmin threw petals over them, and they, in their turn, threw petals back at the marble figure of Krishna, bedecked in fresh flowers, whose eyes stared penetratingly at them, his many arms and hands writhing around his cross-legged form, like so many snakes. Finally Gupta Singh was handed a silken scarf which was wound round both of them to signify the end of the ceremony. He rose, kissed her cheek, and she kissed him back. It meant nothing to her. All it was to her was to mean one step closer to escape and home. She followed him round the holy book three times, and finally they left the temple. The crowd outside started to cheer and wave as they stepped on to an elephant garlanded with marigolds, with a painted forehead and diamonds studded in his great grey ears. Together they sat on the swaying beast staring down at the crowds of villagers who threw up handfuls of pink and yellow petals and handfuls of glittering dust, shouting, clamouring, applauding.

Behind them, in a howdah with hangings of heavy orange silk, Gupta Singh's treasurer threw handfuls of money to the crowd, small gold coins that shimmered in the air like leaves in the autumn before dropping into the clamorous crowd below.

Lizzie started to feel dizzy. In spite of the shade from an enormous silken umbrella fringed with silk, the heat was oppressive as ever. The countryside seemed to spin and she had to grip her seat to stop from fainting. They got down from the elephant before the shore, this time, and Lizzie and Gupta Singh descended from the howdah into an avenue of servants carrying large palmlike fans made of golden hairs and hundreds of blue peacock's feathers. As she and Gupta Singh passed through, each servant dropped to his knees behind them, leaving a carpet of gold and blue.

Finally they got into the boat to take them back, the crowd gave a final roar, and the boatman pushed off.

'At last you are my wife,' said Gupta Singh, looking her in the eyes. 'I am so happy you have made the right decision, Elizabeth. I knew you would. My astrologer is never wrong. I am feeling so healthy, so happy, even now. . . .' But as he said it Lizzie noticed a twinge of pain cross his face and he reached for his phial of powdered rubies. Lizzie laid a hand on his arm. 'As your wife, and your friend, please take my advice. Do not take any more. Let me heal you. Let me find your medicine. This is not good for you.'

208

Gupta Singh hesitated a moment, then put the phial on the pillow beside them. 'There. I will do as you wish,' he said with a smile. 'Throw it, if you like.'

Pulling back the curtains of the boat, Lizzie took the phial and threw it as far as she could into the middle of the lake. It was only as she drew them back that she realized that someone else had seen what she had done. Jamira, who was sitting at the helm of the boat, had noticed the familiar red bottle fly into the air and looked at her sharply as she let the curtain fall back. Suddenly, Lizzie felt filled with dread. Perhaps it was the heat or the ceremony or both; it was as if she had been filled with a wave of depression and unhappiness, a terrible feeling of foreboding. Gupta Singh put his arm around her shoulders and squeezed her to him, and she felt even more trapped. She hated to deceive someone like this; it was no help knowing that she was doing it for his own good.

'My astrologer is saying we must not lie together at the moment,' he said. 'I do not know how I shall be able to resist you, but if I do his bidding my fortunes seem to change.'

'Then you must do as he says,' said Lizzie.

As long as she could escape soon she would be safe, and free of the deception that she felt almost unable to maintain.

By the time they reached the Lake Palace it was dusk and the celebrations were starting up. Fireworks burst into glorious explosions of colour in the night air; shrieking fountains of golden light zig-zagged across the sky, and blue, red and yellow stars suddenly flared up and then vanished. A candle burnt on every lily leaf around the palace lighting it up uncannily, and everywhere lights burned, on the water, in the colonnades, on the quays and balconies or in the sky.

In the main receiving room of the palace a feast had been prepared, and nautch girls were already dancing in the corners, girls dressed in Rajput silk, with splashes of green, blue, red and orange, all adorned with gold necklaces, silver bangles and strings of rubies entwined in their hair.

Their eyes were black with kohl, and their lips stained bright red, enhancing their glowing brown skins. Lizzie and Gupta Singh sat on a raised platform at one end of the room and at a signal from Gupta Singh the meal was served.

Lizzie had never seen such a feast. There were bowls of yoghurt dotted with mint, dishes of curries of all colours, piles of pappadams and breads like towers, plates of dhal and vegetables, and yellow curdlike sweetmeats freckled with pistachio nuts. Jugs of buttermilk flavoured with cinnamon stood by every plate, and napkins drenched in rosewater were handed round between dishes. Some dishes were covered with what seemed like silver paper and scattered with nuts, and it was only when they were broken into and the rich creamy sauce spilled out that the curry was revealed; bowls of crunchy roasted chickpeas and nuts were set everywhere, and whole chickens, nearly red with spicy marinade, were brought in by the servants.

But Lizzie hardly felt like eating. She felt she had betrayed Gupta Singh, and the happier he seemed the more anxious she felt, and she hardly knew how she could bear the agonies of intrigue. A look at Jamira's face, black with rage and loathing, took some of the pain away and replaced it with anger; he seemed to be arguing with the astrologer who, until now, had appeared calm and entirely unruffled.

After the meal, at midnight, they went out to the courtyard. Flaming torches were set in the trees, and snake-charmers appeared to entertain them. They were followed by conjurors, sword-swallowers, clowns, men who danced on fire and walked on nails, and men with mongeese who would fight and kill any snake set before them.

The food still continued to arrive; there was never a moment when there was not a plate of something put in front of the royal guests, and it wasn't until two o'clock that the special drinks were given out, to mark the end of the ceremony. The custom was for all the guests to drink out of the same cup which was finally given to the bride and bridegroom to finish. It took a long time. Lizzie was still dazed and confused, and by the time the cup came to her she could hardly drink she felt so faint and tired. She was about to hand it to Gupta Singh when Jamira suddenly leant forward, holding a cloth.

'You are his wife, you must look after your husband,' he said, taking the cup and giving her the cloth with the other hand. 'You must wipe the sides clean for him to drink or he will become ill.'

Lizzie took the cup back and with a quick gesture wiped the rim clean. Then she handed it to Gupta Singh.

'Now you drink,' she said.

Gupta Singh leant forward and kissed her. The guests clapped. Then he took the cup and drank, deeply, putting it down in front of him. The guests clapped again and were all rising to go when one of them shouted, 'Look! He isn't well!'

Another flash of pain had crossed Gupta Singh's face, and he started to gasp. Lizzie put her arm around him to support him. 'It is all right,' she told the man next to her. 'He is often ill, it is a common attack, it will pass in a few moments.'

But this was a different attack. The symptoms were not the same. Gupta Singh rose. He clutched his chest. He staggered forward, and Jamira instantly leant forward to hold him. The guests, stood, horror-struck, unable to say a word. Gupta Singh choked, then cried out in pain, and slumped forward in his son's arms.

The guests gasped, not quite knowing what had happened. Jamira touched his father's heart, held his wrist, then seized Lizzie's trembling arm and wrenched her up. 'It is her!' he cried. 'She has killed my father. She is British spy and killed my father. You saw her drop the poison in the cup before she gave him the drink! Oh, what shall I do!'

He nearly burst into tears, and Lizzie was unable to make herself heard, but still she leapt aside, screaming: 'It's not me, it's you! You killed him! You put poison in his drink when you gave me the cloth! You wicked . . . oh, Gupta Singh, you can't be dead, please God. . . .' She leant forward to reach his face, and touch him, but Jamira shouted: 'Stay away from my father, you British witch! You will burn, as his widow! And as his murderer! Lock her up!'

And before she could say any more, strong brown arms had seized her, roughly tearing her white wedding gown, and with wails and curses they dragged her back to her room, threw her in and bolted the door.

'You will burn!' hissed one through the door. 'We will watch you!'

Lizzie, nearly hysterical, could only scream through her tears, 'It wasn't me, it was Jamira! Fetch the astrologer! He will believe me!'

'The astrologer?' Jamira's cold voice could be heard laughing outside, 'Why, he was in this plot with you. He will burn too!'

'My baby, where is my baby?'

'We will take care of him!' said Jamira, cruelly. 'Now sleep. It will not be long, so sleep well, Mrs Whittle!'

And Lizzie flung herself on to her bed, wracked with grief and fear.

18

A few miles away a weary trio could be seen on the brow of a hill. A woman rode a half-starved horse and two men walked by her side, one large, rough and burly, the other thin, brown and slight. It was a pitiful threesome, and yet no more pitiful than most of the sights to be seen travelling around Oudh at that time, and if it had not been for the loud, raucous voice of the large man they would not have merited a second glance.

'Well, Emily, no one's come after you yet, so maybe we can rest easy tonight.' The large man drew an enormous red spotted handkerchief from his waistcoat pocket and wiped his brow. 'Gohar, we must find somewhere to sleep. Be a good fellow and talk to a friendly villager, eh? If there *are* any friendly villagers around here,' he added, in an exasperated voice.

'George, I'm sure I can travel further,' Emily's voice was tentative. She had lost all her previous giddiness of spirit and she was much changed. Her bent, weary back showed her pain and exhaustion, her slow movements spelled months of ill-treatment; but the stillness in her eyes showed a new resolution that had not been seen before. 'The further we get away from that dreadful place the better off we will be. I'd rather ride till nightfall and just sleep on the road than risk . . .' she shuddered at the prospect.

'You'll sleep under a roof tonight, Emily,' said Whittle firmly. 'No sister of mine sleeps on the roadside. Anyway, it's dangerous, eh, Gohar?'

Arjun Gohar nodded. 'Very dangerous is being Miss Memsahib,' he said. 'I run ahead. I find.'

He sprinted off in front of them and left the brother and sister, who now drew the horse under a tree and sheltered from the sun. Whittle reached up and lifted his sister down to the ground, tenderly.

'By God, Emily, you look uncommon unwell. You should never have gone to Azimullah. You should have listened to Lizzie. When I think of what he did to you, it makes my blood boil! I'd like to go after him and shoot him from a cannon till every bit of his nigger body was spattered all over his palace!'

Emily sat down, automatically cross-legged after her weeks in an Indian environment. 'Please don't talk of it, George. We have talked enough. I am only glad to be away from there. I can't help but wonder who sent that message, you know.'

Whittle shaded his eyes and looked over the bleak landscape. Then he shrugged. 'God knows. One minute we're virtual prisoners in that Nana's palace, next thing a servant from that rajah is secreting himself round the back and engineering our escape. Who was that rajah, eh? The name was familiar.'

'Gupta Singh, Rajah of the Lake – don't you recall? He was at the Nana's dinner that night when . . . when Lizzie . . .' Emily's eyes filled with tears. 'Oh, I wish to God I'd listened to her,' she whispered. 'Oh, when I think of her, and what happened to her . . . it is too terrible for words.'

Whittle crouched down, squatting on his heels, and put an arm around her. 'Thank God you didn't, Emily, for then you would have been hacked to pieces in Cawnpore.' Whittle and his sister were silent for a moment, as if in thankful prayer.

The silence was broken by Gohar's return. He appeared breathless. 'There is a family I have found – up there.' He gestured through the trees. 'For a little money, some rupees, they will be glad to let us have a room, is not being very clean. . . .'

'Don't worry about clean, lad,' said Whittle, rising up, and helping Emily, too. 'Just lead us there. Water, eh? Some food? That'd be good!'

And so they made their way over the brow of the hill to a small hut, outside which stood a tall Indian in a dirty red turban, presiding over a colony of small children at his feet. He talked a while with Gohar, then, accepting some money from Whittle, he led them to the back of his house to a dingy, windowless room, with matting on the floor. He gestured, then salaamed, humbly.

Whittle and Emily stood aside while Gohar conversed some more in Hindustani. 'Can't understand a word,' said Whittle angrily, as he sat down to pull off his boots, 'Bloody rude, standing there jabbering in front of us . . .'

The low burble of Hindustani continued, Arjun Gohar raising his eyebrows, then laughing, looking crestfallen. . . .

'They're talking of a burning,' said Emily, who was listening, 'Suttee.'

'Huh! That's Indians for you. Not happy with the killing of the British, kill the wives as well. A fine race!'

'No, this is a European woman,' said Emily, her eyes now fixed on the Indian's face as he spoke, 'Something to do with Gupta Singh.'

'Him again!'

Emily slowly turned to Whittle. 'He says there was a European woman who married him last night,' she said, 'and who killed him, they say, at the wedding feast. Now she's going to be burned.'

'Well, if she's a murderess she deserved it. Can't think why anyone would kill a man like that. I thought he liked Europeans. Shows you can never, never trust them.'

Emily leant forward and tapped Gohar on the arm. 'Ask him what her name is, Gohar,' she said. 'It might be someone from Cawnpore, do you think?'

Arjun Gohar asked the Indian, and shrugged. 'It's being like all your names,' he said, 'Mrs Wit, he is saying, all names the same in British . . .'

'Must be a Dutchwoman,' said Whittle, 'de Wit, do you think?'

'Mrs Wit, she is having a baby, yes, she is escaping the massacre, they say she is a witch.'

Emily's hand flew to her mouth. 'George!' she said, 'It's Lizzie! It must be! Gupta Singh always liked her. She has a baby. That's why she sent to save us, it must be, that explains it!'

215

'Come on, Emily, the heat's going to your head,' said Whittle roughly, 'I've never heard such imagination. You women. Lizzie's dead.'

'Did you see her dead?' asked Emily, pulling at his sleeve. 'Did you actually see her body? . . .' Then, looking up, she asked Gohar, 'Ask him, wasn't it Whittle, something like that?'

Gohar asked again, but the Indian shrugged his shoulders and smiled, showing a gold tooth. Then he left the room.

'Lay off, Emily, this is all rumour, and you know it.' Whittle started to get angry. 'Don't you think if I thought it was her I'd want to help her? Of course it's not.'

Arjun Gohar drew a line round his face with a long, brown finger. 'He is saying *very* beautiful, *very* beautiful lady,' he said smiling.

Emily stood up. 'It is her.' Her eyes flashed. 'If you won't go and see, then I will! I don't care what becomes of me! I've got no life left anyway, no one will ever marry *me*. I cannot leave this place until we have found out what is happening!'

'Sit down and shut up!' Whittle's face grew red with anger as he rose to his feet. 'You've been saved, I'm safe – do you want to die? You're mad, Emily. Don't talk nonsense.'

But there was no stopping Emily. She was convinced. 'Very well, she saved us – and you won't save her. No matter. I shall go, with Gohar. Gohar, get the horse! We are going to the palace of the Rajah of the Lake. We will leave Mr Whittle here!'

Whittle sighed. He put his hand on the door and leant against it. 'Emily, you'll regret this,' he said, warningly. 'Now, look, if it's that strongly you feel then I'll go, I'll go and I'll find out a bit more. I'll go as far as I can, without getting myself killed.' He stood up straight. 'Women!' He started to pull his boots on again. 'Nothing but trouble, trouble!'

'You'll have to take Gohar or you won't find anything out,' Emily put her hand on his shoulder in gratitude, 'since you don't speak a word of the language. Take Gohar, I'll explain what he must do. I will stay here for two days, three if you like, and wait for you. I will be safe here. The Indian is kind. I won't be harmed. But I couldn't live with myself if I hadn't felt I'd tried. . . .'

'Probably turn out to be some Indian witch, after all, who deserves to be burnt after killing her husband,' said Whittle. 'Well, I'm not going until I've had some food.'

'Of course not,' said Emily. 'But eat quickly for you must be off.'

And, raising his eyes to heaven in despair, Whittle agreed.

Lizzie had not been allowed to leave her room at all. Sushma had been allowed in, with the baby, who had clung to his mother. She held him close, feeling she loved him even more in this moment than ever before. She stroked his warm head, the silky down of baby hair that covered it, rubbed her cheek against his soft, young skin, kissed his small dimpled fingers and tried very hard not to cry. She hugged him to her, but while his head snuggled comfortably into her shoulder, she could only stare ahead, the room becoming quite distorted as huge tears filled her eyes. She could hardly breathe lest she be overcome with the choking sobs that tore inside her.

'Memsahib! I am sorry!' Sushma looked on, twisting her long thin fingers in despair, her brow knotted in pity. 'I know you have to be burnt . . . but you will be with your husband. I know. I am Hindu. You do not know, but I know. . . .'

Lizzie could hardly hear the words, her heart seemed to be pounding in her ears like drums as she held the baby. Her baby. Richard's baby. They would have to rip him from her arms before she would part with him . . . and, yet, he couldn't burn, too!

'Memsahib,' Sushma's voice continued. 'Can I help you, can I make you feel happier. Oh, do not be crying. . . .'

Lizzie thrust the baby into Sushma's arms and turned her back on her, unable to contain her grief. She buried her head in her hands and her shoulders swayed in time with her sobs. She longed for help, for love, and she was rewarded only with the prospect of death.

'Sushma, you don't believe I murdered him, do you?' she said, finally, pleadingly. She still couldn't look round. Sushma was now the only person she might trust.

'Of course not, memsahib, Jamira did that, I am thinking!' Sushma said, reluctantly. 'But he hates you, memsahib. He is very dangerous and . . .'

'Sushma, please will you do one thing for me?' Lizzie turned round, wiping her eyes with her sari, and putting her hands out to the girl. 'My baby . . . Jamira will kill my baby when I am dead. Will you care for him and protect him? I know it is a very big thing to ask, but I beg you. . . .'

Sushma's white eyes opened in horror at the thought and she held the baby protectively. 'He will not be killing babies, no . . . not even Jamira —'

'He has told me he will,' Lizzie's voice dropped to a whisper. 'He poisoned his father . . . why not kill a British baby? Perhaps if I gave you some money . . . I have some jewels . . . you could take them and go to another village with the baby. Perhaps you could find a European and give the baby to him. I will give you my father's name and address and the European might see that he got back to England . . . will you do this?'

Sushma looked at the door as if frightened that someone might be listening. Then she nodded. 'Very well. I promise. Give me no jewels. I will do this for you.'

Lizzie felt a wave of relief at the words; it was a sign that Sushma could really be trusted. 'No, you must make money, or jewels, or you will starve. Take him, now. Take him away. I will give you a letter later. I cannot bear the agony of seeing him any longer.'

Sushma held the baby tight. She understood and, grasping Lizzie's hand and squeezing it, she turned and left. Lizzie had a last glimpse of the now comforted child and forced herself to wave as he smiled at her over Sushma's shoulder. 'Bye bye,' he said, suddenly, clenching and opening his fist in an imitation of a wave, 'bye bye.'

Lizzie's anguish at the parting was not heard by anyone

outside herself. She felt as if her whole body was being ripped apart, ripped to form a kind of howling void down which she was slipping, losing complete control. The room seemed to circle round her and everything went black.

Much later she regained consciousness. Her head felt as if it had been kicked, as if her whole inner being had been bruised and beaten. Slowly she got up from the floor. Slowly she forced herself to write a letter for Sushma, giving her father's address in England so that any European might understand what had happened. She wrote that the baby's father was Richard Applevale and that he was to be taken to him or his family as soon as possible. And as she wrote his name, she paused, gripping the pen. She would never write that name again. She would never see him again. Now she imagined him, climbing over the walls of the entrenchment at Cawnpore to find her and discovering nothing but the remnants of a deserted siege – if he had survived. She shuddered, praying swiftly that he was alive, and resumed her letter. She tried to write another version in very inadequate German and a passable one in French in case Sushma met someone of a different nationality. She then gathered all the valuables she had, mostly gifts from Gupta Singh, tied them into a handkerchief and waited for Sushma's return.

On the morning of the funeral there was complete silence: all the men had gone ashore to prepare the pyre. Now, at mid-day, accompanying the lapping sound of the water was the noise of men chopping wood from the forests around the lake, cracks of sound that reverberated across the water and back again. Far away she could hear the wailing of the Brahmins as they prepared the ceremony.

They came for her late in the evening. The Brahmins came first, murmuring prayers, swinging the incense around her, marking her forehead with the gash of red that showed she had been blessed. She stood alone, noticing the way they avoided her, as if she were already dead, her blood running cold as the murmurs grew louder and softer as, they prayed and wailed around her. She could already smell the scented oils on their orange gowns, oils that also soaked the wood on the pyre with the sickly smell of death.

When they had retreated, Sushma came in with the simple white sari she was to wear, and they embraced. Lizzie gave her the letters, kissed her, clinging to her like a child, knowing that this was the last time she would touch human flesh.

She felt so utterly alone. The prospect of death seemed to sharpen all her senses, and when she was led out and into the boat that would take her to the shore she was suddenly aware of life as she had never been before. As she looked into the water it seemed to have a life of its own, as if it were almost talking to her. Across the water the trees seemed almost like living beings, swaying in the breeze, and she could swear she almost saw them growing. The fish darted quicker than ever before, the very air she breathed was dancing with life, the leaves of the water hyacinths seemed to curl and uncurl in front of her eyes as if they were saying to her: 'Look! We're alive! Look what we can do!'

When they reached the shore, the track to the funeral pyre was lined with the villagers that only recently had applauded her marriage. It seemed an endless walk. First, when she got ashore, the Brahmins approached with another cloth, drenched in the water of the mother Ganges, and wound it around her, soaking her skin. Then she was made to walk, a living corpse, along the track that she had ridden yesterday, to the main square in front of the temple.

It was all changed. While there had been garlands and celebration songs and crowds, now there was a huge pyramid of wood, hundreds of logs piled on each other, interleaved with sandalwood which let off a sickening odour. At the top of this pyramid was the shape of a body, covered in white silk. How small he looked in death, thought Lizzie, absently. How little he had become. Around the pyre, crammed in every arch and gallery and cloister of the square, were the villagers, some even carrying their chapattis to eat while watching, their eyes glued

220

to the scene, all waiting, their breath held in a kind of unison, to see the *firinghi* burnt alive. Slowly the chant started.

'*Sut! Sut! Sut!*' The chant ebbed and flowed, prayers being intoned all the while. '*Rani . . . sut . . . rani . . .*' A small Indian boy leant forward and tugged at her sari, perhaps to see if she were real, perhaps to be able to say he had touched the living *firinghi* murderess. Tense with fear and horror Lizzie automatically flung out her hand and hit him cruelly to the ground. The minute she had done it she regretted it; he was only seven or eight. One day her baby would grow up to be like that – interested, curious, reaching out to touch life, to feel it in his hands. . . . She bent to help him up, to check that he was not hurt, but his mother had seized him back, looking at her with fearful eyes.

'I am sorry,' said Lizzie, in English. She knew they couldn't understand. But saying it made her feel better. She took another step. A hazy, hissing steam came from the pyre as the hot coals around it started to dry it out. She looked up to the top of the pyre, and the ladder reaching up to it. She turned to the crowd. There were no friendly faces, no escape. It was not only the fear of death that frightened her, it was the method, the slow burning, the terrible pain, the sight of her skin turning black before her. . . . She tried to force the picture from her mind. And yet she could not obliterate the pyre before her, which through the slow smoke seemed to be almost heaving with heat. It would only take one flame to make it catch – one flame from the tall, blue-clad man who stood smiling at the bottom of the steps to the top of the pyre. Jamira.

Lizzie stood transfixed. The crowd stared at her in silence. Jamira looked straight at her, a cunning look of victory on his face. He held a flaming torch and he stood motionless. Behind him a familiar figure stood, smiling also. Lizzie narrowed her eyes and tried to make him out – that slate-grey skin, the cruel nose . . . it was Azimullah come to witness the death of an enemy. For a moment, foolishly, her heart jumped at the sight of a familiar face. But she could expect no mercy there. She took another

221

step. Now she could feel the oppressive heat of the pyre and automatically she winced at the thought of the flames against her flesh. The crowd shifted and a parakeet squawked above as if to hurry her on.

She turned again to the crowd. For one strange moment she seemed to see her father at the back – but looking again she saw it was only an Indian. Then another group caught her eye – it was the Ram family! But then again she looked and it turned out to be a group of youths, hanging on to a pillar. There were Emily and Mrs Jacobi together, with General Wheeler from Cawnpore; but as she blinked they turned into two Indian women accompanied by an old man with a white moustache. Everyone was here – the two men in the carriage from Calcutta, the Nana Sahib, Richard. . . . And as she saw him she opened her mouth as if to speak to him, bringing her arms up pleadingly, when the image changed and it suddenly became George Whittle. Lizzie stared at the vision long and hard – at that coarse skin, the reddened features, the small eyes, and that rough, portly figure. It *was* George . . . and yet it could not possibly be. The sun was playing tricks. She looked again. There was no sign of him now, only the impassive stare of the Indians.

She took another step. Jamira lunged forward, sharply. 'You take your time, you English whore!' he whispered, grabbing her arm. His grasp on her arm hurt Lizzie, and she stumbled foward, then felt his rough hands on her back as he pushed her up the crude wooden steps that led to the top. The crowd now started to move and shift and gasp. It was nearly time. Lizzie turned to look down for the last time. God help me, she thought, automatically making the sign of the cross as she stared below. God help my baby. God help Richard.

Jamira leant forward, the flame licking above his head, bending to start the fire with his torch.

Whittle had not intended to come so far in search of the mysterious European woman until, a few miles down the road from where they had left the last night's camp, Arjun

222

Gohar had talked with some villagers on their way to witness the spectacle. He ran back to the horse.

'Whittle, not Wit, Whittle,' he said. 'Is Whittle, very beautiful.'

Whittle cursed under his breath. He knew it could not possibly be, but at the same time he could hardly face Emily now, for Arjun Gohar would tell her what he knew.

'There are hundreds of Whittles in this damned country,' he shouted at Gohar, spurring his horse. 'It's all madness!'

Luckily Arjun Gohar did not understand, simply ran on ahead.

'Oh, get up, you fool,' shouted Whittle when he caught up with him. 'We'll never get there with you walking. Come on!'

The huge crowd around the temple spilled out into the surrounding fields. Families had come with picnics of dhal and curry and were sitting, eating, before the action began in earnest. In the bright blue sky a vulture circled, attracted by the smell of food; yet Whittle could not help feeling it was a bad omen. Arjun Gohar led him on, and finally they reached the temple as the sun was starting to set. It was hard to push forward, for the Indians had already taken their places and were reluctant to allow these two bedraggled strangers to push in front. However, Whittle was too big and well fed to tolerate any resistance, and they soon took up their places near the front.

The pyre made Whittle feel sick. The sight of the thin, small, white-clad figure appalled him. Death in battle was one thing but death presented so coldly and callously was another.

'That is Gupta Singh!' said Arjun Gohar, pointing him out to Whittle.

Whittle shifted his feet. 'I know it is, you fool! I'm not stupid,' he said. Arjun Gohar was too close to him, smelling of old curry and dirt. He was squeezed on all sides by Indians. He felt claustrophobic and uncomfortable. An Indian next to him stared at him suspiciously. Automatically Whittle's hand reached round his waist to the reassur-

223

ing butt of his gun. He felt better.

The wait seemed endless. The crowd became even more of a crush, and Whittle thought he might faint. Looking up to the rooms along the colonades that bordered the court where they stood he fancied he saw a woman with a baby, a white baby. He narrowed his eyes, but could not make it out. Looking up made him stare into the sun and that meant that his vision was clouded by large green spots of light in front of his eyes.

Suddenly there was the sound of whispering, turning to a rumble of anticipation. She was coming. '*Rani . . . sut . . . rani . . . sut . .*' Everywhere around Whittle the crowd heaved and rocked, all necks craned to see the widow-murderess.

Finally he saw her. A tall slim figure, clad in white, her figure highlighted by the soaking cloth that caught the sweep of her breasts and hips. She walked well, but slowly. Calmly, it seemed.

And then his heart seemed to freeze. He recognized her. The face, now very brown from the sun, was not much changed. Still the proud full lips, the flushed cheeks, the bright eyes and the rich, glowing hair under the sari. Whittle started to cry out but stopped. Gohar looked up at him and, alarmed at the look in his eyes, put a hand out to check any action that might give him away. Whittle didn't even notice the Indian. He felt dizzy as the strangeness of it all hit him. How could she have escaped? What had happened? The crowd around him seemed to press on him even more. She got closer, staring at the crowd as if examining them. Suddenly she stopped and looked him full in the face. He stared back, unable to speak, just looking, transfixed, into her eyes. But there was no sign of recognition in them. She wandered on, as if in a dream.

Slowly she ascended the steps. Whittle started to shake. He could not witness this. He turned to escape, but he could not move. He could only stand and stare. He looked from Lizzie to Jamira, from Jamira to Lizzie, each picture flashing at him like a nightmare. Then behind Jamira he saw the familiar face of Azimullah Khan.

It was this that seemed to galvanize him. Azimullah Khan, the man who had wrecked him and his sister's happiness, was now masterminding the cruel death of his wife! He looked back up at Lizzie, saw her turn to the crowds and make the sign of the cross on her chest, and suddenly he lost control. He hardly knew what he was doing. He saw Jamira lean with the torch. Writhing in fury, he reached for his gun, and with a great howl of revenge he pulled it up with a sweating hand. Aiming straight for Azimullah Khan, he squeezed the trigger.

There was complete uproar. The bullet had grazed Jamira who sprang into the air, screaming in pain, clutching his wound, and the torch flew into the air in an arc into the panicking crowd. The priests chanted, the women screamed, the men yelled: everywhere was smoke and confusion, flames, yells, coughing and screams. The crowd was like an animal let loose, all thoughts of the funeral forgotten in the panic.

Arjun Gohar was stunned for a moment, but when he turned to help George Whittle, he found the crowd had already swallowed him up in a surge of rage and confusion. Looking around in his helplessness, Gohar spotted Lizzie and sprang quick-footed over to the funeral pyre, helping her down the steps.

'Am helping you,' he said, urgently. 'Come with me, I take, we have a horse . . .'

Lizzie stared at him. 'Who are you . . . I can't go . . . the baby . . .'

'Where baby?' Arjun Gohar would have slapped her face to snap her out of her shock had she not been a European. 'Where baby?'

He dragged her through the crowd, pulling her wet winding sheet as they went, keeping with the smoke and the crowd to avoid being spotted. 'There,' said Lizzie suddenly, pointing. 'There is my baby. And Sushma . . .'

Sushma had come running into the forecourt holding the child, and she thrust the screaming child into Lizzie's arms. 'This way!' Arjun Gohar herded the women through the colonnades.

They ran surefooted along the colonnade to the horse. 'Get, get,' Gohar pushed them on, 'I am coming.' He swiftly leapt on to one tethered nearby and pointed ahead. 'Be quickly, quickly, or they will be killing us. . . .'

Lizzie mounted the horse. Fear and shock had paralysed her, making her movements slow. Behind she could hear the sound and roar of the crowd in pursuit of their entertainment, '*Rani! Rani! Rani! Sut! Sut! Sut!*' Then there was a sudden howl of pleasure. Lizzie's blood ran cold. Before galloping off she stopped, looking back briefly at the smoky scene behind her. There was the crowd, chanting with delight. They danced around a head, impaled on a sword.

It was the head of her husband, George Whittle.

Lizzie spurred her horse and together they galloped, looking back no more until nightfall.

There was no time for grief. Relief was soon replaced by fear on the road, though with Arjun Gohar and Sushma Lizzie felt comparatively safe. Very few Indians would want to kill a British woman and her baby, it was true, but very few would even consider helping them; with two Indians her chances were higher.

When night came Gohar insisted they camp by the side of the road.

'Is dangerous, memsahib,' he insisted, when Lizzie protested. 'All the houses will be searched tonight.'

Sushma added, 'Indeed, Miss Lizzie, Jamira will have all his men sent to search the countryside, they will be looking for us. We must hide as best we can until we are out of the area.'

Arjun Gohar agreed, a look of anxiety passing temporarily across his face as he nodded his head and he dismounted by a grove of mango trees. 'I will be finding some food, some blankets, then I return,' he said, when he was sure they were well hidden. 'Wait here.'

The two women sat down on the dusty ground, barely able to see each other in the darkness. Lizzie held the baby, bouncing him up and down to check his restlessness, letting him stand on the ground in front of her, his fingers holding her hands for support.

Lizzie felt she had to express her feelings to the Indian woman.

'Sushma, I have put you in such danger. Because of me you will never be able to go back to your family at the palace. I had no idea things would turn out like this – though why all this has happened I don't know. I want you to keep my money and jewels at least so that you can go off alone if you want and make a new life for yourself. Arjun Gohar will look after me, whoever he is. And if not, I am used to the road on my own. I have used you enough . . .'

Sushma sighed in the darkness beside her. 'Memsahib,' she said, softly, 'if you talk like that much longer I shall believe indeed you are just born from eggs as I said the other day. I cannot rest until see you and the baby safe with your people. Then I will go.'

There was a silence, and Lizzie felt almost unable to grasp the words she spoke. 'But Sushma, the British may be losing the war – you will have no chance afterwards. If you help me you will be killed. You don't understand what you are doing!'

'I do understand, memsahib,' Sushma's reply was soft and reassuring. 'Oh, Miss Lizzie, when I saw you today . . . when I looked from the window and saw the funeral pyre and the people, and Gupta Singh on the top, and the smoke coming up and the smell, I felt I was wrong. Burning, yes, for Indian women, who believe in Krishna, but not for you. I prayed, I prayed to Krishna and my prayers have been answered. You have been saved. I can't leave you, never shall I be leaving you. And the British losing the war – I am not thinking so. Bahadur Shah has been captured in Delhi, he is living in one room, he is old he is sick, he is powerless. Agra has fallen to the British again, and the British are marching towards Lucknow, they say. I do not look to the future, it is not in my religion, for myself. Whatever happens, it is God's will.'

Lizzie felt herself warming to this simple Indian woman.

She put her arm round the baby and lifted him up, and with her other hand she reached into the darkness for Sushma's hand, squeezing it gratefully. 'You are very good to me, Sushma,' she said. 'If we do get to safety somehow, you will be safe with me.'

There was a crackling noise in the bushes nearby and immediately the two women tensed with fear. But it was only Arjun Gohar returning with some wood, some blankets, and two chickens in one hand. He nodded to the women, then swiftly made a fire, and soon they were squatting around it as the chicken roasted in front of them. Arjun Gohar took a water bottle from his side and offered it to Lizzie who gave the baby the first drink. He was getting sleepy now. She rocked him gently, and he leant against her shoulder peacefully.

'We will be leaving tomorrow for Havelock's army,' said Arjun Gohar, decisively. 'There you will be safe.' He turned respectfully to Lizzie.

Lizzie nodded gravely. 'Thank you. But will you tell me now where you come from? Who are you? Did you know that man in the crowd who was killed? Please tell me everything.'

Arjun Gohar reached into the flames with his dark hands and deftly turned the chickens, seemingly immune to the heat. For a moment Lizzie's eyes followed his hand, but on seeing his flesh in the flames had to look away, shivering at the memory of her ordeal.

He rocked back on his heels, quietly dusting the ash from his palms. 'I will tell you. I am with Sahib Whittle, who has gone to get his sister from Azimullah Khan. We are captured as well, and it is impossible to escape until a message comes from Gupta Singh and we are on our way back to Havelock's army where my master is. Then Miss Whittle, she is hearing about you, and she is saying we must go and save you. I am thinking it is impossible, Sahib Whittle is saying you are dead, is not possible, but Miss Whittle she is insisting. So we leave her . . .' He looked away when he said this, anxiously. 'We leave her in a house in a village nearby and come to see you. I am thinking all is lost, you will be burnt, Sahib Whittle is very agitated. I think he sees you, are you not seeing him?'

Lizzie suddenly remembered the sight of the crowd, the sight she was convinced was a vision. She had a brief memory of his eyes, staring into hers. 'Then Jamira is setting fire and Sahib Whittle suddenly is going mad, and he shoots Azimullah Khan. That is all I am knowing.'

Lizzie's head spun. So Whittle had saved her; he had saved her life.

'Where is Emily – Miss Whittle?' she asked. 'We must get back to her. She will be worried on her own.'

'Memsahib, I have tried,' said Arjun Gohar slowly, picking up a stick to poke the fire, 'but there is no sign. I am thinking we must be near her but we must be hidden, and that is why we come here. If we were to join her in the hut we would be discovered instantly. All the village would know. But when I go now to get food I am visiting her to tell her to join us tomorrow to come with us to Havelock's army. But I go to the house and there is no one. Nothing. It is deserted. The family have packed and gone away, and Miss Whittle has vanished. I am very puzzled, no one will tell me what has happened. I am very troubled.'

Lizzie could hardly believe it. She passed a hand over her forehead. 'She was here – only yesterday – and now she's gone?'

'Yes, that is it. But she is knowing where Havelock's army is, I am thinking. She is not dead, for I have not seen any blood. Maybe she has gone on ahead.'

Arjun Gohar's suggestions sounded most unconvincing, probably because he did not believe them himself. He pulled the chicken from the fire and, wrenching a knife from his belt, cut it into quarters, sharing it between them. Lizzie looked down at the sleeping baby and gently set him by her side, stroking his head.

She bit into the hot flesh of the chicken and felt better.

'And where is Havelock's army?' she asked. Around them the night creatures were starting their noises, the crickets chirruped and a jackal wailed pitifully on the horizon.

'It is on its way to Lucknow, memsahib, where it will be victorious,' said Arjun Gohar.

Sushma asked, 'You are with the British army then?' she said. 'You are kitmutghar?'

Gohar turned to her and nodded. He finished chewing his chicken, then spoke. 'Indeed, with a British officer. It is a sad tale. India is full of sad tales, now. All shall become red – indeed how true that has been.'

He was silent for a moment, lost in thought. Beside him the two women stretched out on the ground, the curves in their bodies highlighted by the flames of the fire.

'What is his sad tale?' Sushma asked.

Arjun Gohar smiled, slightly. 'He is a good man, very good. I am with him from the moment he steps off the boat at Calcutta nearly. He is not like the other British officers, he likes the Indians, he is good, he learns our customs, our art, our religion, our language. Why, I have spent many nights helping him with his Hindustani. For the first few months he is like this. Then one day, he changes. I do not know why. But he changes, he goes drinking, he has many, many girls, he is unhappy. Unhappy.

'One day I say to him, why are you unhappy? He says he was in love, he is to be married to a girl in England, and he discovers she has married someone else. Ah, women can be very treacherous!' he said, smiling at both Sushma and Lizzie. 'I tell him, never trust a woman! But it is sad. She is a bad woman. She has driven him mad, quite mad.'

Sushma shook her head. 'Poor man,' she said, sympathetically. 'British women are very bad that way, not Indian women, they stay true, but some British women –'

'Then?' Lizzie could feel the hair on her scalp prickling as Arjun Gohar unfolded the story. Surely this could not be Richard's servant? Her lips parted in breathless eagerness, and she leant forward, her hands on her knees, waiting on every word.

'Then many things happen. We get to Cawnpore. We meet this friend of yours, this Sahib Whittle. You know what has happened at Cawnpore. I think this girl was there. My master, he goes mad. He is wild. Like all the others he knows what has happened, he fears for my safety. I think he fears he might kill me himself, indeed, because at that moment he hates all Indians. He tells me to go. I go. I know I must go. But now I am going back. I think some weeks have passed and he will be greeting me. I hope so.'

Lizzie leant forward in the moonlight. She knew now that it was true. Richard had survived. Not only had Richard survived, but he surely loved her still. She felt a strange warmth spring up inside her as she asked: 'Tell me, Arjun Gohar, was your master's name Richard Applevale?'

The silence was so sudden that it could almost be heard. Arjun Gohar seemed to become rigid, transfixed. He stared at her, almost in horror. 'You *are* a witch!' he said fearfully. 'It is true! You have strange powers!' He shrank away into the darkness, a look of terror crossing his eyes.

Lizzie shook her head. 'No, no, I am not. I am George Whittle's wife. I met Richard Applevale in Calcutta. I – I recognize him from your description.'

Arjun Gohar was not to be convinced. 'No one knows his story except those closest to him. I heard this story just once when he took me into his confidence. He has told me. It is not possible you know him.'

Lizzie nodded, then reached out to take his hand to reassure him. 'I am not a witch,' she said. 'Trust me. When I see him you will understand.'

And as she said it, she could see Gohar was beginning to understand. She noticed his eyes wandering to the baby, then looking back to her.

He pointed to the sleeping child. 'This is your baby,' he said.

Lizzie nodded. 'Yes.'

'Sahib Whittle said something as he left that always puzzled me, something about a baby. . . .' Arjun Gohar got up and walked around the fire, then squatted by the baby, gently stroking his cheek. 'Yes, yes, you are a lovely boy,' he said, his face breaking into a smile. 'Like your father, little one.'

231

Then he got up quickly. 'I am sorry, memsahib, I was frightened. Now we must get rest. We must get you and the baby back to my master, quickly. You have been apart too long, I am thinking.'

Lizzie settled down. She drew the blanket over her. At last she felt nearly at peace.

Now they took the road to Lucknow, the Great Trunk Road branching off to Allahabad; the Lucknow road was much the same, only not so wide, but they travelled quickly and soon found evidence of the army ahead. Each day they seemed to creep closer, each body they saw hanging from a tree was perhaps fresher than the last, a gruesome but accurate sign that they were nearing Havelock's column.

If they were lucky they would find a cooking pot, or a *lota*, left by the camp; once Arjun Gohar found a dead Highlander by the side of the road, his knapsack amazingly still intact, and they helped themselves to his knife, his watch, and Lizzie took his Bible. They made a rough grave for him, and Lizzie said the Lord's Prayer over the sad pile of earth.

But generally they made a happy enough group. Sushma and Arjun Gohar had become friendly and chattered amiably on the roadside; Lizzie usually rode the horse with the baby, but they occasionally switched and Sushma would ride, holding the baby tight while he yelled for his mother down below. He, too, grew into the routine of the journey, but it soon became clear that Sushma and Arjun Gohar were happier walking together. Lizzie started to become light-hearted, hardly daring to hope that she would see Richard again, though fearing that he would still want nothing to do with her.

It was on a day when they felt particularly optimistic, when they had actually come across some camp fires from the army still burning that they were overtaken by a cheerful group of Indians who were singing and marching along the road.

'Where are you headed for?' cried one.

'Lucknow,' said Arjun Gohar.

'To see the British rout the place?' A good-looking young Sikh with an orange turban rode up, and bent respectfully to Lizzie from his horse. 'That'll be a fine sight; we're off to watch, too. That's a nice child you've got there, memsahib. Good day!'

He rode off and somehow the atmosphere became even more pleasant. It was such a change, thought Lizzie, to meet Indians who were friendly on the road, who said pleasant things and smiled, instead of scowling and looking the other way.

'They are nice, no?' she called down to Sushma and Arjun Gohar. Sushma looked up, smiling. 'Yes, things are going well. Everyone is joyful that the British are on their way, even the Indians.' She looked back rather wistfully at the laughing group that had now fallen behind. It would have been nice to join them, she felt. They seemed a happy crowd. But though they waved they made no move to invite them along, so they had to stay on their own.

In the evening when they had had their evening meal the Sikh again rode up. 'Had a good day's journey?' he asked, kindly, and produced a rattle made from a dried fruit. 'Would the baby like this?' he said, getting down from the horse and shaking it so the seeds rattled, just by the child's face. The baby clasped at it gleefully.

'Would you like to join us for some tea?' he asked. 'I hope you do not mind us being familiar, but since we are on the same route perhaps you would like to talk with us and hear of our adventures, as we would like to hear of yours, too. And we have some nice sweetmeats, and some water – but perhaps you are tired.'

He seemed so genuine that even Arjun Gohar nodded his assent, and they took their sleeping things and pitiful possessions over to their camp. There was a band of about twenty, men playing instruments, carving wood, making toys, hollowing out reeds, cooking – a little village on the move. Lizzie thought they must be nomads.

That evening they sang and played and exchanged jokes until, exhausted, they all fell asleep and woke late the next morning.

'Come with us,' said the Sikh, who seemed to have taken over as their host. 'Ride with us – you can share the horses, we have some spare, you will be quicker then. And it is a pleasure to entertain such people as you.'

Sushma readily agreed, and Lizzie, too. It was a relief to be with a crowd of ordinary people at last. It was almost, now, as if the war didn't exist in this good-natured climate of comradeship. Arjun Gohar was the only one who looked worried. But he said nothing as he rode on.

It was only much later, as evening drew near, that he drew up to Lizzie's horse and in a voice full of fear said: 'Memsahib, I fear the worst. I think we have fallen into a trap.'

'Trap? What trap?' asked Lizzie, looking around her.

'Ssh!' said Arjun Gohar, putting a finger to his lips. 'Did you not notice twenty men last night?'

Lizzie shrugged. 'Perhaps, about that – I did not count.'

Arjun Gohar's face looked grim. 'I did. There were twenty last night. Today there are fifteen. Five have gone on ahead on their horses, and I think I see them in the distance . . . look!'

Lizzie strained her eyes through the dusk and saw that Arjun Gohar was right. On the top of a small hill she could just make out the shapes of some men, carrying sticks, it seemed, moving about busily.

'Well, yes, perhaps,' she said impatiently. 'But what if they did go on ahead? What of it?'

Arjun Gohar shook his head. 'I fear they are Thugs, memsahib, and that those five have gone ahead of us to dig our graves. Tonight will be our last. They will entertain us – and kill us.'

'What utter nonsense!' exclaimed Lizzie. 'How could such charming people possibly be Thugs! That man was a Sikh. And anyway the British have banned them, they do not exist on the highway any more.'

'If only you were right, memsahib,' replied Arjun Gohar, nervously, 'but I know there are still some left. And this is how Thugs behave – they are kind to travellers on the road. They are good to them. They sing, they entertain, they tell

234

stories, they give good meals – and then they kill.'

Sushma rode up behind them, and her face paled at hearing Arjun Gohar.

'If you are right, Arjun,' she said, 'what can we do? How can we escape?'

'Now stop it,' said Lizzie. 'This is ridiculous. We are just down the road from Havelock's column. They would not come and kill people so near – they would be found out.'

'By whom? There will be none of us alive to tell anyone.'

'But that Sikh – he is so kind! And a Sikh, surely; the Thugs are a religious group, no?'

'Yes, and he is no Sikh,' said Arjun Gohar grimly. 'I saw him take his turban off today by the stream, and his hair is cut, not long. No Sikh cuts his hair. There is something very wrong.'

'But why would they kill us?'

'It is their belief, memsahib,' explained Arjun Gohar. 'The legend goes that Kali, wife of Siva, fought a monster demon who devoured men as fast as they were born. It was so big that the deepest ocean was coming up to his waist. Kali cut him in two with her sword, but from each drop of his blood arose another demon. She went on destroying them, and grew hot and restless and from the sweat from her arm two men grew and she gave them a yellow scarf to strangle the demons. When they had killed them they offered to return the scarves to her, but she was telling them to keep them and give them to their children and their children's children, telling them to destroy all men who were not like them. And that is what they are doing now – preparing our graves!'

Suddenly the figures on the hill looked sinister and dreadful, silhouettes against the vivid pink and blue sky behind. As Arjun Gohar finished talking, a few of the group came up and cheerfully joined them. Lizzie and Sushma looked at each other. Could this really be true? Were they really Thugs? Or was it all Arjun Gohar's imagination?

Before they could wonder more, Arjun Gohar had suddenly spurred his horse ahead and bolted down the road at

235

an amazing speed, leaving Lizzie and Sushma astonished and the rest of the group apparently equally amazed.

'What on earth has happened to him?' asked the Sikh, looking down the road. 'Has he gone mad?'

Lizzie felt desperate. For one moment she felt like riding off, too, but then she realized it was impossible. It was inconceivable that he could have simply have ridden off leaving them like that – and yet from what she had seen of Indians, loyalty was not their strongest characteristic. She felt both that she could trust him and also that she couldn't, that like all Indians he was only out to save his own skin.

That was certainly Sushma's feeling, anyway. 'Men!' she said to Lizzie, spitting on the ground. 'What rubbish! And I liked him!'

The Sikh came up to Sushma and smiled seductively into her eyes. 'I'm sure I know what he thinks,' he said, laughing. 'He thinks we're Thugs, doesn't he? Oh, we've had so much trouble with travellers thinking we are Thugs, the rumours are quite dreadful. Thank heavens the British have eliminated them from the roads – we surely don't want to meet any, if there are any left, though I doubt it. Colonel Sleeman did an excellent job. I did know a man who knew one, once, a sinister lot they were. Well, it's lucky you're left with us to take care of you, isn't it?' he added, guiding them to the side of the hill. 'We can have a good meal tonight, sing some songs, tell some jokes, and then tomorrow we'll be in Lucknow! Come along! You're safe with us!'

Lizzie would liked to have believed him. But despite his reassurances she was still terrified. She could see, now she looked at his turban, that his hair could not be long for there were some cut ends sticking out. He certainly was not a Sikh. So what was he? There was nothing they could do, however, except join them for supper, and pray.

19

The steady tramp of men's feet still rang in Richard's ears as the army camped that evening. Being with an army on the march was rather like being on board ship – even when the whole column had settled for the night, the rhythm of its relentless, swaying pace stayed with Richard, like the feeling on disembarking from a ship when the whole of the land appears to tilt as if you are still aboard.

This last stretch before Lucknow was not as bad as the rest of the march. Being with Patcham, who was still too wounded to fight or march, but who was getting slowly better, meant that Richard shared the privilege of his tent; now that Arjun Gohar had left with Whittle, he shared Patcham's servants, too, helping them to knock the tent-pegs into the heavy, cloying soil late in the afternoons, helping to pack up each morning before dawn. Quite adept at the task now, they had put up the tent swiftly that evening, lain straw on the ground to prevent the dampness coming through, and the servants had disappeared to make supper.

Richard stood at the entrance to the tent, staring out on to the bleak sight of men tugging off their boots, pulling out their whisky bottles, starting up fires, drinking, joking in the heat. It had now been nearly two years since he had come to India. It was late September. In England the children would be building bonfires, windows would be yellow lights in the darkness and everyone would be wrapping up warm, their breath coming out into the cold night air like puffs of steam. He thought of Regent Street – soon the shops would be preparing for Christmas, and bright green Christmas trees would appear in everyone's sitting rooms while fires blazed in the grates. Damn it. Why had he come to this God-forsaken country? A mosquito buzzed hopefully around his face and he slapped it into a bloody stain on his hand. The whole trip had been pointless. He should have stayed in England, married Lizzie, forgotten about this escapade to prove himself.

Now he had had a letter from his mother telling him about his father's illness − 'He is much better now, my dear, but we did not mention it for it would have worried you so and I know that things must be hard enough in India now without family worries, too . . .' It confirmed everything Lizzie had told him. He should never have left her. He had been so much younger then. The time he had been in India had changed him from an adventuresome wild boy into a wiser man. Had he not come he would never have learnt so much, never known what true poverty was like, never seen the other side of the world, the dark side; he would not have known that there were other ways and customs, not just British ones, he would never have known the close comradeship that soldiers find in war. He would not have known what a sore India was on the side of the world, a putrid boil, a kind of hell − and without that knowledge he would never have known how lucky he had been, in England. He knew, now. If he ever got back there, of course. It was hard to believe he would, with Lucknow ahead of them. He might not even survive this next battle. But he was determined to get back. That determination alone would surely make him survive.

And yet England without Lizzie no longer interested him. True, it would be wonderful to see his father and family again, he ached to ride along the Devon cliffs in the cool rain, to have tea by a roaring fire, to hear those country accents . . . but it would be no life without Lizzie. There was no resolution, now, to his return. It would be a return only to his old home, not the new one he had been hoping for. Any joy that he could imagine about returning to England was instantly erased by the knowledge that Lizzie was dead. If only he had never left her . . . if only he had not been so stupidly proud at Calcutta, perhaps they could have run away! Or he could have taken her with him at Cawnpore! It all seemed so clear and simple when he looked back on what he should have done – and after all those chances now there would not be another.

There was a cough in the tent behind him. It was Patcham, and his concern for his friend stopped his own thoughts.

'Want anything?' Richard turned and lifted the flap of the tent, then went in. It was even hotter inside, despite the damp hangings that had been rigged up to cool them; hot and humid. The lamp poured a yellowish glow around the inside of the tent, giving Patcham, still pale, an almost ghostly appearance, his waxy skin shining slightly in the heat. Although his wound was healing, the blood still seeped through to his mud-stained coat which hung sorrowfully over his armless shoulder.

'Any action?' he asked.

Richard shook his head, brushed the crude bed and sat down, lighting a cheroot. 'No, nothing,' he said, 'but we'll be there in a couple of days. And I imagine we'll see enough action to do us for the rest of our lives.'

'Think we'll make it?'

'I think we will,' said Richard cautiously, 'and I *hope* we will.'

Patcham poured himself a cup of tea from a kettle. Richard leant over to help steady the *lota* for him and Patcham smiled gratefully. Richard was glad. Some soldiers who'd been wounded would suffer agonies refusing aid of any kind, and to see them, these cripples, some without legs, trying to perform daily tasks, was a pitiful, if touching, sight. But they would refuse help. With misguided pride they stumbled on, bitter, wretched, able to endure anything except the feeling of gratitude.

'Have you seen this European woman?' asked Patcham.

'Which European woman?' asked Richard.

'I don't know,' said Patcham, smiling. 'My bearer told me they picked one up today.'

Richard shook his head. 'What do you mean – picked up? Is she dead?'

'No . . . well, that's where I'm worried. She's sick, they say. She escaped from Azimullah's harem and they found

239

her on the road, or so they say. You can't believe any of these stories, however, and this one sounds quite fanciful. But if it's true I pity her. Only the Indians will care for her, y'know. The British soldiers won't have anything to do with her. They say she's tainted as she's been with an Indian.'

'Tainted?' Richard looked up incredulously. 'Good God! One of the reasons we're fighting this war so cruelly is because of what the Indians did to our women! And now here's one who's survived, probably forced to give in to Azimullah, and no one cares for her! Sometimes I don't know which side disgusts me more in this war, to be honest – the British or the Indians. The bad on both sides are equally sickening.'

'They always are,' said Patcham, philosophically. 'Where are you going? I wondered if you could do me a favour?'

Richard had risen, ground his cheroot into the earth and was turning to go out.

'What?'

'Go and see that poor woman, will you? I keep thinking of her and you know it must be very hard on her. I'd go myself if it weren't for my arm. . . .'

'Where did you think I was going, Patcham?' said Richard. 'Of course I'm going to see her! If she's not being treated properly I'll bring her here, but usually the Indians know best how to cure these sicknesses, if she is ill.'

Patcham smiled. 'Thanks,' he said, weakly, and lay back on the charpoy to sleep.

Outside the tent it was completely dark now and it was some time before Richard could find the woman. He only had to mention her and the reaction was bitter. 'Filthy whore!' one soldier shouted after him. 'You officers, you'd touch anything, wouldn't you? Spit on her for me, will you?'

Even the Indians, down at the far end of the line, were reluctant to say anything, knowing the feelings of the British towards the woman. Finally, Richard stopped at a group of servants who were singing, their voices carrying

240

softly into the night air. When they stopped he asked in Hindustani: 'There is a European woman who was picked up today. Where is she? I am looking for her.'

Instantly the group started chattering and he could hear the frightened whisper going round. 'He will kill her . . . he will use her . . . perhaps it is better . . . say nothing, nothing . . .'

'Where is she!' Richard angrily pulled the leader of the group up by his greasy turban. The man muttered curses. 'Look, I can understand every word you're saying. I'm not going to kill her or use her, I want to help her. Tell me where she is or I'll tell Havelock to come and flush her out!'

After more reluctance and lies the man agreed to show Richard where she was. They walked some way down the road beyond the camp until the man pointed to a clump of bushes in the darkness.

'She there. Rupee, rupee.'

'No rupee. Where is she? That's just a bush. She's not in there, is she? Ill?'

'We hide her so no British soldier can kill her or harm her, she very well hidden, rupee, rupee.'

Richard turned round and shook the man by the shoulders. '*No* rupee!' he said, firmly. 'What have you done with her? She can't stay in a bush all night, for God's sake. She'll be dead by tomorrow.' Then he walked forward steadily, half frightened of what he might find. There was a crackling noise behind him. He turned, but there was no one. Perhaps it was a trap. You could never be sure. He slowly pushed apart the branches of the bush and there, in a roughly hewn clearing, was a body. He held his breath and instinctively put his hand on his gun. For all he knew the creature might leap up and stab him. . . .

'You there!' he cried sharply. 'Turn around, I'm armed!'

There was a moaning sound and the body moved, slowly, rolling over towards him. It was indeed a woman, but a very sick, pathetic woman. Richard pushed his gun back into his belt, and swiftly knelt beside her, staring into her face. 'You're not well. Can you walk?'

The woman only moaned some more. 'Spare me . . .' she

wailed, putting up her hands. Richard put his hand on her forehead. She was hot and delirious with fever. He took her hands and gently pulled her to her feet, putting his arm around her. She could hardly stand. And yes, indeed she was ill, dirty and neglected, too.

He called sharply to the Indian outside. There was no reply. Richard cursed as he half pulled, half dragged the woman from the bushes on to the road. He looked around. The Indian had vanished.

Gently, but using all his strength, he helped the woman along the road. She tottered, half fainting, her knees sagging from time to time as she collapsed with the effort. Finally Richard saw a British soldier who reluctantly helped him. Between them they managed to carry her through the muttering groups of soldiers, back to Patcham's tent.

'Get some water, and a woman who knows of these sicknesses to nurse her!' Richard shouted at the servants. 'Hurry, she's delirious, I am sure of it.'

As he laid the woman gently down in the semi-darkness he could feel her sweat on his hands. She was so hot it was almost uncomfortable to hold her for long. He crouched beside her, smoothing her hair from her face.

'It's all right,' he murmured to her, 'we will care for you. We're British. You'll be all right with us. Don't worry. You'll get better.' The moonlight touched her face and Richard was struck by her features. She reminded him of someone. Perhaps he had met her, perhaps he had danced with her in Calcutta. Poor woman! He felt a terrible pity for her, and gently stroked her forehead. At that moment the servants appeared and a hasty shelter was erected from old sacks and poles. An old Indian woman from the travelling bazaar who had sold puppies to the men on the march as pets, offered to help. She squatted down beside Richard and looked at the woman, muttering to herself and shaking her head, reaching for the bowl of water provided by the servants and wiping the sweat from the woman's forehead. She said something in Hindi to the servant who nodded breathlessly, then turned to Richard.

'She has fever, very bad fever. I will make better. I am getting some potions, he will get, rupee, sahib, I beg you rupee, I thank you, sahib. . . .'

Richard got up and pulled some rupees from his pockets and gave them to the old woman. He felt suddenly desperate that this British woman should live. If Lizzie weren't alive at least he could try to save another. 'Here, take it. If she gets better I'll give you more, I promise you,' he said. The woman salaamed, her head near the ground with gratitude. Near the tent Richard could see the faint figure of Patcham, feebly leaning by the opening to see what was happening.

'Get in and lie down,' he said, turning to him and following him into the tent. 'We don't want two invalids. You're in no state to be near a sick woman.'

Patcham grinned ruefully. 'I'm not in much state to be near a fit one, old chap,' he said, turning into the tent. 'No one's going to want me now, old one-arm.'

Richard shook his head impatiently. 'Have a drink and stop talking nonsense,' he said. 'Look, if she's better tomorrow perhaps you can see the old woman stays by her, see she is looked after. I'll have to be on my duties, and you're not such a cripple as you think.'

Patcham poured a drink, offering Richard one, too. 'Of course,' he said. 'And thanks for getting her. I'm glad she's with us, poor soul.'

'I only hope it isn't too late,' Richard stared grimly ahead. Then he knocked back his drink and, pulling off his boots, settled down to a fitful sleep.

When he returned from the day's march the following afternoon he found the woman still ill, and her temperature high. Patcham had been sitting most of the day by her, bathing her forehead, feeding her sips of water.

'Richard, you didn't tell me it was Miss Whittle!' he said, getting feebly to his feet as Richard returned. 'Don't you remember? We met her – well, I met her – in Calcutta. It's George Whittle's sister, don't you remember? I hardly recognize her, I must say, she's mighty changed.'

Richard knelt down beside her and looked. It was true,

he would never have realized who she was if Patcham hadn't told him. She had become fuller, rounder, since he had last seen her and her face seemed less tense, more relaxed – but perhaps that was simply the fever. She was more like a woman than when he remembered her – older, with suffering written in her face, but without the bright tension that used to be so unattractive.

'Emily . . . it's Richard Applevale,' he said, leaning forward, taking her hand. 'Do you remember, Emily? From Devon . . . I knew your brother. . . .'

She tossed on her straw bed, her scarlet cheeks glistening as she snatched her hand away in apparent terror. 'No, not again, Azimullah,' she said, clearly. 'Oh, I can't bear the pain . . . please . . . George, dear, where are you?' Then she opened her eyes and looked at Patcham. 'Why George, you are here,' she said, smiling at him. 'My dear, I was dreaming of Azimullah. I am not well. Have you got Lizzie? Oh, don't burn . . .' She shut her eyes again and rolled on to her side, moaning as yet another delirious attack took hold of her.

Patcham took her other hand and gazed seriously at Richard. 'She's still extremely sick,' he said. 'I only hope that potion the old woman's giving her is going to work. Perhaps the army doctor should see her. . . .'

'And put leeches all over her?' said Richard contemptuously. 'No, stick with the traditional medicines. This infection she has, this is not something our doctors know about. It's not an attack of gout or liverishness, or heart sickness, or a common cold. It is something strange and Indian, and the only people who can cure it are the Indians, I'm sure.'

Patcham stared back at Emily in concern. 'I hope you're right, Applevale,' he said. 'Emily has changed much, hasn't she? Poor dear. She must have been through so much. She's been muttering all day, y'know, and saying some pretty strange things, I'll tell you.'

Richard got up. He stared down at her. In a moment in which he hated himself he found himself suddenly wishing that it were Emily who had died, not Lizzie. Why should

Emily live, Emily who was nothing but a chattering spinster, and Lizzie, his Lizzie, die? He could also feel the affection from Patcham to her, and what might in ordinary circumstances have meant nothing to him, he now felt jealous of. He felt jealous of any sign of the love of a man for a woman, for it only highlighted his own terrible loneliness, a loneliness that he took such pains to disguise but came stabbing at him from time to time at moments like these.

'Well, at least she survived Cawnpore,' he said, almost bitterly, at once regretting the tone of voice in which he had uttered the words.

Emily's eyes flew open, and she struggled up into a sitting position. 'Yes, she survived Cawnpore, George, you see I was right, she survived Cawnpore! She will survive this if only you will hurry. You believe me at last! Oh, hurry, my dear . . . !'

Richard shook his head. 'She's completely delirious, doesn't know what she's talking about,' he said tersely. 'I hope she gets better,' he added, with difficulty, unable to look Patcham in the eyes.

Patcham looked up and smiled at him, knowingly. 'It must be hard for you, Applevale. You may think I don't know anything, but I have a feeling I know more than you think.'

Richard had to turn away, for the pain he felt was almost too much for him to bear. If it had just been Lizzie who had died it would have been bad enough. But the words that Whittle had uttered before he left stayed constantly in his mind. 'That baby. It wasn't mine, you know. It was yours. Bonny lad . . .'

'Bonny lad.' If he ever saw George Whittle again he would kill him. He knew that for certain. Though at least he had saved his sister, somehow. Where was Whittle, anyway? Perhaps he'd been killed on the road. Why wasn't he with his sister?

Emily was still ranting on, but her voice was getting softer and slowly, after soothing noises from Patcham, she relaxed into a delirious sleep. Richard retreated into the tent and poured a large brandy for himself. In the heat the spirits went quickly to his head, but because of the heat their effect lasted only for a short while. But for Richard anything was better than to live in the present.

An hour later Patcham came in and sat down opposite Richard on the charpoy. He poured himself a drink and lifted his glass. He looked happier.

'She's better,' he said, optimistically. 'She's through the worst. I'm sure of it. She's sleeping better now. Her forehead's cooler. My God, Applevale, what a time that woman's had.'

'Well, tell me. Has she told you anything that makes sense?'

'I can only make out bits from her story. It is full of references to Azimullah, of course, and I can only feel he treated her very cruelly indeed. She is terrified of anyone even holding her hand.'

'Not yours, I notice,' said Richard, smiling slightly and leaning back. He'd had a refill and the brandy was going to his head. He felt slightly more relaxed.

Patcham blushed slightly and looked away. 'Not only that but you know I think Whittle did help her escape as far as I can tell, but he seems to have left her.'

'Typical,' said Richard. 'Though I thought he had more loyalty to his sister than his wife.'

'Then she talks a lot of being on her own with an Indian family, and always talking about Lizzie – was that a friend of hers? Perhaps she was another European from Azimullah?'

Richard let it pass. He took another swig of brandy.

'Anyway, I gather she was on her own with this family when people came looking for a European woman in the village, some woman who'd escaped a burning, and all the family left and she went on the road alone to join our army, and she got ill on the way. That's all I can make out.'

Richard shook his head. He kicked at the grey earth beneath his feet and wondered if all this misery was worth it. The canvas of the tent heaved slightly in the hot evening breeze and the smell of the dampness became even more intense. Looking up he could see the mildewed lines where the tent had been folded, and the small insects that had collected there beginning to move as it dried. A beetle suddenly burrowed its way up to the toe of Richard's boot and he pushed it till it rolled on to its back, to lie there struggling That was how he felt, now. Incapable, but trying hopelessly to survive, to right himself, with no possible chance. Coldly he pushed a lump of earth in its direction and it suddenly righted itself and scuttled off into the darkness. Richard could taste the bitter taste of brandy on his tongue and in his throat. It left him thirsty. He lifted the decanter of brownish water from the folding table and helped himself to a glassful, avoiding the fly that had died on the surface. He drew his hand over his brow, feeling it drag across his hot, oily skin, catching where the salt from his sweat had formed hard patches. It was a stinking country. Any acts of kindness or courage – like seeking out Emily or helping Patcham – they were now no longer felt, but simply duty to see that life ticked by as before, or so he saw it. The feeling seemed to have drained from his life like the sand from a glass. Life without Lizzie was hopeless and useless. Life without seeing her again was not worth living. Automatically he reached for the bottle of brandy again and clenched the neck to refill hs glass.

But at that moment the flap of his tent was flung open. There in the moonlight stood Arjun Gohar, breathless, gaunt, his eyes sticking out of his head with terror and urgency.

'Master, sahib, come quickly! I am on the road with some women. We are with the Thugs! You must ride with some men or it will be too late . . . quickly, or they will all be dead!'

20

The sun was sinking rapidly over the horizon, casting long shadows on the ground. Far away the peaceful sound of cowbells could be heard as cattle were being herded back over the fields by a small boy, and an elephant trumpeted as it was led to the river. Otherwise there was quiet, except for the constant hum from the insects and the creak of the drying earth.

Under the group of trees on the hillside Lizzie huddled nearer to one of the trunks for safety. It was shady here, and only the narrowest of the sun's rays penetrated the branches dappling the ground with small pools of yellow. The baby was tottering around by her feet, picking up pieces of earth and staring at them with his big, brown eyes, or stopping, his attention caught by some slow-moving insect crawling in the shade. Sushma sat by her, only her dark eyes showing through the gap in the sari that she had pulled up protectively around her face. Lizzie put out her hand and automatically took Sushma's, squeezing it comfortingly. She turned to her and their eyes met, and Lizzie could see the fear in her small, sharp pupils.

In front of them the group of Indians were busying themselves. One ragged man, darker than the rest, squatted, tuning up an instrument; another man next to him practised low notes on a pipe and occasionally turned it around and blew irritably into the end to clear it. Three more kindled the fire, poking, blowing, so that the blue haze of smoke started to mingle with the last rays of sunlight, drifting up to the cool, dark, green leaves above. Nearby the meal was being prepared, men sifting rice, another rolling curd into yellow balls, another rubbing cinnamon sticks in his dry palms till a fine, dark orange dust fell into the dish below.

248

The Sikh, who was clearly the leader of the group, stood opposite them against a tree and watched them through the smoke. Lizzie could feel his eyes on her and as he stared she grew more frightened. Finally he pushed himself away from the tree and came over to them, a big smile spreading across his features showing his broken, yellowing teeth.

'Ah, you two ladies!' he said, rubbing his hands as he approached. 'You are sad because of the absence of your foolish friend, am I being right? Come and talk to us! Move closer to the fire and let us make a circle. Join us for a song. Here, little baba . . .' He picked up the baby and threw him into the air, catching him deftly as he came down. The baby grinned at him. 'Now you are a big man, baba,' said the Sikh. 'You are walking, you must be looking after your mother and her friend, when you are really big you will chase big lions, bears . . . yes?'

'Bahs,' replied the baby, still smiling, reaching out to touch the Sikh's necklace.

'Oh, no you are not having that,' said the Sikh, laughing with pleasure. 'You like pretty things, you will be having many pretty things when you are big man.' He turned to the women. 'Come along, move in, you are being frightened, come, sit, eat, then we will sing.'

'We aren't hungry,' said Sushma, defensively. 'We are tired. Tomorrow we will eat. We would rather sleep now.'

'Oh, come on, food will do you good!' said the Sikh jovially, giving the baby to Lizzie and reaching out for both of their hands. 'Come along, let me give you a hand up!'

Reluctantly they complied and nervously moved closer to the fire. 'That's more like it,' said the Sikh. 'Come now, let us all eat. Let us be friends. The meal is prepared . . . the smell is delicious.'

Silently a man on the other side of the fire withdrew a steaming dish which had been warming by the embers. The others in the group approached and sat down in a circle. The sun had now disappeared and they were lit by the flames of the fire. Slowly Lizzie began to eat, tearing small strips of her chicken for the baby.

The Sikh laughed and joked and the others joined him,

249

conversationally. Through the blue smoke she could see their features, hard and lined in the harsh light of the fire. Suddenly she noticed one looking at her, a look of cold calculation on his face. Catching his eye she stared back and he immediately changed his expression, clapped his hands and laughed, throwing over a piece of grilled mutton. 'Here! For the baby!' he cried. 'Nice baby!'

Lizzie's mouth went dry with fear, but she picked it up and gave it to the baby, who ate it happily. 'More! More!' he cried, waving at the man opposite, who gave a throaty laugh and shook his head as he chewed a bone.

'Here, chicken leg, make strong teeth.' The Sikh passed a leg to Lizzie, and the baby seized it. It was hardly possible to believe they were Thugs, they were so good to the child. They seemed genuinely to enjoy his presence, to have a way with babies, a kindness about them. But Lizzie knew Indians too well to feel that their kindness to the baby was any reason for trusting them. She ate her own portions as slowly as she could, hardly even taking her eyes off the men around her. She chewed each mouthful again and again before swallowing it, hoping to spin out the time. But she was so fearful she could hardly swallow the meat. As the fire died out, the circle grew smaller as the men moved in towards the embers, smaller and tighter and closer, too close. She could smell them near her now, the dirty smell of people who never washed and slept in the open, night after night.

Finally the Sikh offered tea, saying: 'Now, let us sing tonight. Ladies! Perhaps you would honour us with a song! Perhaps you, memsahib, could sing a song from England! Maybe one day we all be going there. You will be giving us tea in your garden, yes?'

Lizzie shook her head vehemently. 'I have no voice,' she said, feeling the beads of sweat on her forehead. 'I never sing.'

'Nonsense! All British ladies sing,' said the Sikh good-humouredly. 'Of course you will sing!'

'But my throat is hurting, I am not very well, I am not in good voice.'

'Singing will cure you! It is healing, I am promising you. Just a verse! It is our custom to sing in the evenings.' Then, noticing her resolute expression, he added rather more seriously, 'We think it is not good manners, we will be thinking you are not liking us, that you have not enjoyed our meal or our company.'

'Indeed we have enjoyed your meal very much,' said Lizzie, desperately, 'and your company. You have been very good to us. It is just that . . .'

'We are listening. We love to hear. Just a verse . . .' The Sikh drew closer and Lizzie could see the ice behind his eyes, hear the coldness behind that soft, persuasive voice.

There was a hush around the fire. Lizzie looked beside her to Sushma who was staring, nearly paralysed with terror, straight ahead into the fire.

Then Lizzie rose. Perhaps if she could stand she might be able to run. . . . She looked down at the circle of men all staring up at her. Around them was complete blackness now. There was no way of escape. She cleared her voice. She had a sudden memory of the drawing room at Penworth Court, the fire crackling, her father reading the *Barnstaple Gazette*, the whinny of the horses from the stable and the howl of the wind outside. Softly, the sweet words carried on the night air as she sang, soft and resigned.

'The Lord is my shepherd, I shall not want, He makes me down to lie . . . in pastures green he leadeth me . . . the quiet . . .'

But at that point she fell; all she saw was a flash of a yellow scarf and a tearing pain around her neck – but as she clutched at her throat she saw Sushma suddenly rise up from her side, screaming.

'They are coming, there are horses : . . I can hear . . . there is help!'

The yellow scarf fluttered down to her side and the group was in turmoil. Lizzie lay gasping on the ground. Indeed there was the sound of hooves, the blowing of trumpets, the wild yells of the soldiers as they crashed up the hill through the undergrowth. The group scattered, cooking pots smashed as they crashed through the fire to their horses, wailing and screaming in horror, leaving their possessions, their flutes, their rice bowls upturned and pieces of chicken littered over the ground. Through the bushes the crackling sound increased, British voices could be heard, and the high yells of Arjun Gohar: 'In there, sahib, it is in there they are!'

Already one of the Thugs had fallen from his horse, and suddenly they were all scattering as four British soldiers on horses burst into the clearing. 'Where are the women?' A voice from above was reassuringly clear.

'Here . . .' Lizzie seized Sushma's hand and ran, baby on one arm, to the men. 'They are Thugs. . . . Thank heavens you arrived. . . .'

'There's one!' Another voice shouted, and the soldiers charged through the undergrowth after him, one turning on his way to cut another Thug down as he tried to spring from a tree. 'Take the women back, Greenwood,' one of the men shouted as he followed in pursuit. 'Keep them safe, we'll follow Applevale after the men!'

The fourth, who had been following his comrades, stopped and turned with a sigh. 'So much for action,' he said ruefully, helping Lizzie and the baby on to his horse. 'Ah well, some would say it is more pleasant to rescue the ladies. Are you all right? Have they hurt you?'

'You came only just in time,' said Lizzie, in relief, hanging on to the soldier's coat. 'Sushma, are you all right?'

Sushma was mounting Arjun Gohar's horse and Arjun Gohar called over, 'All right, memsahib, Sushma is not harmed.'

Exhausted, Lizzie clung to the back of the soldier and they rode slowly back to camp. Just the sound of an English voice filled her with reassurance. At last, at long last, they were safe. The moon had climbed high into the dark blue sky, and a thousand stars clustered round. When she opened her eyes she could see, far away on the road, the welcoming glimmer of light from Havelock's camp. It was miles away. Lizzie dozed fitfully, and the baby, lulled by

252

the steady movement of the horse, fell asleep as well, his head leaning on the broad back of the soldier. A wild pig surprised them, snuffling along the road in the dark, and by the roadside Lizzie could see the pale outline of a sacred cow, bones from its shoulders and hips sticking up in gawky curves. A squirrel raced across the road, and a monkey chattered from his home in a Hindu shrine at the roadside.

As the horse jogged into the camp Lizzie looked down and saw the British uniforms lit by the flickering fires, heard the groans and snores from the soldiers getting their last hours of sleep. Everything was quiet. Slowly they weaved their way through the camp and finally stopped outside a tent. Arjun Gohar jumped down from his horse and ran in. 'Mr Patcham, sahib, we have the ladies, they are safe. . . .' And shortly a man emerged with a bandage round one shoulder. With his one arm he rubbed his eyes sleepily and stared up at them.

'You're safe? Thank God!' he said, helping them down. 'Where's Applevale, Gohar?'

'He is killing the Thugs, maybe he is killing, they are clever bad men, but I am thinking they are frightened. . . . He will return soon after us, I am thinking, he must be back for tomorrow.'

Gohar looked anxiously at the sky, still black.

'Tomorrow's nearly today, old man,' said Patcham, good-naturedly. 'Well done. Get the ladies something to eat. Why, what have we here – a little chap, eh? A sleepy little chap, too, I see. . . . My name is Mr Patcham, madam, John Patcham, I hope you will forgive my introducing myself. Ah, this is a bonny boy, isn't he?' He helped Lizzie down and looked at her, his eyes covered with that distant veil of one who is trying to remember something. Lizzie stood and stared at him. Was this the elegant young man she had met at the Calcutta ball? He had seemed so pale then, with his small black moustache, so elegant, such a dashing young man; and here he was, months later but seemingly years older, wounded, dark and unshaven, in a dirty uniform, but still with the sweet smile she remembered, still with the perfect manners and the easy charm.

'I am pleased to meet you, Mr Patcham. I think we have met before. I am Elizabeth . . . Elizabeth . . .'

'Elizabeth! I am enchanted!' Patcham clicked his heels. 'We stand on no ceremony here, you will see. We have come to a pretty pass and it is no place for a woman to be, I fear, but tomorrow we march on Lucknow and then we can whip the Indians and be able to give you proper living quarters of your own. In the meantime all I can say is you're welcome to lie down in my tent with the baby, and I'll stay outside. Come this way . . .' He called to a servant who held a tray with tea and biscuits on it, 'Inside here, for the memsahib.'

Lizzie put her hand on his arm and smiled at Patcham. 'Thank you, Mr Patcham,' she said in a low, grateful voice, 'I will lie down if I may. I am tired. I have had such a time you would not believe it. I am so grateful for your kindness. I . . .'

''Fraid it's not comfortable, one bit,' said Patcham, smiling apologetically, 'don't thank me until you see it. I am sure you're used to more comfort.'

For a moment Lizzie thought back to the nights in the Ram family's house, her sleepless hours in the entrenchment in Cawnpore, the bed of grass and straw she was used to on the road. . . . 'This will be most comfortable for me,' she said, 'I promise you.' And she went inside and, aching with relief, lay down. She stared up at the canvas. She was safe. She and the baby were safe. Suddenly she felt as if she were in heaven. She was surrounded by the British, the British army. She would have enough to eat. She might even get back to England, see her father again. She arched her back and stretched out, luxuriously. At last she was with friends. She turned and slept.

It was an hour or so later that she was woken by a noise. She looked up, automatically on guard. She put her hand on the wooden frame of the bed and blinked in the darkness. A figure was at the door, staring in, a black shape against the night sky. He seemed to be peering into the darkness inside. 'Patcham? Is that you?' The voice was

254

familiar and so, suddenly, was the figure at the door. He fumbled in his pocket, found a box of matches and lit one. He came into the tent and Lizzie could see his features in the light of the flame. There were creases round his eyes that used not to be there, his face was worn, and his skin was tanned deep brown, but his eyes were as clear as ever. She held her breath. She couldn't speak. Her eyes covered him, checking, seeing the scarred hands, the torn nails, the broad shoulders, the unmistakable walk. . . .

'By God, a baby!' she heard him mutter as he saw the child, lying on his bed. He knelt down beside it and stroked the hair on its head, pushing it away from the forehead.

'Richard.' Her voice was low and she wondered if he had heard. 'Richard.' She swung out of bed and tiptoed to his side. 'It's me . . . Lizzie.'

He still said nothing. She knelt down beside him, anxiously, and then saw his face. He had recognized the child. Tears poured down his face. He turned to her blindly, unable even to look at her. He put his arms around her and clasped her to him so tightly she thought he would break her bones.

'Don't tell me I'm dreaming,' he said, hoarsely. 'This can't be true. I must be going mad. Oh, Lizzie, is it really you?' He pushed her slowly away and dragged his sleeve across his eyes. She put her hands on his face and stared at him, wonderingly. She felt her heart quicken as he squeezed her shoulders, almost cruelly in his effort to prove that she was real.

'You're not dreaming,' she said, still gazing at him. 'It is me who is dreaming.'

Slowly he shook his head. 'No. This is no dream. I can feel you. I can see you. I'm not asleep, I'm alive. I've woken from a year of horror and wretchedness without you. Forgive me, Lizzie. Don't leave me now, for God's sake.' His voice became desperate. 'Stay with me. Leave Whittle. Just be with me. We can have a life in India if you want it,' he added, shaking her in his earnestness. 'We need never go back if you'd feel ashamed. But don't go back to him. Stay with me.'

Lizzie shook her head. 'There's no need,' she said softly, moving closer to him, feeling the heat from him against her. 'George is dead. I'm alone.'

Richard looked down at her. 'Not any more,' he said, and putting one hand behind her head and pulling her towards him, he kissed her.

Outside, the sun was starting to rise. The soldiers were getting their kit together. The pots from the servants' quarters clattered and jangled and there was the crackle of sticks as fires were started. A horse gave a whinny and the tackle rattled and a soldier somewhere started to whistle 'Auld Lang Syne'. A bugle cracked over the lightening sky, a joyous howl of brass.

Soon the army would be on the march again.

Soon they would fight at Lucknow.

Soon they would be going home.